MODEL MEN

MODEL MEN
GAY EROTIC STORIES

EDITED BY
NEIL PLAKCY

Published in the United States by Cleis Press, Inc., 2246 Sixth Street, Berkeley, California 94710.

Printed in the United States.
Cover design: Scott Idleman/Blink
Cover photograph: Laure LIDJI/Getty Images
Text design: Frank Wiedemann

First Edition.
10 9 8 7 6 5 4 3 2 1

Trade paper ISBN: 978-1-57344-726-3
E-book ISBN: 978-1-57344-745-4

Contents

INTRODUCTION

W ho hasn't experienced a pang of lust or longing at a photo of a male model? Whether a hundred times life-sized on a billboard or romping through the pages of a glossy magazine in his Calvins, Tommys, or Ralphs, the male model is the gold standard for masculine beauty.

The characters in these stories run the gamut from the billboard-gracing Aiden in Cynthia Hamilton's "Big Picture," to life models in drawing classes, to runway models, to ordinary guys immortalized in a catalog shoot in T. Hitman's "When Gary Met Larry." They hook up with artists, photographers, roommates, and lovers, in locations from New York to Miami to a beach in Australia, and many places in between. There are teenagers modeling to pay for college, and in Michael Bracken's "Young Man's Game" a handsome cowboy on the other side of fifty who thought he'd left modeling behind him until a sexy stranger came to town.

One thing all the male models here have in common is sex appeal and a yen for man-on-man action. These aren't the kind of guys who say, "Look but don't touch"—they want to be touched, and in all the right places!

The authors here, some of the best writers in gay erotica today, have taken hold of the idea of the male model and run with it. Here's hoping you enjoy reading these as much as I enjoyed working with the authors and assembling this collection.

MODEL ME

Landon Dixon

Louis gulped, watching as the man came through the door of the classroom, walked up to the front of the class, and stepped onto the raised platform.

"This is Guy," Professor Mansfield said with a slight smile on his face. "He'll be modeling for us the next three classes—in various poses. You'll all get to know him quite...intimately over that time. And, hopefully," he added with an arched eyebrow, "learn to project the human form onto paper with some artistic precision."

Louis stared at Guy, at the tall man's shoulder-length, glossy black hair, his large, liquid brown eyes, the square, dimpled chin, and strong, high-cheek-boned face. He still hadn't taken a breath since the man in the white bathrobe had entered the stuffy, third-floor classroom. And now he almost choked, when Professor Mansfield turned to the model and said, "Guy, if you please." And the man loosened the sashes at his waist and opened his robe, shrugged it off.

The garment sighed to the floor, the women in the room sighing with it, as the man fully revealed himself. Louis tore his eyes off Guy's face and rolled them down Guy's body.

The model was as beautiful as any Old Master painting, an original unveiled right there in front of the class. Shoulders broad and buff and bronze, arms hanging loose and long and corded with muscle, chest humped and cleaved, almost as broad as his shoulders, smooth as his arms, studded with twin, tan nipples. His chiseled torso tapered exquisitely down to a narrow wasp waist, from which his legs poured long and caramel-colored thighs widened with even more muscle.

Louis licked his cracked dry lips, as he studied that which all of the women and men (straight and otherwise) were openly gaping unartistically at—the smooth, cut, hooded cock that dangled from the model's groin to awesome effect. The tan member with the molded crown hung farther down than any flaccid penis had the right to hang, over notably shaven balls.

The stunned silence of the class was shattered by Professor Mansfield clearing his throat and declaring, "All right, class, you may pick up your charcoal and begin drawing."

Everyone did, except Louis. He still stared empty handed and full blooded at the golden Adonis on stage, casually posed now with one foot slightly ahead of the other, one leg bent, back straight and arms hanging, eyes looking out over the heads of the wannabe artists. Louis explored every shining square inch of the model's frame with his unblinking eyes, focusing more often than not on those petulant, puffy nipples, that monster of a cock even unerect. He couldn't see the man's buttocks, but he could picture them—picture-perfect mounded bronze meaty swells.

"A blank sheet?" Professor Mansfield rumbled close by. "This isn't an *abstract* art class, young man."

Louis broke out of his trance. He looked at the professor, grinned nervously, reddened anxiously, applied charcoal to paper happily.

He was a quick draw, and he had the manly model down in detail in half the time it took the rest of the class. The cock was perhaps even more out of proportion than in real life, the nipples flared even more blatantly maybe, but it was still a very good likeness. Louis liked it, a lot, and when Professor Mansfield was otherwise occupied with other budding Rembrandts, he flipped up a couple of sheets on his easel and rapidly went to work on a second rendering of Guy—a representation not just from life, but from fervent imagination as well.

After ten minutes more of feverish drawing, Louis looked up at his golden idol and saw that Guy was looking at him, watching him work surreptitiously. The man smiled, and Louis hastily dropped the sheets of paper to cover up his latest creation, his face shading crimson under the model's warm gaze.

The class was soon over. Guy wrapped himself back up in his robe and padded out of the room, to the audible groans from some of the women, grunts of relief from some of the guys. The professor and the students exited the classroom, as well, leaving Louis behind, all alone—to put some finishing touches on his two compositions. He was planning to hang both sketches in his bathroom that night.

"You really captured me," someone said from behind, making the talented drawer jump.

He spun around, sending the stick of charcoal shooting out of his sweaty hand. Guy was standing there, looking at Louis's sketch of himself in his pose for the class, his brown eyes twinkling, big, strong hands clenching the sashes on his robe.

"Uh, th-thanks," Louis spluttered, even more awed by the man's gorgeousness up close.

Guy displayed his dazzling white teeth in a smile. "But what was that other picture you were working on? Can I see that one?"

Louis fluttered his long fingers up to his pointed chin, bobbed his bony shoulders. "Uh, what other picture? Th-there's just the one—for class."

Guy leaned forward, flipped the well-done drawing of himself over, two more pages. Revealing another fully fleshed-out picture—with someone else now up on the dais with Guy, in front of him, gripping his cock, sucking on his nipples.

"You do have an artistic...bent, don't you?" the model commented.

Louis looked at the lewd drawing, at Guy's strikingly handsome face. He shuffled his feet, opened and closed his mouth, waved his hands around.

Guy put him out of his misery, and into pure ecstasy, by pulling the sashes on his robe open again, shrugging the white garment off his bronzed shoulders for a second time. Louis ceased his dance of nervousness and stared at the naked man, that dangling prick that was the absolute model of male lust.

"Something like this, then," Guy said, gripping Louis's arms and pulling him close, up against his tanned, ripped, heated physique.

Louis just about swooned, his own body temperature skyrocketing, cock leaping in his bohemian black jeans. He was eight inches shorter than the model, so that his mouth was level with the rugged chest, lips in line with those succulent-looking nipples. His hand hung close to that huge appendage down below. He could smell the faint musk of the living god, feel the throb and twitch of the powerful muscles, the tender smoothness of the sun-browned skin.

"Like this, and this," Guy went on, placing one of Louis's

hands on his cock, drawing Louis's lips onto a nipple.

Louis full-body shuddered, thrilling from tip to toe. He encircled Guy's tremendous organ—barely—with his trembling fingers, gripping the massive tool. It pulsed, thickened, lengthened in his soft, damp palm. He flowered his red lips around the proffered nipple, tasting the delightful rubberiness, the swelling rigidness, the pebble-textured areola.

"That's about what you were trying to portray, isn't it?" Guy asked, glancing from the naughty picture to the naughty artist.

Louis bobbed his head slightly, not wanting to break lip contact with that luscious nipple. It was blossoming in his mouth, like Guy's cock was expanding in his hand. He could feel the beat of the man's heart through his tongue and palm. His own heart was racing like a rabbit's, his own nipples buzzing under his black smock, cock bulging his jeans, ballooning with pleasure.

Louis sucked on Guy's nipple. He moved his hand back and forth, stroking Guy's cock. The model of maledom moaned his approval, saying, "I feel what you're getting at."

Then he broke away, scooped up his robe, and slipped it back on. Leaving Louis frozen in despair, his lips pouted and cheeks billowing, hand grasping at air.

"Let's see if you can improve on it next class," Guy said with a wink and a grin.

The next class couldn't come soon enough for Louis, his own frequent coming, as he stared at his drawings and pictured again and again in his mind the encounter they'd engendered, doing nothing to diminish his enthusiasm for his subject.

He was shaking with sheer artistic expression when Guy finally strolled into class, up onto the dais, sat down in the chair Professor Mansfield had placed on the platform. The model looked exactly as before when he disrobed, only sitting now, one arm casually draped over the back of the chair, his head turned to the side in stunning profile, his legs wide apart to reveal the glory of his cock. Louis thought the splendid appendage hung just a little lower, was pumped just a little thicker, thanks to the knowing glance artist and model had exchanged before Guy took the stage.

The class was also swelled by additional members—gawkers there to see the beautiful model everyone in Continuing Ed was talking about. No one was disappointed by what they saw.

"All right, class!" Professor Mansfield shouted about the tumult of appreciative murmuring. "The male nude—seated. You may now begin drawing."

Charcoal scraped against paper. Women stared and blushed and tingled, warmly. Men elbowed and pointed and laughed, uneasily. Louis sketched quickly and boldly, ever more confidently.

"Excellent work," Professor Mansfield remarked.

"I'm, uh, not quite done," Louis said, grinning shyly.

"Yes, I can see that. Well, keep at it."

The second sketch was a detailed, wondrously rendered drawing of Guy seated in his chair like a king on his throne, with another man now bowing down on his knees in front, sucking on the model's cock.

"Like this, you mean," Guy said, later, after the rest of the class had gone, drawing up the chair and sitting down again. He drew Louis close and pushed the quivering artist down onto his knees.

"Exactly like this," Louis breathed, staring at Guy's cock right in front of him, inches away from his burning face. He reached out to grab the semi-erect tool, covet it, worship it.

"Hold on," Guy intervened, stopping Louis's trembling

hand. "Let me put things in the proper perspective, as you've drawn it."

Louis watched with his tongue hanging out, as the model's cock swelled on its own, rose up, hood expanding and sniffing at the air, shaft surging thick and long with blood and desire— the desire to be sucked by Louis. He excitedly reached out and wrapped both of his hands around the throbbing hard shaft, poured his lips over the mushroomed hood, unable to control himself.

Guy grunted and jerked, his pecs jumping, legs clasping the man at his cock in between. Louis swiftly plunged his mouth as far down the wicked dong as he could. He gripped the base, sealed his lips halfway down, letting the member inflate the final few inches inside the warm, wet, velvet-lined cavern of his mouth.

Guy grasped Louis's mouse-brown hair and gently bobbed the man's head up and down in his lap. Louis shook with passion, ablaze with lust, sucking on the model-perfect cock. Its dimensions were the thing of Greek wet dreams. It filled Louis's mouth and part of his throat and all of his soul.

Guy stabilized Louis's head, pumped his hips, fucking the art lover's face. His cock oiled back and forth in between Louis's lips, stroking the man's tongue and mouth, Louis's breath steaming out of his nose and flooding Guy's groin and stomach.

Louis slid a hand up onto Guy's chest, pinched the nipple he'd sucked a week earlier, rolled it. While he slid his other hand down onto Guy's balls, clasping and fondling the man's heavy, shaved sack. Guy's cock glided out to the lips, then plunged back into the mouth as deep as it would go, crowding Louis's throat. It pulsed as it pumped, and Louis tasted a sweet, salty drop of pre-cum sprung from the gaping slit.

That's when Guy suddenly drew his hips all the way back

and eased Louis, gasping, away from his groin. "I can't wait to see your next sketch," the model said with promise.

The next class exhibit was the "reclining nude male" for the eager students to draw. Professor Mansfield had set up a futon on the dais, and to watching, wide eyes Guy shucked his robe and lay down on his side on the padded piece of furniture. His cock hung down his right thigh, hood pressing into the white fabric of the futon like it had pressed into the back of Louis's throat a week earlier.

The muse-filled artist slashed at his easeled paper in a frenzy, sending charcoal sharding off on either side. He captured the built beauty of the reclining model in mere minutes, as the rest of the class labored on around him. Oblivious to the others, he flipped the completed drawing over and attacked the next blank sheet of paper with gusto.

He just about jumped out of his skin when Professor Mansfield stated, "You possess quite the fertile imagination, Louis. And the good taste to go along with it."

The professor smiled, gazing admiringly at Louis's latest, hottest creation.

Guy smiled, as well, when Louis unveiled the picture to him after class. "Let's see if we can create life out of art," he said, taking Louis by the hand.

They climbed up onto the dais, and Guy helped Louis disrobe. The artist's body was thin and pale next to his model's, but fully animated where it counted—between the legs. Louis's cock jutted out long and hard and pink and purple-capped from his loins.

Guy took a tube out of a pocket of his robe before he removed the garment. Then he stretched out on his side on the futon as during class, except now his cock was as hard as Louis's, stroked slick with the lube from the tube.

Louis settled down on his side in front of Guy, replicating the erotic picture he'd drawn. He jerked when he felt Guy's slippery fingers slide in between his quivering buttocks, moaned when the fingers scrubbed up and down, all around his asshole.

"Shall I put the finishing touch on your masterpiece?" Guy breathed in Louis's ear.

Louis nodded, gripping the edge of the futon, feeling the heat of the model's body so close, the heft of the man's cock-head up against his pucker. Guy kissed Louis's neck, pressing forward with his cock, squishing the knob into Louis's starfish. He popped ass ring, plunged chute, plowing his huge tool deep into the heated, gripping confines of Louis's anus.

Louis shook out of control, his ass swelled with Guy's cock inside, his body shimmering with electric sensation.

Guy gripped Louis's shoulder with one strong hand, coiled his other muscular arm around the quivering man's neck, and pumped his hips, fucking Louis's ass. He started slowly, the futon creaking, Louis gasping, cock sluicing sure and sensual. Then he upped the tempo, churning his hips, ramming Louis's butt, sawing the man's chute. The futon scraped to the rocking motion, Louis moaning, Guy breathing hard, thighs slapping against buttocks, cock stretching and stuffing anus.

It went on like that for a blistering minute or so. Before shifting to frenzy level, Guy powerfully pistoning his hips, pile-driving Louis's ass with his hammering cock. Louis almost lost consciousness under the anal onslaught, Guy's arm crushing his neck, cock splitting his bum, banging him to and fro. He desperately grabbed onto his own flapping cock, and stroked, once.

That was all it took under the superheated circumstances. Louis bleated joy, jetted ecstasy. Just as Guy slammed as deep as he could and then shuddered, sprayed, splashing Louis's bowels with searing semen.

Louis's clenching ass muscles clamped down on Guy's shunting, pumping cock, the artist convulsing with orgasm. The model brushed Louis's hand away from his spouting cock and gripped and ripped it himself, sending Louis into further spasms of white-hot delight. Until both men were utterly drained of all artistic and sexual expression.

PHOTO SHOOT
CONFIDENTIAL

Bearmuffin

W hen college football stars Mitch Stormer and Jakooma Jones showed up for the underwear shoot at the studio in Manhattan, the attraction between them was evident to everyone on the set. Tall, commanding, and muscular, Mitch and Jakooma had an eye-popping, jaw-dropping beauty that made them easily the most beautiful men in sports.

At twenty-two, Mitch was six-foot-four and weighed 240 pounds. His brawny chest was carpeted with red fur, and a neatly clipped goatee framed his sexy mouth. His gleaming carrot-colored hair was cut Marine-style on his bullet-shaped head. Mitch had a strong nose and firm chin. His eyes were a dazzling dark green. His deep, powerful voice was thrilling.

Jakooma, twenty-one, stood six-foot-five and weighed just a few more pounds than his buddy. He had keen, angular features, and his mesmerizing eyes were a deep brown. They enhanced his smooth, coffee-colored skin. Jakooma's smooth shaved head made him excitingly masculine. His lips were deep brown, full, sensuous.

Wiry black Brillo peppered Jakooma's broad chest. The fuzz plummeted between his corded abs, tufting around his hefty cock and huge balls.

Mitch and Jakooma had a couple of Buds and smoked some grass to get into the mood, then posed in a assortment of briefs, boxer briefs, and trunks so sheer, so provocative, so tight they barely skimmed the crotch.

They were cheerful and easy to work with and they didn't seem to mind being photographed by the gay photographers or posing with other gay models. The wily makeup artists and hairdressers sensed that something special was going on between Mitch and Jakooma. Everybody seemed to be under the magic spell of their impressive masculinity.

Soon they were caught up in a whirlwind of youthful vitality when nothing is more powerful than the primordial urge to fuck. The photo shoot lasted until the wee hours of the next morning. It was characterized by a sizzling sexual tension between the two studs. They had to restrain themselves from ripping each other's briefs off and fucking.

The photographer put Stormer and Jakooma through one erotic pose after another. Because they were in such close proximity, their powerful homoerotic passions were inflamed to such an extent that they couldn't wait to fuck. Somehow they managed to keep their hands off each other except for one instance when Mitch took one look at Jakooma's meaty bubble butt and licked his lips. "Damn!" he whispered under his breath and he could not resist aiming a playful slap on Jakooma's beautiful black butt.

Though photo shoots can be quite erotic, very little sex happens on the set. It usually happens afterward, off the set. So when the shoot was done, they ambled back to the dressing room and slipped on their clothes. Jakooma slapped Mitch on the butt. A wicked grin lit his handsome black face.

"C'mon, dude," Jakooma hissed. "Let's go back to my place!"

Mitch's hands flew to his crotch. He squeezed his spasming cock that was aching for release. "Fuckin' A!" he said.

They jumped into Jakooma's Jeep and raced back to his apartment located in a fashionable part of Chelsea. Once inside, the studs fell into each other's arms. Mitch plunged his tongue into Jakooma's hot black mouth. Their thick, lust-bloated cocks swelled inside their briefs. They swabbed hot spit. Their grunts and sighs mingled as one.

Mitch and Jakooma interrupted their kissing for a moment to take an opportunity to admire each other. Mitch was white and Jakooma was black, but they could easily have passed for brothers, so alike in body type, handsomeness, and attitude were they: like looking in a mirror. They grinned at each other, filled with mutual pride. They admired each other's athletic prowess, muscularity, and awesome masculine beauty.

"Fuck, dude," Jakooma said to Mitch, his hands massaging on Mitch's broad chest. "You're so hot!"

Mitch grinned back at his buddy. "You too!"

Mitch kissed Jakooma again. His burly hands tore Jakooma's shirt apart, sending several buttons flying into the air. With a savage gleam in his eyes, Mitch pulled Jakooma's shirt right over his huge upper torso and flung it to the floor.

Jakooma's hands instantly flew to Mitch's bulging crotch. The black stud yanked down Mitch's zipper. Mitch's cock was bulging lewdly inside his briefs. Jakooma's eyes grew wide with passion and he couldn't wait to pull Mitch's big cock out.

When he did he let out a deep sigh of astonishment and satisfaction. He couldn't wait to wrap his anxious lips around that cock. Mitch's cock was big, thick, and beautifully pinkish white. Everything that Jakooma had imagined and quite a bit more.

Mitch and Jakooma quickly doffed their clothes and stood naked before each other and took a moment to gaze at each other's beautiful, muscle-bound bodies.

In addition to cocksucking, both Mitch and Jakooma got off on their mutual smells, the perfect aphrodisiac to their love-making. Mitch impatiently proceeded to slam his handsome face into Jakooma's smelly armpits to get a good whiff of his buddy's manly odor.

Mitch jammed his tongue deep into Jakooma's armpits. Jakooma's Brillo-like armpit hairs scratched his tongue. He licked and laved them, savoring the taste of manly musk until they were gleaming with hot spittle. Mitch elicited the maximum enjoyment from the pleasurable sensations radiating throughout Jakooma's body.

Jakooma wrapped a fist around his buddy's spasming cock and began jacking Mitch off as the red-headed quarterback continued to suck on his armpits for a time. Then Mitch moved down over Jakooma's thick paps. He started laving the black nips, twirling his tongue over one in little circles and gently fingering the other. Jakooma responded with one long moan of ecstasy. Mitch sucked hard on Jakooma's swollen nips, see-sawing his teeth over them. Stimulated by Mitch's expert nipple play, Jakooma flung his head back and continued to groan and moan even more.

"Fuck, dude," Jakooma suddenly blurted out, his voice thick with macho pleasure. "Suck them paps, baby, suck 'em good." Jakooma flung his head back farther as deep groans of manly pleasure rumbled in his throat.

Encouraged by Jakooma's overt display of satisfaction and pleasure, Mitch was only too happy to oblige his buddy. He licked Jakooma's nipples some more. Mitch was blowing Jakooma's mind. Jakooma knelt before Mitch and began slurping on his buddy's cock. He relaxed his throat to allow Mitch's hot cock to slide all the way down. Jakooma sucked hard on Mitch's cock while he gently fondled Mitch's big, smooth balls, which elicited more groans on his part.

Mitch tossed his head back, grunts escaping his lips, as his tongue lewdly flopped out of his mouth. Jakooma's mouth felt so good on his cock. Mitch took a moment to beam down with pride at the magnificent black stud who was blowing him. It was one hell of sight. Jakooma's massive head bobbing and swaying over Mitch's thick bloated cock that plunged deep into Jakooma's proud mouth. With every stroke on Mitch's cock and by Jakooma's deep choking grunts as he caressed Mitch's cock with his roaming tongue Jakooma was proving himself to be a fantastic cocksucker.

Ever since they'd met at the team's first practice session a year ago Mitch had wanted to fuck Jakooma. He couldn't help grin wildly with lust, which enhanced the sparkle in his eyes. The realization that now he and Jakooma were about to fuck their brains out made his head spin. It was a fucking dream come true!

"You're a great cocksucker," Mitch said.

Jakooma grinned. He was ready to wolf down even more of Mitch's throbbing cock. Mitch thrust his cock into Jakooma's wide-open mouth until he could feel it bang against the back of his throat. The black stud felt hot drops of pre-cum singe his tonsils. After a few more hard sucks, Jakooma suddenly pulled off his buddy's cock. A sudden impulse overcame him. He wanted to suck Mitch's balls.

And Mitch loved having his big fat balls sucked. He grunted like a pig as Jakooma laved his big fat nuts. His hands flew around his cock, jacking it off in time to Jakooma's noisy grunts.

Mitch howled, his eyes clenched tight, his mouth wide open.

His whole body was burning with an intense desire to cum but he managed to restrain himself because he wanted to suck Jakooma's cock, too, and Mitch loved to suck big black dicks. Jakooma had one of the biggest. Long and fat. Covered with huge blue veins.

It was Mitch's turn to kneel as Jakooma stood up with his mighty black cock jutting out before him. Mitch eagerly took Jakooma's cock into his mouth. He sucked hard for a time paying special attention to the fat glans and teeming black shaft. Virile lust swamped his senses and soon he felt overcome by some inhuman force, as if by some supernatural power he could extract the essence of Jakooma's manhood. Soon, both of them were overwhelmed by their lust, and they both fell to the floor with hands on butts and cocks inside mouths for a wild sixty-nine.

Their noisy grunts and hums of satisfaction filled the room as Jakooma stuck a finger into Mitch's ass and Mitch did the same to his buddy Jakooma. Sensations of macho pleasure flushed their muscular bodies and were swirling inside their heads. Their primordial homoerotic passions were unleashed and they promised to go the limit. They were blowing each other and ramming their fingers into each other's butts until they were both so horny that one wanted to fuck the other.

Mitch pulled off his buddy's cock. It was spasming and rising into the air, slick and wet with his spit. Jakooma kept a firm hand on it, massaging it to keep it good and hard. Mitch looked down at Jakooma's cock filled fist and grinned. His desire for cock was rampant.

"Fuck me dude," Mitch said.

Jakooma laughed. "I want you to fuck me."

"Only one way to solve this, I guess," Mitch replied.

They flipped a coin.

"Heads," Jakooma said.

Mitch laughed. "Tails," he said.

The coin went flying into the air. It landed down between them. Mitch grinned, his eyes filled with desire as he looked at the shiny new penny gleaming on the carpet. It was tails side up.

"Looks like you win, dude," Jakooma said. "How do you want me? Doggie-style or face up?"

Mitch grinned. "Doggie style, dude," he said without a moment's hesitation.

So Jakooma crawled on his hands and knees. He stuck his sweet black butt into the air. "Lube's in the drawer by the bed," Jakooma said.

Mitch found the lube and smeared it on his bobbing cock. By now the black quarterback's hole was pulsing angrily, hungrily twitching like an anxious mouth.

"C'mon, dude," Jakooma hissed impatiently. "Fuck me!"

Mitch was eager to please his buddy. But he wanted to rim him, too. Jakooma had such a gorgeous beefy butt that Mitch became impatient and he couldn't wait to stick his tongue inside it. And though Mitch liked his sex good and rough he could be tender when the occasion called for it, as in this instance when the sight of Jakooma's beautiful black ass, that wonderful vision of beautiful sweaty black butt, inspired a sudden great feeling of love and reverence for the big jock's booty. And so he pried Jakooma's butt cheeks wide apart with his thumbs and parked his face into sweaty cleft and began lightly flicking his tongue over Jakooma's anal puckers. Jakooma felt a shudder of manly lust go through him and a low moan of pleasure escaped his full lips. "Yo, baby, that feels so good. Keep eating my butt!"

Mitch could have rimmed his buddy all night. He ate butt for hours, jacking off his own cock while he sucked ass. He loved the funky taste of his buddy's hot, musky black ass. Jakooma jacked off while Mitch ate his ass. He was in utter bliss, grunting harshly as Mitch's thick tongue fluttered up inside his butt.

Suddenly, Jakooma screamed, "Fuck oh fuck," and he went into spasm, flipping over and grabbing his cock as his hot cum shot forth like a geyser splattering all over the room but not before several jets of Jakooma's hot semen splashed on Mitch's face.

Mitch wiped Jakooma's hot cum off his face, and they both decided that now would be a good a time as any for a little break. So the studs drank some beers and feasted on some snacks Jakooma had in the fridge. Once their appetites were sated the prospect of sex looked better and better. Mitch's cock rose into the air once again, fully erect and rampant. Just one look at Jakooma's spectacular ass and his desire was awakened once again.

"I'm so horny, dude!" Mitch said. "I gotta fuck ya!"

Mitch positioned himself behind Jakooma who, remembering that Mitch wanted to fuck him doggie-style, had very conveniently gotten down on all fours. He quickly smeared more lube on his cock and on Jakooma's asshole. Then he placed his hands on Jakooma's hips and shuttled his lubed cock right into Jakooma's spasming hole. Jakooma screamed when Mitch's cock sliced into his ass crack. In a split second his anal ring popped open wide allowing Mitch's cock to hurtle right up his hole.

Jakooma pushed his ass back. His ass was well lubed so Mitch could easily glide his cock all the way up Jakooma's ass until it banged against a most sensitive spot. Jakooma responded by letting out another low moan of manly pleasure.

"Oh, fuck," Mitch hissed. "Your ass is so tight."

Jakooma knew it would excite Mitch so he clenched his ass muscles even tighter around Mitch's cock. Mitch groaned one long groan of satisfaction and pleasure while his cock was massaged by Jakooma's tight sphincter.

"Oh yeah, that's great," Jakooma hissed. He could feel Mitch's cock swell inside him so he wiggled his tight black butt from side to side. "Fuck me hard dude. Real hard!"

A thrashing, groaning Mitch eagerly fucked the living daylights out of his black buddy. Steaming sweat flew off his head. Hot spittle bubbled from his lips. Mitch grunted and cursed a blue streak as he slammed his mighty cock into the black quarterback's hot, aching hole.

Jakooma fisted his cock furiously. His tongue hung out like a horny dog's. His butt was aflame, his muscles shuddered with lust. They fucked fast and furiously, losing all sense of time as both of them were caught up in the powerful erotic frenzy of fucking.

"Let me have it, stud!" he howled. "Gimme that hot load!"

"You want it now, dude?"

"Yeah, gimme your load!"

"Fuckin' A, dude!"

Mitch pulled back and drove his cock all the way up Jakooma's hot butt.

"I'm gonna fill your ass with cum!" Mitch said.

Mitch clapped his hands on Jakooma's haunches and lunged forward, shoving his mighty cock all the way up Jakooma's sore asshole. His cock exploded, filling Jakooma's ass with burning cum. Jakooma screamed as he shot his wad, spilling his cum on the carpet. They fell into each other's arms, their smooth, muscular bellies sticking together because of all the cum that had splashed on Jakooma's abs. They caressed each other's muscles, and one long, lingering kiss followed another as they basked in the sizzling passion of their homoerotic love.

After that hot fuck, the quarterbacks had beers and ordered a pizza. Their lusty appetites sated once more, Mitch reached over and grabbed Jakooma's cock. He gave it good, healthy squeeze. Jakooma could tell by the gleam in Mitch's eyes that he wanted to be fucked. And that saucy smirk on his face was just too real.

There was no need to toss a coin this time.

Jakooma grinned. He wanted to see Mitch's face when he fucked him.

"On your back, dude," he said to Mitch. Jakooma lubed his cock and Mitch's hot asshole.

"Okay, dude," Mitch said as he lay on his back. "Fuck me!"

Pure hot lust enhanced the sparkle in Jakooma's eyes as he grabbed Mitch's hips and lifted him up as Mitch elevated his beefy legs and plopped his calves on Jakooma's brawny shoulders. Mitch's hole was twitching anxiously, just waiting to be filled with hot, ripe cock. The expression on his face was lively, smiling, boyish. "Go for it, dude!" Mitch said.

"Fuckin' A!" Jakooma replied.

Jakooma carefully inserted his swollen cock into sweaty Mitch's ass. Though it was well lubed, Mitch's ass was barely able to accommodate such a large prick. Mitch howled with a combination of pain and pleasure: *"Yeeeeeeowwwwwww-wwww!!!!"*

Mitch bucked and squirmed finding himself firmly impaled on Jakooma's pumping cock. He held on for dear life to Jakooma's thick biceps. Jakooma's arm muscles flexed and tensed as he started to power-fuck the red-haired quarterback. Jakooma grinned knowingly at Mitch whose eyes were wide open, pupils dilated, staring right back at him.

The studs grinned at each other. Mitch drummed his heels on Jakooma's bold, brawny back as Jakooma's pulsing cock made its way up Mitch's hot hole. Jakooma felt all-powerful as he fucked his buddy. And Mitch was filled with pride that it was

Jakooma, the mighty quarterback, fucking him. They felt like superstars.

Mitch's grunts grew louder. His asshole clutched around Jakooma's cock. It sucked on it like a hungry mouth. Mitch wanted to feel Jakooma's hot sperm inside him. His muscular body rocked back and forth as intense waves of virile pleasure swamped his senses.

"Shoot, buddy. Shoot now!" Mitch cried. He slammed his butt against Jakooma's balls and Jakooma's hot cock flew up his asshole. Mitch's hot asshole felt as smooth as a glove around his pumping cock.

Jakooma could have fucked him all night but he wanted to oblige his buddy.

"Yeah, baby, Yeah! Yo!"

He slammed hard into Mitch, emptying one hot, teeming load after another up his asshole.

"Muthafuck!" Jakooma cried.

Mitch screamed as he spurted his cum all over Jakooma's hard abs.

Afterward, the studs got up and showered. They headed out to Mitch's cabin in a secluded area of upstate New York to celebrate their love and their happiness.

Not long after, their erotic mages were featured in sizzling hot underwear ads in *Vanity Fair, GQ, Sports Illustrated*, and some gay mags.

In these celebrity besotted days, male models are truly gods walking on earth. They have men and women throwing themselves at them, hitting on them incessantly. And anyone would be a fool to pass on all the sexual attention a male model gets.

Even so Mitch and Jakooma had eyes only for each other, and they would spend their time together enjoying the youthful beauty of their superb masculinity and all the delights that homosex has to offer.

Eventually this would lead to a deeper, more profound understanding between them beyond the surface beauty. In time they both became superstars and role models in their own right, not just because they were so beautiful, but because they represented everything that was fresh, clean, and wholesome about homosexuality.

PINK COWBOY HAT

Gavin Atlas

I t's true I borrowed Pete's Mazda without asking, but it was
his fault for leaving me with a set of keys. I did call him from
the road to let him know I had it because that's me. Always
thoughtful.

"What possessed you to leave for Manhattan during
midterms?" His tone was decidedly unamused. I almost snorted.
Since when did Pete care about school?

The answer to his question was a male model, Marc Patrick,
the hottest, handsomest man on Earth, but why tell my ex that?
"Oh, I've just had enough of Handenburg Tech and Rochester
for the moment," I said. "The city is only five hours away,
right?"

"Six and a half."

"Yes, okay, Pete. But you know speed limits aren't my thing."
I noticed he didn't ask why I didn't take my own car. He knows I
don't like risking dinging my Viper in crazy Manhattan traffic.
And my dad would kill me if it got stolen.

My ex sighed with exasperation. "You shouldn't get on Twitter and scream with glee that Pink Cowboy Hat is in the same state if you don't want people to know you're e-stalking him."

Whoops.

"You're not going to get him," Pete said, trying to sound bored. "I told you. You're never going to do better than me."

My anger at Pete reignited. True, with his black hair, ice-blue eyes, and an athletic body shaped by years of hockey, Pete is hot. But I quit doing drugs, and Pete, that asshat, still wanted to party. We're friends still, but that's it. I'm not bitter. Pete's kind of a slut with other guys now, and I sometimes want to put my fist through a wall when I think about it, but I'm totally, totally not bitter. Especially not today, because today I have a plan that, if successful, will ensure I have no reason to bother with Pete again. Except to return his car.

I found my way to the Javits Center where Christiano Bastini's fall collection would be presented, and I hung around the back entrance in the chilly spring air, texting people while waiting for the designer to show up.

I may not be hot enough to stop traffic like Marc Patrick, but in shitkicker boots, a black leather jacket, a tight navy T-shirt, and crotch-hugging black jeans, I thought I'd have a chance to catch the eye of most guys. But a designer who saw models every day might be a different story, so I had on vintage Bastini sunglasses I'd found on eBay. Set me back a thousand. See, if you Google, you find out that Christiano adores it when people wear his father's creations.

I'd been there only half an hour when he arrived in a gray limousine along with a throng of assistants. His bodyguard wasn't going to let me near him, but the designer held up his hand. He was in his sixties, but had enough work done that he only looked old enough to be my dad.

"Where did you get those?" he said, referring to the glasses.

"Oh, these? They've been my favorites for years. Mr. Bastini, I read on your blog that you've had a horrid time finding the right music for this show. I have something for you to hear. It's the perfect tune for the models to walk to."

The designer quirked an eyebrow as he took my headphones.

"It's called 'Whipped Kream' by Fierce Ruling Diva. You'll love it."

His entourage stared at Christiano and waited patiently while he listened for perhaps forty-five seconds.

His eyes grew wide. "This...this is fabulous. I must hear this on the center's sound system. Young man, come in with us. What's your name?"

"Trip," I said. "Trip Masters." Okay, my name is Triptolemus Mickleburg, but that's irrelevant.

We turned to go into the Javits Center when a taxi pulled up, and...and...oh my God, it was Marc Patrick in the flesh. He was wearing his signature pink cowboy hat. Yes, I know. A pink cowboy hat is beyond ridiculous. But he gets away with it. He has golden blond hair, perfect bronzed skin, and green eyes that will literally stun you. I mean, you can't move, they're that mesmerizing. Just looking at him in his hat, a white muscle T-shirt and bright coral jeans made my heart speed up. He seemed to be about six feet tall. Good, I'm six-foot-three if you count my shitkicker boots.

The taxi driver yelled, "Hey!" at Marc because he'd left his phone on the seat.

Christiano chuckled. "That boy would forget his head."

Even though my pulse had gone into overdrive, it wasn't the time to barge over and fawn on Marc. But I couldn't stop looking at him.

I was swept along with the group of models, stylists, assistants on phones, and attendants wheeling racks of clothes into
the building. Christiano rushed my MP3 player over to a guy
who I'm guessing was the sound director for his show. I sat on
a box watching the buzzing activity around me, stealing glances
at Marc as he did pushups, had makeup applied, and gener-
ally smiled at everyone, male or female, who came by to flirt
with him. His teeth were dazzling. Also, as if the pink cowboy
hat didn't already announce he was a total bottom, people kept
grabbing his ass and squeezing. He'd swat hands and laugh a
musical little laugh, eyes dancing. Yeah, he was beyond adorable, but he definitely ate up the attention.

Then, holy shit, people just started changing clothes right
there instead of going into dressing rooms. What total, unbelievable showoffs. Thank goodness. I casually inspected my
nails, pretended I was reading a text, and then "happened" to
catch Marc in just his briefs. His body was perfectly muscled
and smooth, like in the photos. His briefs were aqua, a color
that looks terrible on 99 percent of the world. They were incredible on him. They hugged his fantastic ass so perfectly, I could
scarcely breathe. *God, Trip. Please stop gaping.*

My Fierce Ruling Diva song poured out of the sound system.
It's hard to describe, but it has a shimmying, scratchy beat that
just makes you want to strut, and I saw some of the models start
to dance a bit.

"Hot tune," one of them said.

Christiano came over to the bench I'd claimed and clapped
me on the shoulder. "Thank you, Trip," he said in a thick Euro-
pean accent. "Now those glasses. Are they really your favorite
pair? They're in pristine condition."

"I...uh...save them for special occasions."

Christiano smiled. "May I pay you for them? I don't have a

pair of that style in such good shape."

"Well, I could just give them to you," I said, "if you could be so kind as to introduce me to Marc over there." What was I doing? They cost a grand! Well...anything for love.

Christiano took the glasses from me, giving me a friendly smile, but rolling his eyes at the same time. "I'll do my best, but I'm not a pimp. And I'm sure you know how many fans he has."

"I understand."

"I see you have a keychain from something called Handenburg Tech. You wouldn't be good at math, would you?"

"I've won awards in math," I said, thinking of gold stars I'd received for memorizing my multiplication tables.

"Good," Christiano said. "Be different. Ask him about his family. Ask about school. Don't focus too much on his looks. He can be shy. Guys who only want him for his beauty make him nervous, and they are a dime a dozen."

Christiano pocketed the glasses and walked me over to where a stylist was smoothing down Marc's hair in places it had been ruffled by his cowboy hat. I wanted to re-ruffle it.

Christiano made introductions and my stomach flip-flopped as I shook Marc's hand. He had the softest skin, and he gave me a warm smile.

"So how's...um...math. Christiano said you need a tutor."

Marc's eyes widened. "I do. You can help me?" His real name was Marik Pakorny, and his Slavic accent was mild but detectable. He hit himself in the forehead. "I'm sorry. I'm leaving town tonight to walk in another show."

"Where are you going?"

"Rio de Janeiro."

I put on an "utterly shocked" face. "That's insane! I'm going to Rio, too!"

Well, I was *now.*

Marc appeared startled, but he may have bought it because he said, "Okay. I'll be there a few days. Maybe you can help me then."

"Well, why wait so long? I'll change my flight so we can work on the plane."

I remained in the back while the show was in progress. I made a call.

"Hi, Mom. I suddenly need to go to Brazil. What do you say?"

There was a long pause before she spoke. "I'm afraid to ask, but why do you need to go to Brazil?"

"For love."

"I see," she said. "How long have you known him?"

"About five minutes."

"Trip, be serious."

"He's a model. I'm going to be a photographer. This is how you and Dad met."

She huffed. "Promise me you're not drinking."

"I promise you I'm not drinking."

"No drugs?"

"Absolutely not."

She sighed again. "Put it on my credit card. No first class. Call me from Brazil."

First class was delightful. I'd have to explain later to my mother that the flight had sold out in coach class, but I hoped her bill wouldn't reflect that I'd paid to upgrade Marc to first class as well. Who knew models flew in coach?

Thirty minutes into the flight, Marc got out his math text.

Please don't be calculus. Please don't be calculus.

It was algebra. Phew. However, the book was in Czech. No matter. Math was international.

As I taught him how to solve for *x, y,* and *z,* I inhaled his scent—a light, fruity cologne that reminded me a bit of coconut tanning oil. I had trouble not picturing myself biting him or licking his neck. My dick was so hard, I had to cover it with an in-flight magazine. I wished I could unzip to relieve the pressure. *Math, Trip. Focus on math.*

We finished the assignment in an hour, and thankfully I'd gotten my arousal under control. "Thank you for the first-class ticket," he said. "All this good wine and champagne. But you're only having club soda?"

I looked down, knowing I was about to overshare, but whoever was going to be the guy for me would have to know sooner or later. "I can't drink. I have kind of a crazy family. My dad began taking me to wine tastings when I was fourteen, and...well...I had to quit and my dad did, too. Sober two years."

He patted my shoulder. "Good for you." He motioned for the flight attendant to take his wine away and requested a club soda for himself.

"So what are you doing in college, Marc? You want to do something besides model?"

He nodded. "This is fun, but at some point it will be over, right? I want to be a teacher. Special education I think they call it in English."

I blinked. "Wow. That sounds . . ." *Low paying and dreadful.* "That sounds wonderful." I thought about it for a moment. It really did say a lot about him that I liked, and I mentally kicked myself for my initial reaction. "I'm studying photography because I want to follow in my dad's footsteps—maybe travel photography instead of fashion, but that is how he met my mom—she walked runways like you."

He nodded and smiled, possibly a bit bashful.

"But sometimes when I hear something like 'I want to teach special ed,' I think I should do something else. I mean, what does a photographer offer the world?"

"Beauty," Marc said with a slightly confused look, as if to say, "Surely, you already knew that."

I looked down at my tray table, feeling shy. "You're the one who offers the world beauty."

He laughed, and I could swear he blushed. He started fidgeting. Great, I'd made him nervous just like Christiano warned.

"Should we go back to math?" I asked.

"Okay, but first answer me this. Why are you going to Rio de Janeiro?"

"I...um...honestly? To spend time with you."

He looked down, but I could see a wide smile. He grabbed my hand and squeezed it. "You're very sweet. And you're cute."

Heaven. This was heaven at forty-thousand feet. I'd never been happier.

Neither of us had been to Rio before, and we did the touristy things—took a cable car up Sugarloaf, the famous mountain in the harbor; walked on the beaches of Copacabana, Ipanema, and Leblon watching men play soccer. He told me a secret. There was a publisher in Germany that wanted nude photos of him for a monograph. They'd pay him a small fortune, but he didn't want to do it. All of the photographers they had under contract made him uncomfortable. In return, I told him I didn't want to finish school even though I only had three months left. There was a senior project that seemed impossible, and now I wanted to travel with him instead.

He squeezed my shoulder. "That's crazy, Trip. I don't want to be the reason you don't finish school. Hey! Look at that." He pointed at a rainbow flag up ahead. It turned out there was a small gay section of Ipanema Beach. When we reached it, we shared our first kiss. As our lips met, a shiver of delight rippled down the back of my neck.

We headed for the fanciest hotel on Copacabana I could find, and I sprang for a room with an incredible view of Sugarloaf and the crescent-shaped beach.

The moment the door was closed, I attacked him with kisses. My tongue found his and we shared the longest embrace I've ever known, perhaps a five-minute kiss. I wanted to be inside him that instant. My body screamed, "Now, now, now." But I took a deep breath and moved us to the bed to watch the strands of street lights flicker on as the sun set. I occasionally ran my fingers through his hair, making him close his eyes and smile.

I asked if I could undress him, and he moaned assent. It was unfair. Even his dick was gorgeous. I'm usually not much for blowjobs, but his cock was smooth, straight, and the perfect shape and size for sucking. I felt a deep longing running up my jaw. I had to have him in my mouth.

He groaned as I held his sides and lovingly glided my lips back and forth. I inhaled his clean scent—a mixture of that coconut fragrance and the sea spray we'd been walking past all day. He started to groan louder and grunt, then he pushed back on my head.

"Please stop. I don't want to cum yet. I want to cum with you inside me."

I'd brought condoms with me from home, and it felt surreal that I was actually going to use one of them with the man I'd fantasized about for over a year. I moved an easy chair so Marc could climb in on all fours and watch the glittering bay while I mounted his gorgeous ass and slowly thrust in. Oh. Oh, God. He was so tight and warm.

He gasped. "Gosh, you're big."

I practically purred at the compliment, but I didn't want to hurt him. "Should I pull out?"

"No," he said with effort. "Let me try."

I felt a pleasant ache in my chest and arms caused by my body's need to ravish Marc with abandon. I took long strokes with occasional pauses to bend over him and kiss his back and neck or massage his taut stomach. I had to close my eyes and breathe deep to steady my lust. I didn't want this to be over in three minutes.

Marc still whimpered with each thrust. "Can we try it with me riding you on the bed? Just for a bit. That will be easier for me. And I want to see your face."

I lifted him off the chair and held him in my arms. "Will you wear your pink cowboy hat for me?"

He gave me a mischievous smile. "Sure."

This was miraculous. A picture of this boy (and that hat) was my computer's wallpaper. Now, I was inside him, and from the euphoric look on his face this was just as blissful for him as for me.

He was better able to take me now, and his hole felt even more welcoming than before. Again, I had to restrain my urgent need to pound him senseless, especially considering the way he had begun to grind his hips. Pleasure rippled through my chest and throat as I sank in deeper and deeper.

"Do you want to go faster?" Marc asked, and I saw a look of need in his beautiful eyes.

"You read my mind," I said.

He bent his torso and kissed my lips. "Put me on my back."

Now that I was given free rein, I flipped him over, lifted his legs, and drove my dick into his ass.

Marc cried out with each stroke as I sped my pace—faster,

deeper, harder. Sweat dripped from my forehead. Marc thrashed like a wild animal, and he jerked his cock feverishly.

Watching him writhe in ecstasy was more than I could bear. I exploded deep inside him, filling the condom with my seed. At the same time he reached his peak, howling as jets of his cum hit his neck and cheek.

I reluctantly pulled out of him while my dick was still hard. He lay there panting for at least a minute.

"Can we shower and then cuddle?" he asked.

I kissed his mouth. "I'd like nothing more."

"Then after...can we have sex again?"

"Oh, God. Absolutely."

The fashion show featured underwear and bathing suits—I should have figured since it was Rio. I was in the audience watching for Marc. Holy cow, he came out in black briefs that were mostly sheer. His body was oiled. His face oozed confidence. He couldn't have looked more amazing. I wanted to fall at his feet and worship.

He gave me a mischievous look before turning and pacing down the catwalk. Damn, if his ass did not look perfect. I felt the heat rise in the room as the entire audience watched his miraculous backside shifting with every step. I barely had the presence of mind to take pictures with my phone.

Of course I sent them to Pete. I couldn't help but brag. "We spent the night together," I said in a text. "He's amazing."

Marc and I were at a steakhouse for dinner when Pete buzzed me back. "Fine. You win and you're right. He is amazing."

I felt a triumphant smirk come over my face, and Marc asked me what was up. Before I could stop myself, I explained how Pete said I would never do better, and now I had. Clearly and absolutely.

Marc frowned. "So...this is about a competition? About getting back at someone?"

Shit. "No! Not at all! I've wanted to meet you for months and months! I'm crazy about you."

He got up from his chair. "I feel like a conquest. I don't like that."

"I don't see you that way. I promise."

He put some money on the table. "Finish your meal. I want to be alone for a while."

I closed my eyes in anguish. Was he right? Was I using him because of his looks? Was that all that mattered to me?

I thought about it. Is it really so wrong to want someone because he's beautiful? Looking at Marc makes me happy. It's fair to want that, isn't it? It's only shallow if that's all I cared about. If Marc had been a conceited asshole instead of a sweetheart, I wouldn't have done all this. I would have gone back to Rochester right after the show.

I arrived at the hotel, prepared to plead my case, when something pink caught my eye. On one of the lobby couches, Marc had left his hat, his phone, and his math book. I collected them and brought them upstairs. All I found was a note. He said he was sorry, but he'd decided to go back to Prague early. God damn.

I called my mom again. She wasn't happy.

"Prague, now? If you're this reckless with money, Trip, we're not going to get you a condo when you graduate. You're going to have to live with us until you calm down."

I didn't hesitate. "I understand. I'll live with you guys if it means I can go."

I could hear my mom's disbelief. "Wow, Trip. Really? Well, if it's that important to you."

We hung up, and I called the concierge.

"Could you find me the first flight to Prague? First class? No, wait...coach."

Maybe it's because I live in a blocky brick dorm on a drab campus, but to me, Prague was almost as insanely beautiful as Rio. Gorgeous orange rooftops and church spires as far as I could see. Well, almost that far. Way in the distance there were some ugly Communist-era high-rise apartments, but if you ignored them, it was breathtaking. I felt a pain in my chest that I wasn't discovering this city with Marc the way we had in Rio. I'd known him less than two days, and I already missed him more than anything.

I decided it wasn't an invasion of privacy to turn on his phone and find his home number. I had to ask a passerby for help since his entries were in Czech. I called and his mom answered. He lived with his family? She told me he was at school, but I could stop by later. I found out they lived in the ugly high-rise neighborhood on the outskirts. I wondered if his family was poor. It was no big deal to me, but I knew from experience that a lot of regular folk are turned off by how I drop cash left and right. I guess just because you have a glamorous job, it doesn't mean you always make glamorous bucks. I hoped he didn't think I was trying to buy him.

I took a cab to his apartment, feeling beyond depressed. His family lived on the eleventh floor. The building look clean and in adequate condition, but I was surprised when his mother opened the door. They had sleek, modern furniture and a flat-screen TV. I suspected Marc's mother was wearing real pearls.

She clapped her hands. "You have his hat! He'll be so happy." She yelled for him, I think, and then motioned for me to sit on their black velvet couch. I did come in, but I remained standing.

Marc came out wearing a baby blue T-shirt and old jeans. He looked like he hadn't slept, but he was still breathtaking. I sighed.

"Here's your stuff," I said, handing him his textbook, phone, and hat.

He gave me a sweet smile and said "Thank you" in a quiet voice.

"I had to switch planes in Madrid," I continued, aware that I was almost mumbling, "and I bought you something so you won't lose your phone anymore. Attach this to your jeans." I handed him a black leather holster. It was designed by Christiano Bastini, of course. I hoped it would remind Marc of me.

"Well...I don't want to intrude," I said. "I just wanted to do something nice for you and to say I'm sorry. I'll get out of your hair now."

"Wait," he said and he ushered me out into the hallway. He pulled me into a tight hug. "That's the nicest thing anyone's ever done for me," he whispered. "I can't believe you flew thousands of kilometers to return my hat." He kissed me on the cheek.

My heart leaped. "Do you think you could give me a second chance?

"I want to, but we live so far apart. Perhaps—"

"Oh, I forgot to tell you. I'm moving to Prague today. I hear there's a shortage of algebra tutors." Good, I was back to my old self, and I made him laugh. "Seriously, though, I can visit you. A lot. If things work out, I could try to find a job here."

Marc smiled but gave me a scrutinizing look. "Do you promise to graduate first?"

"Yes, I promise."

"In that case..." Marc ran his hand down my side, and his lip curled in a grin. "There's a certain photography contract I may be able to get for you."

I tilted my head and smirked. "Oh, yeah?"
"Yes."
I kissed him on the lips. "I can't wait to start."

TIED UP

Emily Moreton

I'm just saying," Matt said, hoisting himself onto the counter in the tiny kitchen tacked onto Simon's studio and stealing a red apple. "This one's real, right?" he asked, checking, and bit into it when Simon looked up from his cameras and nodded.

"Just saying what?" Simon prompted after a couple of bites.

"Hmm?" Matt asked. "That I don't get the point of Christmas-themed erotic art. What are you going to do with these, put them on Christmas cards?"

Simon shrugged, eyes brightening in amusement. "I could. You could send them out to your family, with one of those 'Here's what I've been doing all year' letters."

"Oh yeah, I can just imagine it," Matt said, putting his apple down so he could type on an imaginary keyboard. "Dear Mom and Dad, Merry Christmas, hope Zoë and her kids are well. Here's a picture of me at my last job—it pays much better than painting. Please give Nanna and Pops the additional enclosed card when you see them, I'll call Christmas Day...."

Simon laughed. "Maybe not. Loretta commissioned them, for her gallery. She seems to think they'll sell."

Matt knew Loretta, a little, from displaying a series of his cityscape paintings there a few months back. "I think that's actually more disturbing than the thought of you putting them on Christmas cards," he said. "Remind me to turn her down if she invites me to any of the benefits."

The studio intercom buzzed, and Simon patted Matt's knee on his way to answer it. "I'm sure she wouldn't make you go naked," he said over his shoulder.

"I hate you," Matt called after him cheerfully, and hopped down, throwing his half-eaten apple away.

Simon's other model wasn't one Matt had met before—taller than him by a couple of inches, not quite lean enough to be mistaken for a bean pole, but closing in on it, with light brown hair and green eyes, skin pale where Matt's was darker. He grinned and reached out to shake Matt's hand. "Danny West."

"Matt Alvarez. Good to meet you."

"You too."

Simon rolled his eyes. "Always so polite. You make me want to break out the tea and crumpets."

"Do you have tea and crumpets?" Matt asked, prepared to be less than surprised if Simon said yes. Even for an erotic art photographer, he could be pretty strange.

"No. I'll take you for coffee when we're done if you like." Simon met his eyes for a long moment, then looked away to Danny. "You too, of course."

"Great," Danny said, sounding a little doubtful.

"All right," Simon said, after a moment of silence. "You two want to get ready?"

* * *

Simon hadn't bothered to make the whole room up to look like a bedroom, just set a bed with dark matte covers in the middle, a small table to the side with their props, the rest of the room empty but for Simon's equipment.

Matt had gotten over feeling weird about being naked in front of a total stranger and an old college friend with a camera after the first time, and at least Simon kept the heat up. The addition of mistletoe over the elaborate iron-framed bed made the whole thing a little stranger, but at least they weren't wearing Santa hats or reindeer antlers.

"Be thankful for small mercies," he muttered.

"Imagining jingle bell restraints?" Danny asked, wandering into the room behind Matt.

"Something like that," Matt agreed. Unsurprisingly, given his pallor and the time of year, Danny didn't have any tan lines, just darker pink around his nipples and an arrow of brown hair pointing down to his—okay, kind of impressive—cock. *This could be fun.*

"Ask me some time about a shoot I did in the UK, for Comic Relief," Danny said, then, in response to Matt's blank look, "Red Nose Day."

Matt could already imagine. "Maybe not."

The door to Simon's office opened and he came in, armed with a couple of cameras. He fixed one to the tripod and hung the other round his neck, glancing up to smile at them both, hovering by the bed. "I'm going to take some general shots, check the angles. Why don't the two of you get comfortable?"

Which was, ironically, the only time Matt felt really uncomfortable doing this—the change from naked-stranger-I'm-working-with to guy-I'm-getting-it-on-with was always awkward. "I'll just—" he said, and gave up, sitting on the edge of the bed and shuffling back until he was reclining against the pillows.

"Yeah," Danny said. His own smile was a little uncertain, but he crawled between Matt's legs willingly enough, resting one hand at Matt's side, and sliding the other up his neck to cup the back of his head. "You smell nice," he said, and leaned in to kiss Matt, light and soft.

That was hardly conducive to what Simon wanted from the photographs. Matt wrapped his arms around Danny's back, pulled him close so they could kiss properly, mouths opening against each other, Matt's tongue sliding against Danny's. He heard the click of Simon's camera, somewhere close, and shifted slightly, till Danny's leg slid between his, Danny's soft cock against his thigh. He moved a little against Danny, felt the first twitch of interest.

"That's good," Simon said softly. "You two look good."

"Say I'm pretty," Matt said, not looking away from Danny, "and I'm leaving."

Danny laughed, low enough to send a shiver through Matt's nerves, and the camera clicked. "Pretty's not the word," Simon said. "Lie flat, okay, Matt."

Danny lifted himself up on his arms, enough for Matt to wriggle down under him, skin against skin in all the right places, and it didn't seem like either of them were going to struggle to get it up this time. Danny settled over him again, cocks sliding together, and touched Matt's face softly. Matt turned into it, kissed his palm. It still wasn't really the right tone for what Simon wanted from his pictures, but it was kind of nice, and Danny seemed to like it.

Matt wondered if he should have taken Simon up on the offer to have the two of them meet before the shoot. These things were always easier if he'd slept with his co-model in advance.

"That's good," Simon said, sounding like he was moving. "I'm gonna switch cameras, then we'll shift to the real thing."

"Sounds good," Danny said, using the hand on Matt's cheek to turn him so they could kiss again. Matt closed his eyes, listened to Simon moving around somewhere close, and rubbed his hands down Danny's muscled back, the curve of his ass, figuring it was probably the last chance he was going to get to touch. Skin under his palms felt good, starting up a low burn of arousal that he knew would just get more as they went on.

He hoped Danny was one for happy endings.

"Okay," Simon said, close again.

Matt opened his eyes, turned his head to see Simon crouched by the bed, hands empty on his knees. The position pulled his pants tight in all the right places, and Matt felt the same flare of arousal he always did at seeing his friend in his element like this. It wasn't like he'd never slept with a photographer before— between the set-up and the camera, most shoots felt more like foreplay than work—but Simon had never seemed interested.

Matt forced himself to focus on the job, letting his eyes drift slightly to the camera on a tripod behind Simon, angled toward the head of the bed.

"Matt, bend your far leg," Simon said, nodding as Matt complied. "Little less. Danny, sit across him, turn your back to the camera slightly. These won't show anything below the waist, okay? That's it, good. Can you balance like that, leaning forward, no hands?"

Danny tried, tilted forward, and caught his balance on the wrought iron headboard. "Hold on," he said, shifting, dropping a little more weight onto Matt, who hissed without meaning to, Danny's balls pressing against his stiffening cock. Danny ignored it, and said, "Like this is okay."

Simon stood up, went behind the camera. "Yeah, all right.

Don't lean too far to the right, you'll block the shot. Matt, put your arms above your head, hands around the railings."

Matt complied, feeling the stretch in his ribs. When he glanced down, he could see Danny's cock resting against his stomach, half-hard. He thought about Danny pushing into him and shivered.

"Nice," Simon said. "Now if you could just look at his face, maybe," he added, sounding like he was laughing.

"Fuck off," Matt said pleasantly, meeting Danny's eyes, bright green, nothing like the mistletoe Matt could just see above them.

"Yeah, yeah." The camera clicked a couple of times. "Okay, Danny, let's go. His left hand needs to be low enough that we can see his face still, and the knots need to look real, please."

Danny leaned over, picked up one of the red satin scarves lying on the table, and ran it through his hands, not looking away from Matt. "I think I can manage that," he said.

The first loop of the material around his wrists was like an electric shock, same as always, straight down his spine and into his cock, his balls, everything going tight. Matt would be the first to admit it was a kink he was maybe a little too into to be putting on film, but Simon had asked, and it felt good. Really good, with the world narrowing down to Danny over him, the metal under his clenched fingers, the smooth material of the scarves against his skin, and the click of the camera, Simon's low voice, somewhere far away but still feeling like one more set of hands on him.

He was aware that he was breathing fast, his cock pressing against Danny's ass, but it was okay; Danny's pupils were blown wide, and it was clear he was far from unaffected.

"That okay?" Danny asked, fingertips light over Matt's curled fingers.

Matt tugged. There was a little give, but not enough for him to move, even when he unclenched his fingers and created more. He nodded.

"Matt, look at me," Simon said. He was still behind the camera, but he smiled. "Danny..."

Danny ran his hand down Matt's arm, bent to kiss his neck, the wrong side for the camera.

"Something like that, yeah," Simon said. He sounded slightly breathless, Matt thought, though it was hard to tell when his face was mostly hidden. Probably it was a good thing; meant the pictures were working. "That's nice."

Danny kissed Matt's neck again, hand sliding even further down to run a dry finger over his nipple. Danny's hips were moving, a tiny rocking motion that slid his cock against Matt's stomach, and Matt couldn't remember when he'd started doing it, only that it felt hot against his skin, burning him.

"That's good," Simon said again. "I'm gonna switch camera positions. Danny, there's condoms on the table, like usual, and lube. Close-ups, no faces—your fingers in him, then your cock. All right?"

"Yeah," Danny said, sounding hesitant.

"What?" Matt asked, trying to pull out of the headspace he could feel himself dropping into, remember that this wasn't all about him, even though it felt like it.

Danny hesitated, then shook his head. "It's nothing." He smiled, and it didn't seem forced. "Everything's fine. You need anything?"

Matt shook his head, since none of the things he wanted to ask for were appropriate for a professional relationship, and mostly weren't things he wanted to ask Danny for anyway.

Danny nodded, and moved off of Matt, sitting on the edge of the bed to reach for the condom packet. Matt shifted, glad for the restraints so he couldn't reach down and get himself off. No orgasms in this shoot—one of the models for a different set of pictures in the same theme had made a cum/snow joke that had given Simon a complex about it.

"All right," Simon said, back behind the camera. "Matt, bend your far leg again, right up this time, and slide the other one over. Danny, between his legs. I want to see both of you."

Danny knelt up again, the thin condom nearly invisible, though Matt knew Simon would Photoshop out any evidence of it, and slid one bent leg under Matt's. His fingers were slick with lube as they skimmed over Matt's balls, making him hiss again, and he slid two into Matt with an ease that obviously surprised him.

"Proper pre-planning," Matt started, not bothering to finish when Danny laughed. He didn't add that he'd learned the hard way, with photographers who weren't like Simon, weren't careful of their models the way he was.

Danny had nice fingers, long and thin, and it felt better than it had when Matt had done it to himself, alone in the tiny changing room, even though Danny was going too slow. Danny rubbed his thumb against the patch of skin behind Matt's balls, then over them, circling at the same rhythm as his fingers were moving in Matt's ass, and Matt turned his head from the camera, his breathing speeding up all over again. "Easy," Danny said softly.

"Yeah," Matt gasped. His cock ached, and his skin was hot enough that Danny's thumb felt like ice on him. "Keep going."

Danny added another finger, and the camera clicked, and Matt moaned, even knowing he'd be humiliated at the memory of this, when Danny, for all that he was hard, barely seemed to be emotionally affected at all. Matt twisted his hands, banged his thumb against the headboard and hardly felt it. The click of the camera felt like another pair of hands on his body, stronger than it ever had before, multiplied by it being Simon behind the camera, by how easy it was to imagine Simon himself touching.

"Matt, you ready?" Simon asked, and Matt realized he'd closed his eyes at some point. He couldn't quite make them open, just turned his head and nodded. "Danny?"

Danny must have done the same, because his fingers went away, and he shifted, hands on Matt's knees, pushing his legs open and back, until they were pressed almost to Matt's chest, held in place more by Danny's hands than by anything Matt was doing.

Matt clenched his hands tight on the iron bars, and felt the head of Danny's cock against his ass. He took a deep breath, tried to relax a little more, like he wasn't already plenty relaxed, and then Danny was pushing into him, huge and hot, filling him up until his balls were pressed against Matt's ass and his cock was against Matt's prostate and he could hardly breathe through it. He felt a dab of something cool against his stomach, realized it was his cock, leaking fluid.

"Just like that," Simon said, too close to be at the tripod still. "You're so hot."

Matt's hands were shaking, from arousal, from how tight they were clenched on the bars, from Simon and the compliment, even if it was just professional. He felt like he might explode if something didn't happen. "God, please, move," he gasped.

Danny squeezed his knee, but didn't say anything.

"Danny, fuck me, please, I won't cum, I just need..." He tried to shift his hips, couldn't, with the way he was bent.

"I can't," Danny said, voice strained.

"It's okay," Matt managed. "I just need something...."

"No, I really can't," Danny said again. "My boyfriend and I

made a deal, he doesn't object to me doing this as long as I don't
have sex."

Matt swallowed hard, wishing Simon would hurry up, call it
done. "You've got your cock in my ass."

"It's only sex if I move," Danny said. Matt wanted to look
at him, see if he really believed what he was saying, because
if he did, his boyfriend was one dumb fuck, but his eyes were
burning. "This is just—another way to touch you."

"Christ," Matt moaned, and turned his head back the other
way, panting for breath. His whole body ached with the need to
cum, the need for someone to move, in him, on him.

"I'm sorry," Danny said. He sounded genuine, enough for
Matt to nod, okay, sure, if you say so.

"Few more seconds," Simon said. "You're nearly done,
you're perfect, both of you, you're amazing," and then it was
over, Simon stepping back and saying, "That's it, all done."

Danny squeezed Matt's knee again, starting to pull out.

"Untie me," Matt gasped, letting his legs drop back onto the
bed. He must have been in position longer than he'd realized,
his thigh muscles burning.

Danny slid the rest of the way out, already moving away, the
head of his cock bumping Matt's balls, and Matt groaned, tried
to thrust up into it, except Danny was already gone.

Matt felt someone move, sit on the edge of the bed. He made
himself open his eyes, look up at Simon, who, yeah, was definitely into the photographs. Behind Simon, at the edge of the
room, he could just see Danny, one hand braced on the wall, the
other moving in an unmistakable rhythm. He wondered what
Danny's boyfriend had to say about him getting off on having
his cock in Matt's ass.

"Untie me," he said again. "God, please, I need…"

Simon ran one finger round the scarf over Matt's right wrist, watching his own hand. "I could," he said idly. "Or I could leave you like this. I think you like it."

"Fuck you," Matt groaned. His hips jerked up without him meaning to, trying to find something to rub against when there was nothing but air. "Simon, come on."

"I think I like you like this," Simon said. Distantly, Matt heard the door open and close. "I think I like it very much," Simon added, and he moved, so fast Matt barely registered it, and then Simon was crouched over him, over his legs. "And I think you will too."

Matt cried out at the first touch of Simon's mouth on his cock, taking his whole length into warm and wet and, fuck, so good he thought he'd cum immediately, so much better than he'd ever imagined. Simon didn't mess about, just sucked him, hard, bringing one hand down to roll Matt's balls in his palm, making Matt shout again, so turned on he could hardly stand it. He tried to reach for Simon, automatic, and the restraints held, snapped his hands back. He twisted his whole upper body instead, not even sure what he was trying to get when he had Simon sucking his cock, Simon's hand on his balls, Simon, oh God, shoving three fingers into his ass, fucking him with them, and it was too much.

Matt shouted, back arching off the bed, and felt Simon pull back off his cock, but it didn't matter, because he was coming, so hard he thought he might pass out, his whole body one long pulse of pleasure.

When it was over, he collapsed back onto the bed, feeling weak, aftershocks still zinging through his extremities. He opened his eyes, Simon fuzzy around the edges above him. "That was," he said, and couldn't think of the end. He'd never even realized Simon was interested, had always told himself he was seeing something he wanted to see that wasn't there.

"That was your turn," Simon said, hands on the buttons of his dark shirt. "Now it's mine."

"Oh God," Matt moaned, letting his head fall back against the pillow. His cock twitched, expressing its own interest in the proceedings. "You want me to suck you like this?"

"No." Simon kneed his way up the bed, naked, cock sticking up between his legs, and it should have looked funny, but it just made Matt a little dizzy. He wondered if this was how Simon saw the world, through his camera lens. "I want you to let me untie you, turn over, and lie still while I hold you down and fuck you."

Matt's world blurred out a little, images tumbling through his mind so fast he got even more dizzy. Simon's hand on the scarves was enough to pull him back though, everything suddenly sharp and bright. He rolled his right wrist as his hand came free, then his left, but that was all he had a chance to do before Simon was turning him onto his stomach and pushing him down, hands on his biceps. He breathed, felt Simon breathe somewhere above and behind him, and then Simon was pushing into him, same place Danny's thick cock had just been.

Simon shifted forward, putting more weight onto his hands, letting his cock sink a little deeper into Matt, who moaned, feeling himself getting hard again, not that he'd ever really gone soft after his orgasm.

"Do it," he said, muffled into the pillow.

That seemed to be all the encouragement Simon needed; he pulled out nearly all the way, then pushed back in, hard and deep, enough to shift Matt's hips against the mattress, to rub his cock and balls on thick cotton sheets. He groaned, then again when Simon repeated it, again, again, fucking him hard and fast, almost careless, balls slapping Matt's ass with every thrust. Matt curled his fingers tight around the pillow, trying to move

against Simon's thrusts, but his second orgasm was already fluttering on the edges of his vision, in the base of his spine, and it
was all he could do to hold on and take it.

"God, God," Simon panted, rhythm breaking up, and Matt
went with it, fucking himself on Simon's cock, fucking his own
into the mattress, until his second orgasm broke over him, his
ass clenching around Simon's length inside him, and Simon gave
a broken moan, hips stuttering, and came as well.

Matt felt like he was floating back down to full awareness from
somewhere very far away. His whole body felt like an overcooked
noodle, his cock and balls stung, and his ass ached around the
soft length of Simon's cock, still in him, Simon's weight still on
him where he'd collapsed as he rode out what had felt, to Matt,
like a pretty intense orgasm.

"You okay?" Simon asked, patting haphazardly at Matt's
shoulder.

"Better if I wasn't breathing through a pillow," Matt said.

Simon moved, sliding out of him, and fumbled the condom
off. Matt reached out one limp, exhausted arm, and caught his
wrist before he could get up, pulling him back down so they
were curled together, skin against sweat damp skin. Simon
looked worried, even as he mirrored Matt's hold on him.

"Kiss me," Matt said, already leaning in. It wasn't like
kissing Danny had been, as much a performance as something
for them. It was more, better, even though they were both too
worn out to do a great job of it. Affectionate, ten years of friend-
ship behind it.

"Okay?" Matt said, feeling the tug of exhaustion.

"Yeah," Simon said, pulling him closer. "Perfect."

* * *

Three months later:

Pretty much the last thing Matt wanted to hear was the rattle of his curtains being opened, not least because it was followed by way too much daylight for the blanket over his head to take care of.

"I hate you," he said, squinting his eyes shut to see if that helped. All it did was make his head ache more.

"No you don't," Simon said cheerfully, the bed shifting as he sat down. "It's Christmas, I've got coffee and painkillers, you love me."

"I'd love you more if you had breakfast," Matt said, turning so he could rest his head, still under the blanket, against Simon's thigh. "Or if you hadn't let me drink so much last night."

"I'm not the one who thought he could out-drink John's Marine friends," Simon pointed out, patting Matt's shoulder through the blankets. "I didn't want to spoil your fun."

"You just wanted me at your mercy this morning so I'd agree to something ridiculous like, I don't know, lunch with your sister or carol singing with Mrs. Williams from downstairs."

"My sister's a five-hour flight away, and your singing voice is appalling." Simon rubbed Matt's shoulder again, then started easing the blankets away. "Come on, get up, we've got a Christmas present."

"I'm kind of hoping we've got more than one," Matt grumbled, giving up his half-hearted fight with the covers. Coffee did sound awfully appealing.

"This is for both of us—a joint present." Simon, when Matt emerged, was dressed already in soft jeans and a black sweatshirt, but still barefoot.

"It better not be china," Matt said firmly. They weren't even technically living together yet, he so wasn't ready for the implications of picking out china patterns, especially when they both had a full set already.

"It's not," Simon promised. "Guess again."

He gestured to a brown paper parcel leaning against the bedroom wall—maybe three feet by four, and flat, with a "Fragile" label stuck on it.

"Who's it from?" Matt asked, suspecting he already knew the answer.

"Loretta," Simon said, somewhere between bashful and pleased.

"Oh God," Matt groaned, falling back onto the bed and pulling a pillow over his eyes.

Though he would admit, under duress, that there were worse ways to spend Christmas than reenacting that photo shoot.

THOSE
ALMOND EYES

Jay Starre

I t started with a kiss, totally unexpected and totally smoking hot.

Kevin had been looking forward to the photo shoot ever since he'd scored the gig. An avid surfer himself, shooting a layout for *Surfside* magazine was a dream come true. Then, he was given the model's name and he was really stoked.

Blaze Li.

The first time he became aware of the hot young model was only six months earlier as he flipped through the pages of a trendy New York magazine called *Uptown*. A glossy ad featured Blaze alone. Dressed in cream and beige loungewear, his golden skin and sleek black mane stood out, as did his eyes. The most amazing almond in both color and shape, they stared directly out at him from the page, smoldering and intimate.

The second time was only a month later. On this occasion there wasn't much left to the imagination as Blaze's body was revealed in its rippled, sleek entirety. It was an underwear ad on a downtown New York City billboard. And it was enormous.

The third time was a few weeks earlier, in Rome at a haute couture show. A photographer buddy of his had conned him into attending, and in the end he was glad he did. The show was ridiculous and outrageous as expected, but fun, and he was enjoying himself thoroughly until out strolled Blaze Li.

Naked from the waist up, his smooth torso was dappled with silver and jade glitter, while woven into the sleek strands of his long black hair were matching silver and green feathers. His amazing eyes were accented by outlandish swirls of jade-green makeup. His pants were striped in the same silver and green and clung to his body like a second skin. He was barefoot and padded along the runway like some exotic Asian tiger about to pounce.

When he turned and headed in the opposite direction, Kevin got a good long look at the compact globes of his perfect ass. A raging hard-on throbbed in his jeans. That stiff dick only subsided temporarily, resurfacing shortly afterward when he was face to face with the hot model backstage.

His buddy took him behind the scenes into the chaos of the dressing room where he, along with a half-dozen others, was introduced to Blaze. It was a brief encounter, a mere nod and a hint of a smile from the sexy model, but their eyes met and held. Kevin's cock strained against the inside of his fly.

That was it. Now, they were scheduled to spend the morning together. Just the two of them.

The beach at Noosa he'd chosen for their photo shoot was clothing-optional and a bit of a hike from the road, which suited him perfectly. It was January and the height of Queensland's summer. The Australian gums and eucalyptus that lined the shore offered some protective shade, and a morning breeze off the surf felt deliciously soothing.

It was only 7:00 A.M. and Kevin was wondering if the model

was going to be fashionably late when a light tap on the shoulder
from behind startled him.

"You're quiet! Hey, how ya doin'? I'm Kevin Grant, your
photographer for the day."

"Yeah. We met a few weeks ago in Rome."

The voice was subdued. Just a ghost of a smile pursed the
bowed lips, but those eyes met his with direct intensity and held
them.

"Yeah, right. Uhhh, let's get started while it's still relatively
cool and the light's how I want it."

Blaze merely nodded. Neither were big talkers, and with no
nonsense and no bullshit, they got to work.

Kevin had his own style. He worked alone with one camera,
no lighting, and no attending makeup artists to fuss over his
models. Some of them refused to be shot that way, but Blaze had
been fine with it.

No wonder. As he donned one swimsuit after the other, from
skimpy pairs of nut-huggers to baggy knee-length surf shorts,
every square inch of flesh revealed was without blemish and
perfectly sculpted in rippling muscle.

His body was lean without being emaciated, muscular
without being muscle-bound, and at all times gracefully masculine. Kevin ate it up with his camera, while enjoying a pleasantly
throbbing stiffie under his own surf shorts all the while.

They chatted only intermittently. Blaze revealed he was not a
native New Yorker but was born and raised in Hawaii. And like
many people there, he was the result of the island's racial melting
pot. His mother was Chinese and his father Portuguese. He had
been a college gymnast and had given it up only when modeling
offered him good money and a chance to move to New York.

Kevin offered a bit of his own history. He too had been a
college athlete. A swimmer, he still swam regularly, and of

course he loved surfing. But his true love was photography, and he was happy to be making his own mark in the industry.

The kiss that started it all happened just after a dozen or so changes.

Ensconced in the shade of the woods just up from the sandy beach, Blaze stripped off one suit before donning the other right there in the open. It was a nude beach after all, and none of the few sunbathers lounging nearby took noticeable heed.

Of course, Kevin couldn't take his eyes off the luscious sight of the hot model in the buff. His golden skin was nearly hairless. Only a scant and obviously trimmed patch of black fuzz grew above his cock and balls.

And they were very nice cock and balls. Full nads snuggled tight below a slim but lengthy tube of caramel-brown meat. With Kevin's eyes on him, and the camera, that slim tube did seem to swell slightly, which did nothing to deter from the sensuality of the pics Kevin was taking. Nothing wrong with a bit of a bulge under the swimsuit being featured.

Kevin had just managed to catch that tantalizing bulge in the perfect light as a beam of morning sunlight zeroed in on it through the dappled shade. He lowered the camera, a big smile plastered all over his face.

Blaze came at him with quiet but determined grace. One moment he was five paces away, the next he was right there in Kevin's face. Hands came up, one slid behind his neck and the other cupped his chin. Those amazing almond eyes stared into his as pursed lips gently came forward and landed on his own wide mouth.

It was soft and gentle, supple lips just touching his own. He gasped, opening his mouth, and just like that a tongue slipped into him.

Clutching his camera in one trembling hand, he managed

to reach around with the other and grab hold of one cheek of
Blaze's compact ass. Solid heat emanated through the thin material of the swimsuit while the round cheek itself pushed back
and rolled against his spread fingers.

Totally dumbfounded, and totally spellbound, Kevin surren-
dered to the tongue-stabbing kiss. Blaze continued to hold his
head and face with his slender hands as he devoured his mouth.
It was a wet, sloppy, and deep kiss, but it was languidly gentle
for all that.

And it was driving Kevin crazy. His hand on that rock-solid
butt cheek squeezed and kneaded almost frantically. Now that
the likelihood of exploring that gorgeous body was literally
within his grasp, he could hardly hold back. He wanted desperately to drag the hot model back into the quiet of the woods and
ravage him.

Blaze's eyes were half-shut, soft and warm as he stared
into Kevin's big blue ones. His hands were firm as he held the
photographer's face immobile and continued to suck, lick, and
tongue his lips and gaping mouth.

Then, Blaze pressed forward, just enough to mash his crotch
against Kevin's. The blond photographer gurgled around the
tongue sliding toward his tonsils and pressed back. A throbbing
tube of heat ground against his own swollen shank.

Although he was wearing board shorts and a tank top, Blaze
wore only that skimpy green swimsuit. Kevin wanted nothing
more than to tear that suit off!

Blaze broke the kiss with a sloppy smack. Pulling away only
slightly and with eyes still half-closed, he offered just a hint of a
smile. "There's a quiet place close by. I checked it out yesterday.
Want to?"

"Fuck yeah...but I need to take some more photos. Can we
do that there?"

Kevin was astounded at his own ability to remain focused on the job, with that lean, hot body pressing against him.

"Absolutely. You can take some of me in the buff too, if you like."

That decided, they stepped apart, and without saying more than a few necessary words, scooped up Kevin's camera bag, the tote bag with the swimsuits in it, and Blaze's own small pack and headed down the beach hand in hand.

Kevin felt like a kid off on an adventure when Blaze had taken his hand and led him down the sandy shore, that barely discernible smile on his wet lips and wearing just that skimpy suit. Together they passed the score of scattered nude sunbathers before they reached the end of the beach and headed off on a sandy trail through the woods.

Five minutes was all it took. A side trail rose to a stepping-stone path around some jumbled boulders and then back down to a tiny cove surrounded by densely wooded rocky bluffs.

A massive flat stone jutted out over the sea a few feet below.

Blaze spoke quietly, and directly. "I'd love it if you rimmed me. Then fucked me."

Fortunately the sun was prevented from frying them by one of the wooded outcroppings to their right. The breeze was stiff off the water and the waves splashed energetically below, spray coming up now and then to coat the slab in scattered shallow pools. It was perfect.

Perfect for eating out the perfect ass. Kevin couldn't help chuckling with nervous excitement. "Sure, Blaze. Want to show me that awesome, photogenic ass of yours?"

The sexy model offered an outright grin for the first time that morning before he dropped his armload on a dry spot on the rocks and turned to face the ocean. Tall and slender, with broad shoulders, a muscular back, and a narrow waist that emphasized his jutting butt, he was outlined by a clear blue sky and an endless ocean before he bent over and spread his feet wide apart.

"How's it look?"

He wriggled the suited ass teasingly before grabbing the waistband of his trunks and shoving downward. He stepped out of it and kicked it aside.

Kevin was awestruck. What a divine ass! Taut and smooth, creamy brown and divided by a deep crack, it was almost too good to be true. He dropped his stuff beside Blaze's and lunged forward to drop to his knees behind that gorgeous butt and begin to worship it.

"It looks pretty darn tasty," he replied with a grunt as he reached out to seize the firm cheeks and pull them apart.

Deep in that valley, a hairless hole pouted. The blond photographer dove for it.

Just like Blaze had kissed his mouth, Kevin kissed that sweet asshole. He planted his lips on the puckered rim and kissed gently at first, holding the cheeks open, then as Blaze wriggled back against his lips, he began to tease and lick at the entrance.

"Oh yeah...take your time. I love it."

The voice was sultry and low, eager but not demanding. The quaver Kevin detected in it only encouraged him to test the hole's resistance. After sucking on it with wet slurps, he began to probe with the pointed end of his tongue.

"Ohhh! Yeah! Please!"

The lips pushed outward and the inner flesh yawned. Kevin stabbed deep and twirled his tongue. That amazing ass squirmed and heaved in his hands. The compact globes tensed and convulsed, ramming back against his face and then riding it up and down.

As requested, he took his time, lapping, probing, and sucking as the heated-up model pushed backward and humped his mouth and nose with wilder and wilder abandon. Eventually he was sitting over Kevin as the photographer leaned backward on his knees and clung to the taut mounds of his satin-smooth ass.

It was more than a little gratifying to have the subdued model getting so worked up. Kevin ate out his ass much longer than he might have otherwise. It really seemed to get Blaze steamed up, and all that wriggling was opening up that snug asshole too.

By the time he came up for air, the puckered slot was dripping spit and snapping open and shut with frenetic greed. He was pleased to see how pink and swollen it had grown, and was more than ready to pound his aching cock home if Blaze was ready for it.

He asked. "Can I fuck you now Blaze?"

He held that beautiful butt apart with his hands, staring at the wet slot as it continued to open and close like a gulping mouth and bit his lip with anticipation. Blaze wriggled again and arched his back, obviously teasing as he pushed outward with his sphincter and showed off a slippery pink gap that quivered delightfully.

Blaze chuckled as he replied. "Yep. Go for it. Get naked while I get some lube from my pack. I brought some along just in case you fell for my charms."

"Who wouldn't?" Kevin said with a snort as he abandoned that butt temporarily and got to his feet.

He kicked off his shorts and sandals while throwing off his tank top. Barefoot, he splashed through the warm puddles of salt water as he approached Blaze again. The model had quickly rummaged through his bag and found the lube he'd brought.

With lithe athleticism, he dropped to his hands and knees and presented himself to the approaching photographer. "Lube me up. I'm all yours."

That direct offer spoken in that sultry, almost solemn tone were steamy hot, but hotter yet were the wink and smirk Blaze offered as he craned his head around and looked back at the blond photographer.

The dude was not only built like a lean god, he was handsome as hell too. High cheekbones emphasized the wide-set big eyes. A long finely shaped nose divided them while pointing directly down at the small but lush mouth and lips. A dimple in the chin added a sweetness to the angular shape.

It was a little intimidating to be getting ready to fuck such a gorgeous creature, but with that perky ass waving at him and that gentle smirk egging him on, he got down on his knees in a warm puddle of salt water and went for it.

His released cock reared up like a threatening tower of purple purpose. A blond, he was fair-skinned but his cock when it was hard grew thick and dark. At the moment, it was so stiff it hurt. Blaze had handed him a condom along with the lube and he quickly tore it open and wrapped up, feeling how hard and eager his cock was. Then, he planted it between the spread ass cheeks while he upended the bottle of lube and squirted a generous stream of the clear goo all over ass and dick.

His hands shook as he tossed the lube aside and grabbed hold of that offered ass. The cheeks were so damn firm he could hardly get over it. He squeezed them not all that gently and pulled them as wide apart as he could. Blaze chuckled as he dropped his head down to nestle in his folded arms and slid his knees wider on the slick slab.

The strands of his midnight-black hair fell around his neck and onto the wet rock. Even his hair was gorgeous, long and straight with just a hint of a wave. Seized with a nearly overpowering lust, Kevin reached forward and grasped a handful of those silky strands. He pulled back as he planted the knobbed head of his cock at the entrance to Blaze's puckered, well-licked hole and drove inward.

"Yeah! Perfect!"

The sultry cry of encouragement had Kevin groaning. The hole, wet with spit and coated with lube, was still snug enough to put up a clamping resistance to the plunge of his flared cock-head, but it hardly mattered as he shoved deep and watched it disappear entirely between the oozing pink ass-lips.

Once he had the knob buried, the shank that followed was easier to feed into that pulsing shaft. He buried half of it before he pulled back out so that the flange of his knob tickled the snapping sphincter again and Blaze was squirming around it with open-mouthed moans.

He held onto a thick strand of dark hair in one hand while he squeezed the solid cheek of the model's butt with the other and slowly fed him back the thick meat he'd withdrawn, and then some.

His cock was a good ten inches long and thick besides. He had to be feeling it! From the way he moaned, it wasn't a bad feeling he was getting either. Kevin began to pump in and out, each time a little deeper. Blaze only moaned louder while he allowed his knees to slide father apart in the slippery slab and gobbled up cock with his willing asshole.

Spray from the splashing surf hit them with the occasional dousing, while the sun played tag with the overhanging gum trees and the temperature varied dramatically, steamy hot one moment, pleasantly cool the next.

But there was no variation in the steamy pump-and-grind of cock burrowing its way home in that gorgeous amber ass that willingly sucked it deep. Kevin released his hold on Blaze's hair and leaned backward on his calves, holding the model by the slender waist and lunging back and forth with his hips.

Blaze met his thrusts with a rhythmic drive of his own hips. Face still down on his arms, his ass rose up in the air behind him, sleek and round and quivering as he rode the cock pumping his hot asshole.

The kneeling body was so beautiful it wasn't enough just to fuck it, Kevin had to feel it too. He ran his hands up the firm back, feeling the solid muscle on either side of the deep divide on the backbone. The skin was smooth as silk. He found his way to the broad shoulders and gripped them with each hand. Pulling back on those muscular shoulders, he drove forward with his cock, slamming it balls-deep with every lunge.

Blaze took it at first with a mixture of groans and grunts, pushing back with that lush round ass to swallow all that was offered, until he all at once reared up and back. On his knees, he squatted over the thrusting pole and reached back to pull Kevin's face against his. Greedy mouth clamped over his and sucked in his tongue as the model craned his head around and kissed him.

It was unbelievable. Kevin rammed his cock in and out while he sucked in Blaze's tongue and gurgled incoherently. But now he also had the model's sleek torso to play with.

The stomach was amazing. Flat except for the rippled muscle of his abs, there was no hint of hair, and somehow Kevin knew it was natural and not shaved. Above the long stomach, the slabs of his chest flared outward like the broad muscles of his back. Each firm pec was punctuated by a small brown nipple he just had to tweak and tug on.

Quickly those nubs grew swollen and erect. He teased them mercilessly as Blaze groaned louder and began to drive his round ass down over the cock fucking it.

They both got wilder, writhing and lunging, until a particularly lusty wave managed to leap up and drench them. They broke their kiss, laughing and gasping before clamping their mouths together again and continuing their vigorous grind-and-pump, albeit dripping salt water.

Kevin had resisted the call of release, because he sensed it would be the end of their romp, but eventually he couldn't stand it any longer. He let go of one quivering nipple and dropped his hand to the jutting cock at Blaze's waist.

It was definitely not as thick as Kevin's but it was nearly as long. It reared up stiff and twitching to slap against that firm belly. The photographer merely stroked it at first with teasing fingers, smiling around Blaze's tongue in his mouth as it lurched violently and drooled copiously.

With one nipple being tweaked, his cock being teased with tantalizing fingertips, and cock ramming up into him from behind, Blaze finally abandoned any semblance of graceful aplomb.

He broke their kiss and cried out. "Jerk me off, Kevin! Now!"

Kevin choked up with laughter—and sheer joy—and did as he was asked. He wrapped his hand around the rigid pole and began to pump it rapidly, thrusting upward with his hips at the same time.

Cock ramming deep into his ass and a fist yanking on his own cock, Blaze rose to the occasion and humped that thrusting shaft with equal force. He slammed down over Kevin's cock, his firm ass cheeks jiggling now and his lean torso heaving as he gasped for air.

"Too damn good, Kevin. I'm done in!"

Kevin felt the cock in his hand swell into quivering rigidity just before a surge of cum rose up the column and exited the straining purple head. Goo shot straight in the air to splatter that lean torso in a violent spray.

Equally violent were the convulsions wracking Blaze's asshole. Kevin felt those spasms gripping and massaging his thrusting cock like a gulping mouth. He let out a savage grunt and let loose.

His cum filled the condom encasing it. His shaft throbbed and pulsed in time with the spasms of the steamy asshole surrounding it. Blaze rode their mutual orgasm to the very end, slamming down with his firm ass until every drop had been sucked out of both their cocks.

Spray from another energetic wave hit them. Laughing, they disengaged and rose to face each other.

"We still have to get some more shots," Blaze reminded him with a smile and a wink.

"Absolutely. Let's not waste any time. Grab a suit and strike a pose."

This time around, the shots Kevin got had a definite sexual innuendo to them. Blaze offered smoldering smiles and spread his lean thighs apart as he thrust his hips forward, or turned and jutted out his amazing ass with one hand planted on a perky cheek. And those were the ones where he was wearing a suit!

Kevin had to grin as he realized that many of them would not do for *Surfside* magazine, but there were other buyers he could approach. He and Blaze could make some good money off the results of the steamy day's work!

Blaze called an end to the photo shoot in a particularly exciting way. Discarding the last pair of board shorts he'd paraded around in for the camera, the almond-eyed model dropped to his knees and leaned forward on his flattened palms. Head back and dark hair flowing down his shoulders, his round ass jutted out from his slender waist, perfect and alluring.

Between the solid cheeks, the pink hole quivered, leaking lube and nicely swollen from their wild fuck earlier.

"Get a quick photo of that, slave-driver, then are we done for the day? I'd like to retire to my air-conditioned hotel room for a well-deserved shower. And if you care to join me, a well-deserved second round!"

Kevin was busy snapping shots of that gorgeous pose, the white-capped sea and azure sky framing the amber body and that inviting, fuck-hole being offered up for round two.

BIG PICTURE

Cynthia Hamilton

The night I brought Aiden home to my Park Slope apartment, to my bed, I had no idea who he was. I only knew that everything about him looked familiar, but I didn't know why.

It wasn't just that I'd seen the icy blue of his eyes before, or the way he wore stubble so well on his chiseled jaw. It was the ripple of muscles on his torso and the kissable, lone freckle that rested above his navel like a beauty mark, a constellation. It was the tempting hollow between firm oblique and hip.

He was shaved where it counted. A neatly groomed stripe of dark curls provided a bed of contrast for his swollen cock, but the root of the perfect organ was smooth. His balls were completely bare, hot like warmed satin against my lips.

He moaned, and I realized I'd been so busy wondering where I might know him from that I hadn't been paying attention to the way I was mouthing at his dick. Now I wasn't sure what I'd just done to provoke the sound, or how to get him to make it again. I hummed encouragement and took his shaft in my hand

while I suckled long, wet kisses at the tender flesh where cock
and balls met, pulling playfully with my lips.

That was it.

His body arched, straining, his dick throbbing against my
fingers, and another sound—this time a smooth growl—left his
throat.

Still in my briefs, I ached.

I got up to my knees and kissed my way up the underside of
his shaft, then took his swollen crown into my mouth. A deep
breath through my nose, a careful alignment over him, and his
smooth, warm glans slid all the way along my tongue. He tasted
clean, that genuine smell of soap and good, pure sweat, and a
hint of some earthy cologne. And for as good as he smelled, he
felt even better. Thick, smooth, that tiny vein pulsing with his
elevated heartbeat.

He reached down and tangled his hands into my hair, bucking
his hips and thrusting along my hard upper palate, all the way
to the softness at the back of my throat. I guided the base of his
shaft with my other hand. He moaned for me again, fucking my
throat with rising urgency, bending his knees and planting his
feet on the bed for leverage.

A sheen of sweat glowed bronze on his skin, and the contrac-
tions of his abs were hypnotic. He curled his hips upward, sharp
thrust after thrust. He was gorgeous, and he was in me, swelling
and straining now. So fucking close. I dug my nails into the
back of his thigh and pulled at his cock with a tight tug of
suction. Yes. There it was. He strangled back a groan, and hot
jets of seed pulsed up his length, spilling down the back of my
throat where I could easily swallow. I cradled him in the heat of
my mouth, shifting slightly and sweeping slow passes with my
tongue until his hips jerked and he protested in a breathy voice
that he couldn't take any more.

We lay together, fondling and kissing absently. His gaze was still dreamy when he nudged me over to take me.

I awoke briefly to the alarm chiming on his phone and the first reluctant purples of sunrise. He kissed me, murmured something that didn't quite register, and was gone. I rolled over into the warmth his body had left behind, asleep again before my front door closed behind him.

An hour later I awoke again, alone in my bed. The whole thing felt like it had been a dream. But there were two empty glasses on the table and the spent foil packets on the nightstand to remind me that it had been real—I'd really picked up a guy at Rachel's TriBeCa loft party and brought him home. It wasn't the sort of thing I usually did. It was rare for me to even go out on a weeknight. Stopping at the gym on my way home from work didn't count.

On the train, I replayed the evening over and over, my hands remembering how he felt, my tongue sweeping the roof of my mouth with memories of the firmness of him thrusting into me. My balls felt heavy. I tingled when I thought of the smell of him. I tried to distract myself with reading and then nudging my finger around the pointless games on my phone, but all thoughts wandered back to Aiden.

I got off the subway a stop early, counting on the brisk walk to clear my mind so that I could focus. Turning up my collar against the wind, I stepped up to the corner of Broadway and Houston, waiting for the light to change. And there was Aiden—his sultry eyes and his perfect stubble and the rippling expanse of his abs.

Now I knew where I'd seen him.

"Holy crap," I muttered out loud. The light changed, beckoning the crowd across the lanes of paused cars and yellow cabs, but I couldn't move. Foot traffic shifted around me like a stream parting to flow around a rock, then joining seamlessly back together, oblivious to the interruption.

The canvas billboard had to be fifty feet tall, pulled sleek and taut to the building by the reinforced rings along its edge. His leg was bent at the knee, elbow resting on it, torso twisted toward the camera to show the curl of his tanned body. His stubble, writ so large I could almost feel its texture under my palms again, looked barely a day old. Lips that had kissed mine just a few hours before were parted just slightly with a hint of a sly smile—as if, as long as I'd happened upon him in only his underwear, he might as well invite me to stay.

The wind picked up, and before I could think about how absurd a thing it was to do, I found myself looking for the rise of gooseflesh on his arms. I felt tugged to join him, like his expression seemed to want me to do, to shield his perfect skin against the blustery morning.

He'd been looking right into the camera, so he was looking right out at me. I could see the texture in his eyes, the little flecks of gray and gold. His hair was tousled, like the wind had taken it. No—like he'd just woken up in a stranger's bed after a brisk late-night tumble. Like he'd been caught by the lens before he had a chance to run his hands through it and was too sated to care.

My knees were trembling. In my slacks, I was hard again.

I turned my phone over in my hands, tracing my thumb around the circular recess of the power button. Aiden's name glowed in centered white text, with no last name to push it off to the side. Below it, in slightly smaller font, a string of digits waited to connect me to him.

My thumb hovered over the green Call button, then retreated

to the safety of the black circle. I couldn't do it. Yet I nudged the screen back to life every time inactivity turned it dark. I watched the minutes tick silently past.

Fade. Nudge. Brighten. Fade. Nudge.

It had been one thing when I hadn't known who he was or why I'd recognized him. To call him now, with his fifty-foot likeness not a block from my office window, was something else. *Star-fucker*, my head called me, over and over. What could I say to him now? How could I talk to him without mentioning the billboard? There was no way to pretend I didn't know. I couldn't just say, "So, what do you do?" over drinks, like I hadn't seen it. And if I played it that way, I couldn't backpedal later and admit that I had.

I couldn't decide.

I would work late. That would bury the urge to call Aiden. It would also delay my walk past the corner with his bedroom eyes looking right into me and his sleek, tight briefs and that little ghost of a sly grin that made my stomach flutter just to think about it. Not that I *had* to walk past his corner at all— Was I thinking of it that way already?—but detouring to avoid his likeness seemed even more absurd than not wanting to lock eyes with a photograph that couldn't see me back.

I took a deep breath.

He was gorgeous, and it had been great, and I half-remembered a tender good-bye kiss and nothing to indicate that it should be anything but a positive memory. There was no reason to ruin a good thing by thinking about it too hard.

The phone buzzed in my hands. Startled, I jerked and it fell to the carpet, face up, vibrating insistently and still displaying Aiden's name. For a moment, I was stunned enough to wonder why it showed his name instead of the caller's. Then: *Oh.*

I scrambled to pick it up before the buzzing ended and my

voicemail began. "Aiden? Hi."

"Hey." His voice was warm, and having it amplified so close to my ear was just like seeing him on the billboard—larger than life. "Thanks again for last night."

I laughed, despite myself. It was relief, and flattery, and a bunch of other things I wasn't sure I could name. "Thank *you*, for coming over," I answered. Then I flushed. That had been lame.

"I know it's soon, but I've got a shoot tomorrow afternoon that's not far from your place. I wondered if you might want to catch dinner, and…?"

My cheeks were burning, the flush spreading down my chest. *Yes, fuck yes*, I thought, but instead I said, "Yeah. Yeah, I'd like that. 'Dinner and' sounds great."

"Mm." A quiet sound to show he was pleased. It reminded me of the little noise he'd made when I'd kissed him below his cock. I felt it all the way through me. "If I stay over, I'll have to leave early again. Is that okay?"

"Sure, I don't mind." Curiosity flared in me, but I didn't ask where he had to run off to. I didn't know how to say it without sounding suspicious or insecure. And, I wasn't. Really, just knowing that he wanted more of me, more nights in my bed, was enough. "I'll even let you get to sleep earlier this time, if you need to."

He laughed. "Don't you dare."

"Sunrise yoga."

It was what Aiden had muttered against my lips that first morning. As the weather grew colder, it became as much an expletive as an apology, but it was part of his commitment to keeping every part of his body in immaculate condition, along with manicures, salon treatments, and an admirably careful diet. Some mornings he resented the commitment more than others; some, he tried to drag me along with him; and, once, he succeeded. It was worth it—once—to be invited into his world; to watch his beautiful body in fluid motion; to catch his sly winks and his own appreciative glances toward my ass. But once was enough to fuel weeks of early morning fantasy time, and my body was too greedy to relinquish those quiet, dream-like hours when my pillow was still warm from him and my skin still smelled of his sweat.

Once a week, or sometimes twice, we would steal each other for an evening. "Dinner and," or sometimes just the "and." Each time he left my bed in the predawn glimmer, and his face and body would greet me at the corner on my way to work, as though he'd saved up one last knowing grin for me—one last quiet moment together—before I started my day.

It was surreal, seeing him like that before the feel of him had left my fingertips, but I got used to it, even looked forward to it. I watched the other commuters, men and women alike, and the way they would glance up at the billboard, at my lover with his tight briefs and bedroom eyes. Sometimes they would barely register the advertisement. It was assessed just long enough to be deemed less than vital, filtered out in favor of more pressing visual information: the flow of the traffic, the turn of signals at the crosswalk. Sometimes someone would frown fleetingly with distaste. Because of something about his body? Or the fact of his near-nudity? Or perhaps just because they preferred a man in boxers? But sometimes they'd would linger a moment on him, seeking out something particular. The ripple of abs, maybe. The line of his jaw.

Did they imagine his cock? I would wonder. And if so, I wondered, did they imagine it accurately? Circumcised, perfectly long and thick, with its pronounced ridge. Did they picture it twitching against his smooth, flat belly with each heated breath that crossed the delta of his frenulum? I often caught myself staring at the bulge of potential hiding inside the smooth gray fabric.

I had never been so willing to go to work in the mornings, or to go out for walks at lunch. My productivity and mood, my bosses noted in my yearly review, had soared.

But I knew billboards didn't stay up forever. They retired; they rotated. They moved on. And who knows how long it had been there before I'd met him—back when I'd been one of those blank-eyed commuters who'd seen his giant likeness as an unattainable fantasy, out of reach, and also frivolous advertising, not requiring my immediate attention.

One day, I knew, I would turn the corner and not see him there. The thought settled hollowly in my stomach and turned the morning and evening spottings into something different again. Sighting him still gave me a little boost, but now it gave me a flood of relief as well. Still there for one more day. How long did I have before I would lose my stolen moments with Aiden's likeness? Would it happen before or after he moved on, too?

"I'm going to LA for a couple weeks," Aiden said one night. He took his time with my shirt buttons, kissing his way down my chest. "That jeans shoot came through, and my agent lined up a couple more jobs as long as I'm out there." He continued unbuttoning when he got to my slacks and used the two loose ends of my open belt to pull me forward to his waiting mouth.

We celebrated, long and enthusiastically. In the morning, I'd forgotten about his trip until he reminded me, lips lingering on mine at the sunrise kiss.

"Don't get into trouble," I teased. I slid my fingers into his hair and tightened them, drawing him close, kissing him until he hummed his little "Mm" into my lips and perched a knee on the bed for balance. He reached under the sheet, hand closing around my cock, cool from the air compared to the heat of my shaft. His thumb swept a retaliating tease across my glans and I groaned.

"Get into lots of trouble," he murmured back, his voice as sly as the secret grin he wore on the billboard. "And tell me all about it."

He squeezed. My back arched and my cock surged in his hand, already primed for the morning-after release I usually gave it. I pulled him back into bed without much resistance, kissing him hard, pausing the needy jerks of my hips only long enough to tug down the exercise pants he'd just put on.

Back and forth, tighter, faster, until his hand was just a blur pushing my foreskin up and down my swollen crown. I came in sticky arcs across his chest, and he only rested in his accomplishment for a few moments before scooping up the pearly cum with his fingers. He guided my head to his lap and reached around me, stroking up and down the cleft of my ass with my own slickness, gliding slippery circles around my tight, willing pucker. While I slid my lips up and down his shaft, with heady suction and swirls of my tongue, his strong fingers fucked me. Powerful, jerking thrusts pumped his fist against my ass, harder and faster as I got him closer.

Aiden was late for yoga.

When I passed his corner, the simmer in his eyes made me remember his instructions. *Get into lots of trouble.* Maybe he expected to be partying it up in LA and he didn't want me thinking we were exclusive. I wasn't sure how I felt about that. Maybe hearing about his lovers' erotic adventures was just something that turned him on.

I looked up at the icy-blue eyes for an answer, but his likeness didn't offer any hints. It looked into me with the same knowing expression it always had.

The light changed, and I walked on.

Rachel was having another loft party at the weekend, and I decided I would go. It would keep me occupied, at the least; keep me from wondering where Aiden was, and what or who he might be doing.

On Rachel's roof, I met Chris. Dark-skinned, slight where Aiden was toned, he was in town from Miami and had never seen snow. We made small talk and our bodies drifted closer while we squinted into the sky, watching for the flurries that the forecast had warned about. His hand slid into my pocket seeking a haven from the cold. About half an hour later, his tongue slid into my mouth.

Chris's hotel was closer than my apartment. He was disoriented by the scale of the city, but I knew where we were going, so I led the way. It was an older building, narrow and historic. I passed it frequently and knew it by name. It was around the corner from my office.

I filled my lungs with the chilled night air and let my breath out slowly. Aiden was lit from above and below, casting long shadows on his face and making his pale eyes seem to glow. It was his touch that I felt lingering on my skin, the sense memory of him; his scent. His warmly lit bare chest and sculpted thigh had been visible from Chris's window, and I hadn't been able to look away.

Absently, I turned my phone over in my hand. A few stray flurries had started to filter down from above. One landed on my sleeve. I wondered if Chris was watching them. If maybe he was waiting for me to leave the corner so that he could get back to the party and pick up another guy. I hadn't meant to lead him on, and he'd been gracious enough for the walk back to his hotel to "find his bearings" and "learn the city." It just hadn't felt right to go through with it when Aiden filled my vision...and my thoughts.

Aiden's name—first and last—glowed white on my screen, and I pressed Call before I could have second thoughts. It wasn't early, even in west coast time. I was surprised enough that he answered but even more surprised that I didn't hear the thumping bass of a loud club behind his voice.

"Hey..." He sounded quiet. Tired, maybe, but his tone was warm. "I was just thinking about you."

"Hey," I answered, cupping my hand around my earpiece and straining to catch background noise over the sparse late-night traffic. "Are you busy?"

"Just sitting alone in my room. I...actually, I have your Face-book page up on my laptop. I was looking at your photo," he said.

Suddenly, the air around me felt too warm. "Yeah?"

Silence met me for a moment, long enough for me to wonder if the connection had dropped. "Yeah," he said. "Like it makes you any closer to being here, right?"

I looked up, seeking out his eyes again. They met mine, sharing their secret warmth and assurance with me as always. His lips still held a hint of a grin. Maybe I'd been too busy bracing myself for the day that I would turn the corner and find him gone. I'd been looking at the billboard instead of the big picture. "No, it's okay," I whispered. "I know just what you mean."

MEDICAL
MODEL

Logan Zachary

I s it time to play doctor yet?"

"All you have to do is allow the students to perform their tests on you. Answer their questions and try to relax as they work on you. You are evaluating them as much as they are evaluating you," Dr. James said. "We need you to be a medical model for these students. But unlike the untouchable models on the runway and in the magazine with the *Don't touch me* attitude, you'll be touched, poked, probed, prodded, palpated, and examined."

I sat on the exam table, naked, except for a paper gown. Why did they always keep these exam rooms so cold? The hair on my legs stood on end and brushed against each other as I rubbed them together. "What?"

"I hate using the rubber arms and body parts for the physical exams. A real medical model forces the intern to problem-solve and interact. I want them to treat the patient, not the problem." Dr. James smiled at me.

"How does this work?"

"Nate, the intern will hand you a folder that'll have information about your condition and answers to most of the questions they'll ask. Feel free to do any acting you want, but don't overdo it. They're scared as it is. Don't freak them out any more than you have to."

"I know..."

"The seizure you faked was brilliant and was very convincing, but you scared the instructor more than the medical student." Dr. James peeked behind me to see if he could get a peek at my ass.

I slapped at his hand. "I'll behave. Cross my heart." I pulled the gown down as far as it could go to cover my knees. "Will you be in to grade any of them? I love your watchful eye." I batted my lashes at him.

"I'll see what I can do, but we'll see how the day plays out."

There was a knock on the door. A young female in a white lab coat opened the door. "Oh, excuse me," she said.

"Dr. Martin, I was just leaving." Dr. James left the room and waved her in.

She handed me a folder, and I flipped it open.

"Nathanial Thomas," her voice cracked with nerves, "how are you doing today?"

The folder read "Migraine headaches." *I can do this.*

The next time the door opened, a handsome young man who looked like a football jock wearing a white coat entered the exam room.

I felt a stirring under the paper gown and sweat started to flow. This was not the time to get aroused. I opened the folder. Prostate cancer.

Fuck.

"Mr. Thomas, what seems to be your problem today?"

I looked down at his hands. He had large, thick, fat fingers. His index finger was going to have to enter me...there. I swallowed hard. "I've noticed some blood in my stools..."

Dr. Jock reached over and pulled out a purple rubber glove from the X-Large box. He opened a drawer and took out a tube of KY jelly. He asked a question, but my eyes couldn't stop looking at his index finger. My balls pulled up and my cock started to swell.

"I...I..."

"I know you think this is my first time, but I have completed this examination may times." And then he winked at me.

What the hell was that for? Was he playing me to put me at ease? Or...I looked at him. Oh, so handsome, oh so perfect, oh so gay? How many guys' asses had he explored? Probed? Prodded? Fucked?

Had Dr. James done this on purpose?

"If I could have you stand up and support yourself against the table..." He stepped back and allowed me to stand. He pointed to the table and waited.

"I'm not...," I started as I pushed the paper gown down and hoped my cock would stop growing.

"It's fine. Trust me."

There was a knock on the door.

Fuck.

The door opened and Dr. James came in. "I'm just stopping in to see how things are going. You don't mind, do you?"

I'm sure my eyes screamed at him to leave, since I couldn't say anything.

"So what test are you performing?"

Dr. Jock snapped the rubber glove and worked the lube down his index finger. "He said he had blood in his stool, so I figured I'd need to do a rectal."

"Good idea. Did you need any help with that? I can show you some techniques, if you'd like."

Dr. Jock stepped behind me and said, "Watch how I do it, and then you can show me how to do it better."

If I wasn't hard before, I was now.

"If you could turn around and bend over...," Dr. Jock said.

"There may be a problem," I started, as I turned around.

"That's all normal," Dr. James said waving his hand at me.

I felt one of the flaps open up and revealed one cheek. A cool breeze rushed up my gown, and my cock jumped and bounced. This wasn't supposed to be happening.

Dr. James touched my shoulder. "It will be over before you know it."

"Fine." I faced the exam table and set my hands on the edge.

Dr. Jock moved behind me and opened up my gown.

"Notice the solid muscle tone," Dr. James said, as he ran his finger over the curve of my ass.

I felt my knees threaten to give out.

Dr. Jock touched my shoulder and said, "Relax and take a deep breath." He slipped his finger between my cheeks and sought out my opening. The KY was warm as his finger explored. He found the tight sphincter and pressed in. Inch by inch his finger sank into my butt. He wiggled it back and forth, reaching for my prostate gland. He pulled back and forth a few times.

My cock jumped and I felt some wetness at the tip. My balls jumped and the hair tickled them as the air moved over them.

Dr. Jock's finger found my prostate and pressed down firmly on it. He palpated it and fingered it from all sides.

Pre-cum flowed out of my dick and pleasure soared over my body. I pushed back against his finger. My ass sucked on his finger, begging for more.

"His prostate feels round and firm, not hard or mushy. No abnormal masses felt."

He kept his finger inside me as he spoke. He pressed down on it over and over again.

"Very good," Dr. James said, as he pulled on a rubber glove. It snapped into place as he stepped next to Dr. Jock. "Let me feel and then I can show you a little trick I've learned."

Shit!

I felt Dr. Jock withdraw from my ass and step back.

"As you can see he has a very muscular butt, and those strong muscles may make it hard to insert your finger, so asking him to breathe deeply was a great idea. That helps him relax. Are you relaxed?"

Bastard!

I felt him slip his finger into my crease and work its way to my hole. He pumped into me several times as he searched for my prostate. Usually I was taken out for dinner first, but I did volunteer for this, and I was getting paid for it. I pressed back against Dr. James and moaned as he dug.

"Am I hurting you?" he asked, pressing in deeper and poked my prostate.

Bingo!

More pre-cum oozed out of me and dripped onto the floor, I felt one drop land on my foot, hot and wet and slick.

"He has an amazing prostate, and he is the perfect test subject. Notice if you grab his testicles, it blocks his butt from relaxing." Dr. James grabbed my balls and pulled them down.

My ass clamped down on his finger, and he probed and twisted. My cock flapped up and down as he milked my low hangers. His bare hand was warm, and I felt him roll my balls between his fingers.

Oh my god!

I dropped my head forward and closed my eyes. Was he trying to jack me off here?

He pulled his finger out of my butt but continued squeezing my balls. "This could be the perfect time to check for testicular cancer. Nate, could you sit down on the table and we'll check for a hernia and cancer at the same time. How often do you examine your testicles?"

"I try once a month." I sat down on the edge of the table, and that piece of paper crinkled under my backside.

Dr. Jock asked, "When do you do that? In the shower?"

"Nate, that is a great time to examine your balls," Dr. James said as he lifted my gown to reveal my knees, still respecting my modesty.

My cock was standing straight up and rested against my belly. The paper garment flipped up and my hairy balls fell into view.

Dr. James folded the gown back and grabbed one testicle. He pulled it, rolled it, and pulled the skin tight. "Notice the rich color and healthy hair. And one testicle usually hangs lower than the other one."

Dr. Jock moved to the table and grabbed my other ball. He rolled it in his fingers. "It is warm, healthy, and well developed."

"Both have descended and if we pull them up, we can make sure that he doesn't have a hernia. The inguinal canal is a weak spot in the abdominal wall and can tear open..."

"And could cause a problem if a piece of his intestine slipped through and got stuck, cutting the blood supply off and causing tissue death." Dr. Jock continued to play with my ball. He then pulled it up and inserted his finger underneath to feel for a hernia.

My dick rocked back and forth. The stimulation rose in my

pelvis, and I felt more fluid pour down my shaft.

Shit!

"I feel that so many men are embarrassed about these exams and they could save a life. This is an important thing that we need to instill into our patients."

Dr. Jock nodded but didn't let go of my testicle.

Dr. James looked at his watch. "It looks like we have some extra time, so what else should we work on? Have you ever cathed a man?"

Oh crap!

"I think I need to use the restroom," I said.

"Perfect, we'll catherize it out of you." He turned and pulled out a kit from one of the cabinets. "Can you lie back on the table and bring your feet up?"

"I didn't agree to this."

Dr. James pushed me back as Dr. Jock slid out the leg rest on the exam table. Dr. James set the plastic box on the table and opened it. He pulled up my gown, ripping the paper in the process.

My erection sprang up and bounced up and down.

Kill me now.

Both doctors stopped and stared. "You sure are a healthy man, Nate," Dr. Jock said as he pulled out a red cathing tube and applied lube to it. He grabbed my cock and pulled the slit open. He guided the tip of the tube in and slowly pushed. The rubber tube entered my penis and filled me. I could feel the pressure as it slid deeper into me. My hard cock started to swell even bigger as it slid down my shaft. "Having an erection will help the tube slide in easier, but it will be a lot longer. A real long, long tube." His hand massaged my erection and worked the tube in.

I felt my dick grow thicker in his hand. His stroke felt so

good, despite the pressure of the tube being inserted deeper and deeper inside my shaft. The tube stopped and refused to go farther. Pain started, but I took a deep breath, and the tube continued in. The inserted end must have entered my bladder because warm urine started to flow out.

Dr. Jock aimed the end of the cath into a urinal and caught the output.

It felt great to empty my bladder. As the flow stopped, Dr. Jock started to pull the tube out. "What an amazing job you're doing." He poured the urine down the drain and threw the used cath kit in the garbage.

Dr. James stepped in front of me. "I hate to waste that erection. How about getting a semen sample? Doctor, would you like to assist?"

"I could demonstrate several techniques to obtain a sample," Dr. Jock offered. "He seems motivated enough." Dr. Jock stepped to the head of the table. He pulled open his lab coat and started to unbuckle his belt. He drew down his fly and let his pants drop to the floor. His tightie-whities were bulging on his football player's body. His hand grabbed his basket and pulled on it. A wet spot soaked through the cotton and the fat mushroom head was visible.

Oh yes.

Dr. James moved between my legs and spread them. His hand stroked my balls and worked up my shaft. He ran one finger up to my tip and spread the pearl of cream over its end. He brought his finger to his mouth and tasted me. "Delicious."

I couldn't decide who to watch. Dr. James started to open his pants, but Dr. Jock was removing his briefs. A thick bush of brown hair flowed out of his waistband, followed by a huge, thick eight-inch cock. He pushed the underwear down to his knees and moved closer. He grabbed his cock and said, "You can stroke the whole penis, but some men prefer to only work the tip." He demonstrated both techniques, milking out a pearl of pre-cum.

The musky male scent of sweat and semen entered my nose. I brought my head back, licked my lips, and Dr. Jock guided his cock to them. He traced my mouth with his dick, smearing the clear fluid along them and then circled around and around.

Dr. James pulled down his pants and moved closer to my ass. "We had such great success when we stimulated your prostate." I felt his cock rub along my butt. He pressed against my hole; the lube from the previous exam made his entry easy. His tip slid in, and he buried himself to the hilt, prodding my gland again.

Dr. Jock saw him enter me, and he did the same with my mouth. His thick cock tasted of salt and man. Inch by inch he filled my mouth until his thick bush touched my nose. I inhaled and savored him. I was filled from both ends and basked in the warmth that flooded my body.

Dr. James grasped my dick and started stroking. His hand spread my pre-cum and lubed my shaft. His touch made my hips rock back and forth, push my cock into his hand as his dick slipped in and out of my ass.

I sucked on Dr. Jock and felt his hairy balls bounce.
Thank you Jesus.

He reached down and squeezed my pecs. His fingers combed through my hair and played down my torso. He humped my face and moaned with pleasure.

Dr. James increased his speed in my ass and on my cock.

I reached up and pulled on Dr. Jock's tight end, increasing his speed into my mouth.

His cock seemed to swell and grow as my mouth worked on it, pre-cum started to flow out of his dick and mixed with my saliva. The mixture increased the depth of his thrusts and my lips sealed around him, drawing out more.

My balls started to ascend as Dr. James plowed into me.

"I'm...get...ting...close." He drove into me with each syllable. He pulled out of my ass and surged forward. He grabbed his cock with mine and jacked them together. His pre-cum mixed with mine as our two thick shafts rubbed along each other.

Dr. Jock grabbed my head and held it in place as he fucked my mouth.

Dr. James humped and jacked faster.

I felt a hot, wet gush explode out of his cock. It mixed and ran along my shaft and I knew my load would explode soon.

Dr. James groaned with pleasure and squeezed my cock.

I rose up and pushed my dick against him. My balls let loose, releasing the force they had been building. I sucked harder on Dr. Jock and felt him shoot deep into my throat. I swallowed and swallowed, trying to prevent from drowning in this sea of semen.

Dr. James milked my cock for all that remained and wiped the excess across my abs. He massaged his cock and mine together.

Dr. Jock pulled out of my mouth and shot another wave of cum across my chest. His load mixed with ours.

I closed my eyes for a second, and the next thing I felt was a wet, warm washcloth wiped across my torso, over my cock and around my balls.

Dr. Jock dressed and left the room, as Dr. James cleaned me up and dried me off. He opened a cabinet and pulled out a new paper gown. "Your next doctor will be with you in a minute." He pulled off the cum-soaked paper on the table and threw it away. He pulled a new, fresh piece to cover the table, and he patted the spot.

I donned the new gown and tied the strings at the neck as Dr.

James finished readying the exam room and left. My bare ass sat on the paper and waited.

"Knock, knock." The door opened and Dr. Yummy entered. Thick black hair that fell down to his shoulders in waves, brown eyes, tan skin, white, even teeth on a perfect model's body. He handed me a folder. Prostate cancer.

There was another knock on the door. Dr. James entered and smiled. "I came to help." He grabbed a purple rubber glove and snapped it into place. "Turn around and bend over."

Oh fuck, here we go again...

DOUG

Garland

D oug was eighteen, just out of high school. The youngest guy who had ever posed for the magazine. He was from a small town in northern California, posing to get money for school. With his shoulder-length hair the color of burnt cinnamon and frat-boy good looks I was instantly smitten, though I was forty-five, old enough to be his father.

"So have you ever done this before?" I asked him.

"No," he confessed, in a soft lyrical tenor, on the brink of manhood yet still filled with childlike innocence.

"Well don't be nervous. We won't do anything you're not comfortable with."

"Thanks," Doug said. "So how does this work? What do I do?" He ran his hand nervously through his luscious locks.

"First just relax. Be yourself and don't be nervous. I know, easy for me to say. I get to keep my clothes on."

Doug laughed, showing off those perfect ivory-colored teeth, and I snapped my first picture.

"See? Not so bad."

He smiled and nodded.

"First I'm going to get some clothed shots of you and then we'll work our way down. Shirtless. Underwear. Nude. Sound good?"

"Sounds good," he responded.

I could see him relax. Good. My job was always easier if they were relaxed. Not that I blamed any of my boys for being nervous. What they were doing took a lot of guts. I could never pose nude no matter how much you paid me.

"So what brought you to LA?" I asked as I clicked my camera. I found that if I talked to them they became more themselves and forgot about the camera and posing. "Acting? Modeling?"

"No," he laughed. "That stuff really isn't for me." He caught me off-guard. I thought those were the only reasons good looking young people came to LA. "I'm going to USC."

"What are you studying?"

"Business communications."

"Nice. Can you lift up your shirt a little and give us a peek at your stomach?"

He did and my heart raced at seeing his flat, smooth stomach, evenly tanned by the sun.

"How long have you been doing this?" he asked.

"About twenty-five years."

"Wow," he said impressed. "I can't imagine doing any job that long."

"That's because you still have mother's milk on your breath."

He laughed as if this was the funniest joke in the world. I loved his laugh. It was warm. Friendly. Genuine.

"Want to take off the shirt?" I asked. Truth be told I couldn't wait to get him naked.

"Sure," he answered casually as if I had asked if he wanted to go to a ball game.

Slowly he peeled off his shirt. His pecs were hard and meticulously developed. His nipples, a virginal pink color, were the size of silver dollars. Like his stomach, his chest was devoid of hair. Two small tufts of a darker cinnamon-colored hair lived under his arms.

As the day wore on Doug and I grew more and more comfortable with each other. He definitely had more personality than most of the other no-brain egomaniacs I had to deal with. Plus he looked really good in his tight briefs.

"So how are you feeling?" I asked as I changed the film in my camera.

"Great," he answered. "This is easy."

"Glad you're enjoying yourself. So...ready to ditch the undies?"

"Okay," he said starting to pull his briefs down.

"Wait," I stopped him.

"What?"

"Turn around. Let's get some shots of your butt first."

"Okay."

Turning around he exposed his butt and my dick got instantly hard. Doug had one of the roundest, tightest bubble-butts I had ever seen!

"Doug, look over your shoulder and smirk at the camera. Pretend you're flirting with someone you like."

He did and I almost melted like butter on hot bread. The big flirt even winked. I wondered how many girls—or guys—he had done that to.

"Was that okay?" he asked, voice tainted with just a hint of self-consciousness.

"Great. Now I want you to look away from me, flex and clench your butt."

He did, and damn if I didn't almost cum! Closing my eyes I

counted to ten and reminded myself that I was a professional.

"Okay," I said once I had regained my composure. "Ready to show the world your dick?"

"I guess," he answered, still facing away from me. I could hear the blush in his voice and I couldn't help but grin.

Doug turned around and you'd have thought it was the first time I'd ever seen a naked man. My heart stopped and my dick got even harder.

I couldn't tear my eyes from his body. His neatly trimmed pubic hair. His fat dick that rested on two of the biggest bull balls I had ever seen. I loved balls, and Doug's were perfect. I'm amazed I didn't lick my lips. Or fuck him.

"Is my body okay? Is my dick big enough? Do you think they'll like my body?"

His boyhood insecurities turned me on even more.

"You're fine. Everyone's going to love you."

"Really?" he asked, perking up.

"Really," I answered honestly.

I must have snapped a million pictures of him. I have never taken that many shots of any model. He was just so yummy. I didn't want our session to end. It should be illegal to cover that body.

"I'm glad you think your readers will like me."

His words made my chest swell up with pride. "I'm sure you have no problem getting one-night stands."

As soon as I said that I froze. My eyes bugged out. I hadn't meant to say that out loud. I was supposed to be a professional. One of the top photographers in LA.

Much to my surprise he merely smiled and said, "Thanks. I don't really do one-night stands though. I gotta be really horny or really into someone to sleep with 'em right away."

"That's nice," I replied honestly. "You don't meet a lot of young guys with those values."

Doug grinned, showing those dimples that must have broken a hundred hearts.

The sun was just setting, staining the sky a brilliant blood-red. Unfortunately it was almost time for him to leave.

"Are there anymore shots you need, Paul?" Doug asked.

"Well…and you only have to do this if you're comfortable, but Mr. Cundy does like to have a couple shots of the guys hard."

We were silent for several minutes. It felt like a lifetime. I could see his brain weighing the pros and cons. I always hated asking my boys this question. It was always 50–50. Half said yes. Half said no.

"Okay," Doug finally said.

"Really?" I was a little surprised but very happy. I was curious to see what his dick looked like hard.

"Sure." He shrugged like it was no big deal. "Might as well go all the way."

I'd like to go all the way with you, I thought devilishly, and I had to use extra restraint not to smile.

"There's some porn over there if you need some help," I said gesturing over to a bookshelf with some magazines on it. Most of the guys did experience performance anxiety.

"It's fine. Give me a couple seconds," he answered tugging on his cock.

Within seconds he was rock hard. Ahhhh…to be that young again.

"Is it hard enough?" he asked. I couldn't help but blush. No man had ever asked me that before.

"It's great."

Doug smiled.

He really did have a beautiful boner. It was the perfect size. I snapped a whole roll of film on it.

"Okay," I said bittersweetly after I had run out of film. "That's a wrap." It was the first time I was ever sad a session had ended.

"Already? Wow. That went by fast."

"Glad you enjoyed yourself," I answered unable to rip my eyes from his hard-on.

"I had fun." He looked down at his dick and smirked. "Shame to waste a good boner."

"Bathroom's over there," I said pointing. "There's some lube in there. Go nuts."

"Want to help me?" He asked stepping toward me.

"Ex-excuse me?" I was sure I'd heard him wrong. Or at least was daydreaming.

"You heard me," he said taking the camera from my hands and wrapping them around his silky smooth shaft. "I saw the way you looked at me today. The way you're still looking at me," he whispered, sending shivers up and down my spine.

"I..." I didn't know what to say. All I could do was blush.

"Like that dick?" he asked.

"Yes," I answered, breathless. I couldn't believe this was really happening. I had never messed around with a subject before. It was like something out of a late night cable movie. "So Mr. I-don't-really-do-one-night-stands....Are you really horny?...Or do you really like me?"

"Both," he whispered.

Doug brought his lips to mine. In all my years of messing around with guys on the side I had never kissed a man. I liked it. Doug's lips were soft. Moist. They made my heart flutter. His thick tongue entered my mouth and flicked against mine. Soon our tongues were joined together in an erotic tango.

Before long I was naked and on my knees. Cupping his balls, I slowly ran my tongue over his dick, licking it like an ice cream cone.

Unhinging my jaw like a serpent I easily deep-throated him.

Holding onto my head he groaned and rose on his toes like a ballet dancer when the tip of his dick hit my tonsils. Closing my eyes I savored the way his dick filled my mouth and the taste of his salty-sweet pre-cum sliding down my throat. Slowly I sucked his dick. Judging by the way he moaned I knew no one had ever given him a blowjob as good as mine.

"You do that so good," he complimented.

Grinning up at him I squeezed his slippery mushroom head. "Married men in their forties give the best head," I promised winking at him.

Holding my head in place, he fucked my mouth like a champ. His balls gleefully slapped against my chin. My hands squeezed his hard ass, fingers teasing his long deep crack.

"Wanna fuck?" he asked.

Hell yeah I did.

Doug got on his hands and knees, catching me off-guard. I never would have pegged him as a bottom. Maybe that's why his ass was so round.

Spreading his cheeks I flicked my tongue against his smooth hole. Doug's body shuddered and his hole puckered. Spitting on it I stuck a couple fingers inside him, preparing him for my cock.

"Spit on my dick," I told him. "Get it ready for your ass."

Turning around Doug spit on my hard-on, making it glisten. He loudly slurped my cock, and goddamn the things that boy could do with his mouth! If business communications didn't work out he'd make a fortune in the porn industry.

Mounting him, I slowly slid my dick inside his ass. "Your cock feels so good," Doug moaned.

"Your ass feels so good," I responded, slapping it and making the flesh jiggle.

Slowly I pumped in and out of him, finding my rhythm.

Doug's ass squeezed my dick. I felt my balls tighten.

"I'm close," I moaned. "Where do you want me to cum?"

"Inside me," he groaned.

Massaging his back, I couldn't hold off any longer and shot deep inside him with a long satisfied *Ahhhhhhh*. I always loved cumming in guys. There was nothing as satisfying as that feeling.

"My turn," Doug said.

"I've never bottomed before," I confessed.

"Don't worry. I'll be gentle," he promised, laying me on my back. "I want to see you as I take your ass virginity."

Rubbing his cock against my hole it wasn't long before it opened for him like a blossoming rose.

My mouth opened in a silent orgasmic *o*. His dick felt so good stretching out my ass.

"Like that?" he asked.

"Yeah."

Doug was a very good, very skilled, lover. His dick awakened g-spots I didn't even know existed.

He pounded in and out of me furiously. My hands roamed over his body. He never took his eyes off me. It was like we had a connection. This felt like more than a casual fuck. Doug's hot cum filled my ass to overflowing.

"That was great," he gasped, continuing to kiss me.

"Yeah," I sighed.

We were silent as we dressed. We kept stealing glances at each other and smiling. Kissing me once more Doug walked out of the studio. That was the last time I ever saw him.

IT'S ALL ABOUT THE ATTITUDE

Aaron Michaels

The photographer stepped away from his camera, hands on his hips, and glared at Jesse. "We're aiming for drop-dead, fuck-me-six-ways-to-Sunday, if-I-buy-the-same-clothes-he's-wearing-I'm-gonna-get-laid gorgeous here. What's so difficult to understand about that?"

Jesse crossed his arms in front of himself and kept his mouth shut. The photographer's assistant, a mousey young woman somewhere in her twenties, busied herself making notes on a clipboard, her back to Jesse and her boss. Trying to make herself invisible, no doubt. Standing alone against a silver-gray studio backdrop and illuminated by all sorts of megawatt-light umbrellas, Jesse didn't have that option.

"They assured me they'd found a wonderful model for me this time. An actor, they said. Easy to work with." The photographer wasn't yelling—yet—but the vein running across his forehead was definitely more prominent than it had been when Jesse started posing a half-hour ago. If the guy wasn't careful, he'd give himself a heart attack. "If this is what you call acting, my friend, don't quit your day job."

Okay, that really hurt. And to think, Jesse'd been looking forward to working with this guy. Sure, Tefford Saks (no relation to the store) had a reputation for ranting up a storm when he wasn't getting the exact shot he had in mind, but everyone still wanted to work with him because he was damn brilliant with a camera.

That's why Jesse agreed to audition for this job in the first place. He didn't really care about being the Face of Fortunadi Fashions, an upstart, high-end men's clothing line, but he was in desperate need of some publicity. What better way to advertize himself than on a thirty-foot-high billboard in Times Square? Especially a thirty-foot high billboard he didn't have to pay for.

So far Jesse Chance's acting career had consisted of a few B horror movies (where he'd been the pretty boy first to die shortly after having sex with the film's blonde teenage bimbo) and a couple of forgettable movies of the week on the Syfy channel. Jesse's agent was about to drop him, the only callback he'd had was for a soap opera so bad not even his mom would watch it, and if he screwed up this gig, Saks would make sure the only modeling job Jesse ever got again was Poster Boy for the Disease of the Week handouts at the free clinic in West Hollywood.

The sole bright spot in Jesse's world at the moment was the new man in his life. Tall, dark, and smoldering, Greg Simmons was a personal trainer at the gym where Jesse had a thirty-day free trial membership.

Jesse was pretty sure all Greg wanted was a pretty boy to fuck every now and then, which was fine with Jesse. Actors who "had ambitions," as Jesse's agent liked to say, didn't "have relationships" with other men. Jesse had heard the speech from her so often that he almost saw the air quotes hovering over her frizzy red-haired head.

"You can't be Neil Patrick Harris unless you *are* Neil Patrick Harris," she liked to say. "Not in this town."

Okay, fine. But it wasn't like TMZ followed him around anyway.

And they never would, not if he couldn't even nail the emotions required for a simple photo shoot.

Jesse took a deep breath. If Saks wanted fuck-me-six-ways-to-Sunday emotion, Jesse knew one quick way to get it.

"I need five minutes," he said.

The photographer's eyes widened in surprise. "What? You fuck up my shooting schedule 'cause you can't do your damn job, and now you want five minutes?" The vein in Saks's forehead had started to throb. Maybe the guy was such a jerk because he had a constant migraine.

"Yeah," Jesse said. If he couldn't pretend to be sexy, at least he could pretend he had enough balls to stand up for himself like he didn't need this job to survive. "Five minutes, then you'll get your shots."

Saks grabbed his assistant's clipboard and threw it on the floor. His assistant never made a sound, even when the plastic shattered on the bare concrete floor.

"Take your damn five minutes," Saks said. "I need a smoke."

The assistant watched her boss stalk out of studio, then she glanced over at Jesse. "He'll be back here in exactly five," she said. "I hope you know what you're doing."

Jesse did, too.

He trotted back to the small changing room at the rear of the studio. He made sure the door was shut behind him. It didn't have a lock, but he'd have to make do. He retrieved his cell from the pocket of his jeans (a nondesigner brand) and selected a number from his list of contacts.

Please be there.

Greg answered after three rings. "Hello, lover."

That deep, raspy growl never ceased to turn Jesse on. That's what he was counting on, among other things, like Greg being a good sport and playing along.

"What are you wearing?" Jesse asked.

After a short beat, Greg's low chuckle resonated over the phone. "My, my, my. I didn't know you were into this sort of thing."

"Not usually, but I'm desperate. I'm supposed to 'exude sex' here, but the guy's a dick, and all I keep thinking about is my dwindling bank account and the possibility of a career asking people if they'd like dessert or should I bring the check."

"Ah, the fashion shoot. So does this mean I'm your go-to guy for all things sexy?"

"Yeah. Pretty much my go-to guy period."

Oops. Where did that come from? Jesse glanced at the clock on the wall. Shit. He didn't have time to worry about what he'd just inadvertently said.

"Look," Jesse said. "I've only got three minutes to get sexy or I'm dead meat."

"Three minutes. Nothing like working under pressure."

Greg went quiet, and Jesse got worried. They didn't really have a relationship, just a lot of fun, hot sex. He could really be pushing Greg too hard, no pun intended.

Then he heard Greg grunt. Jesse recognized that grunt.

"You know what I got here in my hand?" Greg asked.

A flush went through Jesse. "Yeah. A cock the size of Milwaukee."

"Hard and hot, just for you, baby."

Jesse swallowed hard. "Tell me what you're going to do with it."

"Fuck you till you scream. Fuck you so hard you'll feel me in your throat and you'll be begging me to let you cum." Odd sounds came from the phone, a rubbing, scratchy sound, then Greg's voice came back. "Feel how hard I am for you?"

Good God, he'd touched himself with the phone. Jesse closed his eyes and imagined that. His own cock was getting heavy. He wanted to touch himself, but he held off. The look he was going for was erotic, not postcoital.

"I want to suck that cock of yours," he told Greg. "Make you scream. Make you so crazy for me you'll fuck me all night."

Greg groaned. "You're doing a damn good job of it now."

"Yeah?"

"Want me to jerk myself off and let you listen? You could imagine it's your hand doing me while my tongue's up your ass."

Jesse's cock twitched. If he wasn't careful here, he'd be going back in front of the camera with a raging hard-on.

"Think about this," Greg said. "You know what we're gonna do when we get together tonight? All of what we're talking about here, and that's only for starters."

Jesse glanced at the clock again. Thirty seconds. Damn. "I don't want to wait till then, but I have to."

"Knock 'em dead, stud," Greg said. Then he added, "Make 'em all jealous that I'm the only one gets to fuck you."

The call disconnected. Jesse blinked at the phone. Wow. He'd called Greg hoping for a little dirty talk, but Greg had gone above and beyond, and all at a moment's notice.

A knock at the door interrupted his thoughts. "You've got about ten seconds," came the assistant's voice.

Jesse thought about Greg on the other end of the call. Greg, in a tight wife-beater T-shirt with his cock sticking up hard out of his workout shorts.

"Yeah," he said to the assistant. "I'm ready."

He opened the dressing room door. The assistant took one look at him, a quick head to toe glance, pausing only briefly at his crotch. "I believe you are," she said. "Now go make that asshole your bitch."

Jesse didn't know if he made Tefford Saks his bitch, but the photographer was smart enough not to say one word to Jesse for the rest of the shoot. Instead, he had his assistant turn on some sort of techno dance mix and had her tell Jesse to move however he wanted.

Jesse let the beat play out against the movie unreeling in his mind, a XXX feature starring his hot-as-hell lover and his big cock. Jesse moved and posed, mouth half-open, eyes heavy lidded and soft-focused. He ran his hands through his hair, disrupting the makeup artist's earlier attempts to tame his curls, and let his hair fly where it wanted to.

At some point the assistant must have adjusted the intensity of the umbrella lights, because when she finally said they had everything they needed, the studio seemed darker than it had been when they started.

It took Jesse a few moments to come back to the here and now. Somehow he'd managed not to cum in his fancy Fortunadi clothes. Amazing, considering he'd just had the most intense waking almost-wet dream of his life.

The assistant was scribbling on a new clipboard she must have had stashed somewhere. She'd also apparently cloned herself because three more mid-twenties women were standing around behind the lights, ogling Jesse.

Saks checked his camera equipment, nodding to himself, and—was that an actual smile? Jesse took a deep breath, somewhat surprised that he'd managed to work up a sweat.

"You're free to go," the assistant said to Jesse. "We'll have proofs sent over to your agent, just so you see what we're sending off to Fortunadi. If any of the rest end up being publicity stills, we'll let you know."

"Publicity?" Jesse was confused. He had no rights to any of the photos. Saks was way out of Jesse's price league.

"For our website," the assistant said.

"Uh…" Jesse didn't know what to say. The people Saks put up on his website were top models. Sports megastars. A-list actors. Not a B-list wannabe pretending to be a fashion model just to keep himself afloat.

The assistant nodded at her clones, who were trying to make themselves look busy while still sneaking glances at Jesse. "You did good," she said. "You made a few fans here. My guess is they're going to look you up on IMDB, and there will be a run on your movies after they tell all their friends about you."

Jesse almost laughed. He didn't think his movies were even out anywhere.

Saks stepped away from his camera, and the assistant faded into the background. "Good job, young man," Saks said to Jesse. "If you can bottle what you did today, combined with your looks…you've got a career ahead of you."

Okay, this was getting surreal. "Thank you," Jesse managed to say. "Now if you could just convince a casting agent that I'm—"

"I didn't mean acting," Saks said.

Huh?

Before Jesse could think of a response that wouldn't make him sound like an idiot, the photographer nodded at him and left. The three assistant clones who'd been hovering retrieved the camera equipment and proceeded to lock it away.

"Uhm, did he mean modeling? A career in modeling?" Jesse said to no one in particular.

The assistant with the clipboard smiled at him. "When you get the proofs, take a good look. Then you decide what he meant."

Greg practically ripped Jesse's clothes off that night. "I've been hard for you all day," he said, propelling Jesse into the bedroom.

Jesse's apartment was little more than walk-in closet-sized, but he did have a bedroom with a queen-sized bed that took up almost all the floor space. It looked like Greg intended to give the bed—and Jesse—one hell of a workout.

Not that Jesse minded one bit. He'd managed—barely—to keep from embarrassing himself at the shoot. The minute he'd heard Greg's knock at the door, Jesse's cock decided it was time to take over.

Greg hadn't called, he'd just shown up at Jesse's with a six-pack of beer and a smile that would have melted steel. He'd taken one look at Jesse's crotch, and the beer had gone in the fridge. That was for later. Now was all about sex.

"So, did I do it for you?" Greg asked in that same sultry voice he'd used on the phone.

Greg was spread out on top of Jesse, bare chested. He had the kind of muscular body that Jesse only dreamed of having one day. Not that Jesse was a slouch in that department, but his own body type ran to lean muscle, not washboard abs.

Jesse grabbed Greg's hand and pressed it down on his aching cock. "What do you think?"

Greg chuckled and squeezed, and Jesse moaned. "I think I like when you call me up and talk dirty to me," Greg said.

"Even if I get you all hot and bothered?"

"Especially when you get me all hot and bothered."

"Like now."

"Lover, I am beyond bothered now." Greg squeezed again, then he let go of Jesse just long enough to strip off his own jeans.

Jesse hadn't been exaggerating, at least not much, when he'd said Greg had a cock the size of Milwaukee. Jesse didn't think of himself as a size queen, but Greg was built. Long and thick and cut, Greg's cock was a thing of beauty to behold. He could have made a fortune in the porn industry. Jesse had no idea what Greg saw in him, other than a pretty face. As far as Jesse was concerned, Greg could have had his pick of any of the people at the gym—men or women.

Jesse leaned forward and took Greg in his mouth, just like he'd promised. The man had saved his ass this afternoon. Giving the man a good blow was the least he could do.

But after less than a minute, Greg pulled him off. "You know what? I don't think that's what I want. Not tonight."

Greg had never said no to a blowjob, but if he wanted something else, Jesse was happy to oblige.

"Tell me what you want," Jesse said.

"Uh-uh." Greg sat back on his heels. His cock jutted up from his lap, still slick from Jesse's mouth. "That's not how tonight's gonna be."

Most of Jesse's blood was in his own cock, which made it hard for him to think under the best of circumstances, but tonight Greg was really confusing him. "I don't understand. Are you annoyed with me about today?" What if he'd interrupted something important when he called? "Did I...did you get in trouble because of me?"

"Nope. But you called me because you needed something from me. Now I need something from you."

Okay, fair was fair. "What do you need?"

"The real you."

"What?"

"I've been with actors before, and I'm never sure who I'm with. You all make a living playing parts, I get that. I even get that you've been playing a part with me. You might not know you're doing it. Most of the time I'm okay with that."

Greg thought Jesse was playing a part? "What part?"

"The pretty boy slut who can't wait to catch a ride on the next big cock in town."

Jesse blinked. Greg thought he was a slut? "That really hurt."

Greg shrugged. "Didn't mean for it to. Look, we hook up and we fuck. Like I said, I'm okay with that most of the time. I thought I'd be okay with it tonight, too. But this afternoon I got a glimpse of the real you."

"Because I talked dirty to you on the phone."

"Nope." Greg leaned forward and grabbed Jesse's hand. "Because you babbled to me on the phone about being scared of fucking up your job. That's the real you, and I like it. Just like the real me's more than my big dick."

The words would have stung if Greg hadn't said them gently and with a grin on his face.

"Careful," Jesse said. "We actors tend to be a big bag of insecurities and neuroses. You let that genie out of the bottle, I might not be able to put it back."

"I think I can handle your insecurities. I did pretty good this afternoon, didn't I?"

Jesse looked down at Greg's hand holding his. They'd never held hands before. Had he read what Greg really wanted all wrong? Fuck buddies didn't hold hands or talk about their feelings and insecurities.

"Yes, you did wonderfully," Jesse said. "I almost came right in my expensive Fortunadi men's trousers."

"I did cum in mine," Greg said. "Good thing I was in my car."

Jesse's eyes widened. "You were *driving*?"

"Oh, hell, no. I was in the parking garage next to the gym. I just drove myself back home and cleaned up before I went back to work. Smiled real nice at my favorite client...."

"I thought I was your favorite client."

"My favorite middle-aged housewife client, and she forgave me for being late."

"She probably has a crush on you."

"Probably. But she tips me well."

Jesse squeezed Greg's hand. "Would she tip you as well if she knew about this?"

"Doesn't matter. Besides, it's not about who we are out there." Greg gestured with his free hand to Jesse's tiny bedroom window. "It's in here, when it's just the two of us, that's when I want you to feel like you can be yourself."

"And you can be yourself."

"Absolutely."

A new idea occurred to Jesse. "Have you been playing a part with me?" Greg didn't have any acting aspirations, at least none that Jesse knew about.

"The personal trainer with a big dick, you mean?"

Well, that wasn't exactly what Jesse meant. "Something like that. Maybe."

A slow flush rose to color Greg's cheeks. "You got me there, but in my defense, I do have a big dick. Besides, I thought that's what you wanted."

And Jesse had thought Greg only wanted a pretty-boy fuck buddy. "Man, are we pathetic or what?"

"At least we're talking about this shit."

True.

Jesse glanced down at Greg's lap. His big dick wasn't quite as hard as it had been a minute ago, but it was still pointing out its interest in Jesse. "So, are we going to do more than talk tonight?"

Greg grinned at him. "I wouldn't be sitting naked on your bed if all I wanted to do was talk."

"Then what do you want?"

"Let me show you."

This time when Greg leaned Jesse back on the bed, it was with a tenderness he'd never shown before. Greg cupped one hand on the side of Jesse's face and kissed him for a long time. Deep kisses. Unhurried and thorough, and with a kind of gentle passion Jesse had never experienced.

That was just the beginning.

Jesse couldn't remember the last time someone had made love to him, but that was, without a doubt, what Greg was doing. His hands moved up and down Jesse's body in long, flowing strokes that excited Jesse more than he would have thought possible. Greg didn't go near Jesse's cock, even though Jesse was so hard he desperately needed to be touched. Instead, Greg kissed nearly every square inch of Jesse's body except his cock.

"You're driving me nuts, here," Jesse finally said. He was squirming on the bed. He'd tried touching himself, but Greg had captured both his wrists and was now doing amazing things to his bellybutton. If Jesse lifted his hips just the right way, the tip of his cock grazed Greg's hair. That was only serving to drive him more insane with need. "If you want to see me, the real me, beg for it, here I am." He lifted his head and looked Greg in the eyes. "Will you please fuck me already?"

"No," Greg said. "But I will make love to you."

He lifted Jesse's legs on his shoulders, then pushed them back until Jesse's ass lifted off the bed. Jesse felt thoroughly exposed, but he didn't care because the next moment Greg's mouth was on him and his tongue was in him. Jesse shouted with the pure, raw, live-wire amazing sensation of it all.

Jesse's cock was dripping on his own stomach by the time Greg pushed himself inside. Jesse was pretty far gone, so wrapped up in the sensations running through his body, he couldn't have pretended to be anyone else other than who he was. Greg was unraveling him, bit by exquisite bit. When Jesse finally came, eyes rolled back in his head, his entire body felt wrung out. He wasn't even sure when Greg came or when he rolled off, or how Jesse ended up enfolded in Greg's strong arms.

They both napped, or at least Jesse thought they did. When he woke up, Greg was still holding him.

"Just so you know, I can't be Neil Patrick Harris," Jesse said. "Not that I want to be, but you get my drift, right?"

Greg nuzzled Jesse's head. "Out there doesn't matter. All I care about is what happens in here."

"Well, here's me being me being insecure." Jesse took a deep breath. "The photographer thinks I could have a career as a model. Not as an actor. As a model."

Greg had begun to trail one hand up and down Jesse's arm. "What do you think of that?"

"My acting career's going nowhere fast. To Hollywood, I'm just another pretty face, and pretty faces are a dime a dozen. I don't do comedy well, and I don't get callbacks for anything with a decent budget. I could probably get by on the kind of work I've been doing and go on and on into obscurity and no one but my mother would care."

"I'd care," Greg said, and he placed a kiss on the top of Jesse's head.

"You have to care," Jesse said. "We're no longer fuck buddies. Non-fuck buddies have to care. It's in the handbook."

Greg chuckled. "So you think you might be interested in fashion modeling?"

Jesse wrinkled his nose. "I'm not sure they call it fashion modeling if you're a man, but yes, I think it might be good to keep my options open."

"Smart man," Greg said.

"Well-fucked man."

"That all?" Greg sounded disappointed.

"Well-made-love-to man," Jesse said.

The smile that stole over Greg's face warmed Jesse in a way he hadn't felt in a long, long time. "Most definitely," Greg said.

Jesse did keep his options open, right up until the Face of Fortunadi Fashions billboards started to go up and the fall catalog hit the stands. According to the trades, Jesse had "cheekbones to die for" and "a bedroom stare that would set any girl's panties on fire." Jesse and Greg had a good laugh about that last one.

When Jesse's agent started fielding twice as many calls for modeling jobs as acting jobs, Jesse took the hint. He was pretty good in front of a still camera by then. All he had to do was think of Greg making love to him. After all, he had a lot of firsthand experience to draw on.

He might never be Neil Patrick Harris, but Jesse was okay with that. He had Greg, who showed every sign of wanting to stick around for the indefinite future. So what if he didn't have the acting career he'd dreamed of. Spending a few hours a day in front of a still camera was way better than pretending to die over and over again at the hands of the deranged killer of the week in a movie so forgettable it would never be released on DVD. Going home at night to Greg was even better.

Fortunadi Fashions flew them both to New York for the unveiling of Jesse's billboard on Times Square. Jesse looked up at the thirty-foot version of himself, all bedroom eyes and come-fuck-me stance, and was flat-out awestruck. He'd seen the proofs, but the real thing was overwhelming. The only thing that kept him grounded was Greg's strong hand in his.

Just be yourself with me, Greg had said. As it turned out, being himself was a damn fine thing to be. If he'd gone with his first love, acting, he'd never be able to hold hands with his actual love in the middle of Times Square. It was all just a matter of adjusting his attitude.

"Bite me, Neil," Jesse said to the New York City night.

Greg turned to look at him. "You say something?"

Jesse shook his head and smiled. "Nothing important." He squeezed Greg's hand, and Greg squeezed back. "Nothing important at all."

TEDDY IN
MY BRIEFS

R. W. Clinger

Teddy Crew's bulky crotch was next to my face by accident, which prompted me to take in his pungent, sweaty man-smell that I found sexy. The guy would try anything on for attention. He found my navy Aussiebum briefs in my dresser, liked them, undressed down to his bare bottom, and put them on. Before I knew it, he was standing on a desk chair for my inspection. Teddy accidentally bumped his pounder into my mouth, sort of chuckled, and teased, "Hey, dude, watch what you're doing down there."

Problem one: Teddy was major straight. Even though all the dudes in my queer circle imagined him with a harem of hot girls, that wasn't so. Teddy wasn't getting busy with anyone, including me: Evan Donnelly at your service, his blond college roommate who won this year's Tightest Ass award down at the Queer Factory, a gay bar on Rosensteel Street.

"Earth to Evan, did you hear me?" He bumped my mouth with his cock again, pushing the navy-colored briefs into my face. The briefs had brought out the naughty in him. He seemed to turn into a completely different person as soon as the fabric touched his succulent package. He managed a couple thrusts forward, bouncing his six inches of limp rod against my face, teasing me.

I was ready for whatever the twenty-year-old jock with the aqua-blue eyes and suntanned skin wanted to surprise me with. I opened my mouth, wrapped lips around his cotton-covered protein and held his hips with my palms, ready and willing to carry out some naughty stuff that gym buddies just might carry out together after maybe drinking too much beer.

Problem two: Teddy had a history of modeling underwear in local newspaper ads, and the things were his weakness. Thongs. Briefs. Boxers. Jockstraps. By Papi, Body Tech, Clever, Rufskin, Diesel, Mundo Unico, Candyman, and Aussiebum. Whatever the style or brand, Teddy liked to try them on. His gigs paid well too, from what I understood. Enough to pay his college tuition. Plenty for him to go out on the town and spend a fortune drinking.

"You're being naughty, Evan."

"Stop pushing your cock in my face and I won't."

"You know you want to lick it."

"I really don't. I have cock all the time," I said, which was total bullshit.

Problem three: Teddy was a tease, with both the guys and the girls. The dude was a pure angel, inside and out. One hundred percent moral and decent. Mormon all the way. Just because he modeled part-time didn't mean he slept around, even if he had the rocking body for it, of course. My roommate was a flirt. You could look at him, but rarely could you touch him, if ever.

We were both crossing a line by my manhandling. His six inches of semi-hard beef popped out of the cotton's elastic rim and greeted my lips. I took advantage of the situation and licked his cut head and caused him to grow fully hard. Before I knew it, Teddy sported a nine-incher that was all mine.

He let out a sudden moan, pulled the briefs down a little, pushed his cock into my mouth, and confessed, "These briefs are amazing."

I sucked, licked, choked, and gagged. Teddy thrust forward and backward, held onto my blond hair and head for balance, and moaned like the wind outside. He crammed all of his nine inches into the depths of my throat, pulled out, slapped my cheeks with the beef, laughed down at me in a crazy-sexy manner and...

The desk chair cracked, giving out under his jockish weight. He fell away from me, toppling on his bed like a semi-naked gymnast. As the chair splintered to the floor, I rated Teddy's landing a 5.9 mark and said, "That was so hot, dude."

Positioned on his back and holding his cock, which had warily deflated, Teddy inquired, "What was hot, the blowjob or my fall?"

"Both," I supplied, studying the splintered chair. I then apologized for my impromptu action and said, "Teddy, I don't know what came over me. A guy gets in front of me and I tend to go crazy with my mouth." I wiped my lips with the back of my right hand and eyed the jock's rocking body.

He ignored me and pushed his goods into the briefs. He asked, "Do you think they're too small for me?"

"Briefs can never be too small."

"Will you let me try these out for a day?"

"I want a full report tomorrow morning over breakfast."

Teddy saluted me from his bed, shared a beaming smile, and slipped into his gym shorts as quickly as I could remove them.

(Click: I always took pictures of him, making him my

*model. I lusted for his skin, hungry for what he had to offer
me as a man, even if he was straight. My personal junior at
Yullin College. My meat. I didn't want him any other way. I
took pictures of him when he was asleep, firm between his legs
and with dots of pre-ooze on his Timoteo red classic briefs.
I focused on his swollen and sleeping package and perspiration-covered chest and semi-parted lips. I took pictures of his
muscular chest and underarms: narrow patches of blond hair
in both areas. I took pictures of him...)*

The next morning Teddy was walking funny, which made
me believe that he had spent a hot night with a sexy Russian guy
named Sasha he had been talking to at the bar. That wasn't the
case, though. Teddy complained that the briefs were a little too
snug and he needed a larger size.

"Let me check for any marks on your ass," I supplied, happy
to help.

Before I knew it, he was stripping off his running shoes,
jeans, and even his cotton T-shirt. He stood in front of me,
posing with his legs slightly separated.

I was on my knees in front of his cock, again. I directed,
"Turn around and let me have a look."

Teddy listened like a good jock/model/roommate.

My fingers pulled down on the briefs as I admired his bulbous,
perfectly fuckable bottom. I saw the red lines on his thighs from
where the briefs' elastic had etched into his muscular and hairless
flesh. I then took a whiff of his bottom, became sexually dizzy
from his male perspiration, and confessed, "You're right....The
briefs are too small. Take these off and relax your goods."

The roomie was happy to oblige. He slipped out of the briefs
and dropped them to the floor, taking a breather.

Before he had time to turn around, I couldn't help myself
and dabbed my tongue against his bottom. Mouth met his tight

rump for the very first time, which surprised the Mormon and caused him to jump.

Teddy spun around and asked, "Dude, what happened back there?"

"Sorry, I couldn't help it."

He shared a provocative look with me that was innocent and sexy. Teddy then turned around and asked, "So, this is what you want?" and grabbed his cock with his right hand, showing off.

I admit, he caught me off-guard. The semi-swollen tube of tasty sirloin was just staring at me, as well as its owner. I licked my lips, shared a smile, and confessed rather boyishly, "You must be reading my mind."

"I don't do guys," he confessed. "Shame on you for thinking about it."

"Sorry about that, Teddy," I shared, rising from the floor.

He pushed down on my shoulders and said, "Don't ever try to hit on me again, okay?"

"I won't," I confessed, peering at his upright tool in front of me.

"And don't ever think about sucking it, either," he whispered, pushing the head of his swollen rock to my lips, directing it into my mouth.

(Click: He didn't know I was in the bathroom with him while he was showering. Didn't know I photographed him under his hot spray after he played tackle football with his straight buddies. Didn't know I liked it when he lathered his torso with Irish Spring and soap dripped off of his taut nipples. Didn't know I watched him soap up his junk: swirling the bar of green and white soap over his droopy and hairy balls, and along the limp length of his wide cock. Didn't know...)

The joys of consensual blowjobs between college roomies

was desired to obtain the most ample grades, in my opinion. No wonder I was greedy for Teddy Crew.

I felt his palms on my shoulders and began to lap the length of his pulsing pole.

Teddy was in licking luxury, moaning and murmuring above me. After a minute of our connection, he pleaded, "I'm straight. Don't think this is something you're going to get every day."

I placed my palms on his strong hips for balance, felt his tool push to the back of my throat and his balls slap against my furred chin. He jammed his fleshy device inside me as far as it could plunge, pulled out, and jammed it in again. I heard him gurgle above me as he held the back of my head. And together we worked like diligent boyfriends, no longer fearing each other, breaking the wall down between queer and straight.

The lavishness of to and fro didn't stop for twenty minutes. I was in dick-delight as he agreed to our guy-with-guy motion. He murmured things I didn't understand, dizzy above me. He pulled at my hair, banged my face in a careful manner, and obeyed his hearty thirst for my mouthy pleasure.

I didn't have to tell him to pull out of my mouth before an orgasm twisted through his sculpted frame. Following a symposium of gyrations and undecipherable garbles, Teddy freed his harpoon from my oral suction, yanked on it a few times with his right hand in an up-and-down frenzy. The model grunted and groaned like a triple-X star and directed hot guy-syrup up and over his chest, ornamenting nipples, shoulders, and neck.

To top off his moment of bliss, he maneuvered his hose against my face, slapped my right cheek with his meat, then my left cheek, and chanted, "If you tell anyone about this I'll fuck you into next week."

Problem four: I was a total gossip-whore about everything. If you wanted a secret kept, you didn't tell Evan Donnelly. So, in truth, I told Stan Maleski about my gig with Teddy in my briefs. I told Paul Showendale, Jake Jonowsky, Sam Carlton...and ten other guys. Oops, my bad.

(Click: I photographed him jerking off in his bed with his legs spread apart and his nine-inch spike aiming at the dorm room's ceiling. Teddy was unaware that I was snapping pictures of his work: Stroke 29-covered palms shifting wildly up and down on his tool; hips rising and falling on his mattress; perspiration clinging to his abs and nipples and forehead; man-sap jetting out of his veined spike and pooling on his chiseled, model-boy chest.)

I was out of briefs by the end of two weeks. Teddy invaded my private drawers on a daily basis and sported the cotton with all smiles, which prompted problem five: rumor had it that Teddy in my briefs turned wild, coveting the Yullin Yellowtail swim team and sweaty wrestlers, enjoying Bobby and Brian York, twins from Memphis, and whomever else he could nail.

His sexual antics were crazy to realize: taking on three guys at the same time at a frat house; jerking dudes off in the showers; blowing Sammy Aster and Zach Marlin in their shared dorm; filming his sexual escapades and broadcasting his scenes on the Internet; making money from a few of his male-connected-to-male gigs and...

In reality, the briefs had to be taken away from him because he had spiraled out of control. No longer was he a quiet Mormon boy with manners from Salt Lake City, Utah. Teddy was now a needy and frisky man-on-man machine. I had pummeled him into that position...and now I had to get him out of it.

Jealousy found me. How dare he go on a sexual rampage? Who had he turned into? Why?

Truth was, I didn't want to share him with anyone. His flesh was mine...and no one else's. He belonged to me. He was my model. My subject. All mine.

(Click: I photographed him eating his own cock-sap after he jacked himself off. One fingertip...two fingertips...three fingertips were lathered in his own thick cream and entered his mouth. He sucked on them up to their first knuckles as if he were a porn star, enjoying his model role. And following his sucking and cleaning and sucking again, he licked his lips, starting with his bottom one first, rolling his tongue from right to left, and then the upper lip, finishing his rolling from left to right and...)

"I want all of my briefs back, Teddy," I implored, threatening him with cockeyed brows and a serious tone in our dorm room, ready for battle.

"What for?" His rakish smile melted me. Dammit, why'd he have to smile like that?

"You have a problem wearing my briefs. You're a chronic brief abuser."

He shyly shook his head and shared, "The rumors aren't true. I've been a very good boy."

"You deny fucking half the wrestling team?"

"I do."

"What about the York twins?"

"I don't even know the York twins."

Problem six: my eight inches of boner was snug in my Rufskin workout shorts and it wanted to be played with, sucked, jacked off, or consumed by a hot ass that just happened to look like Teddy's. I wanted/desired/needed my roommate more than any other man in my life. And nothing was going to stand in my way of having him.

The model moved up to me, locked his chest to my chest, and breathed me in. Before I could back away, my eyes connected with him, I felt his tongue on my cheek and then on my neck. Teddy clamped his lips to my lips, pulled me to his naked and ripped torso, and caused me to feel perplexed, unsure of the moment, but safe against him, unharmed.

The kiss lasted for two minutes. Tongues tangled as we shared guy-saliva. Eventually he pulled off and away, leaned his forehead against mine, kept his glare locked to my glare, and stated, "Don't blame me for being out of control, Evan. I'm new at this and it feels right. I've put a lot of trust in you and..."

I touched his chest with a palm, flush against his heart, and chanted, "You're so naughty."

"But I like to be naughty."

"Of course you do. Maybe it has nothing to do with the briefs, right?"

He gave me a look of discontent. "It has *everything* to do with the briefs. I'll tell you what, I know about your pictures of me and how you think I'm your model. You give me copies of your pics and I'll give you your briefs back."

"You know about the pics?"

"Fuck yeah."

"You just want copies? I still can keep them?"

"I wouldn't dare take your pleasure away from you, Evan."

"That's hot."

"I am hot, aren't I?"

I didn't have enough time or control to escape his spell or answer his question because he quickly removed my T-shirt and jeans, dropping them to the dorm room floor. He kissed my chest with his opened mouth, tasted my salty skin, and devoured my right shoulder blade. I felt his tongue against one of my underarms, against my ribs, next to my navel, and then he fell to the floor, bare knees on hard wood, and cupped his lips over my briefs.

I was growing hard against his mouth. Five inches grew into six inches...seven inches...and then into eight full inches. A throbbing mass twitched in front of my torso, all by itself, welcoming Teddy's gratification.

As expected, the model dove onto me and plunged my plug into the back of his mouth, gagging on my shaft. In doing so, he rolled his fingertips up and down my perspiration-covered chest, driving my skin crazy. He slurped at my cock, slobbering over its capped head, totally enjoying himself. Festively, he pulled me toward his face, pushed me away with delicate force, and pulled me toward him again. He digested my skin with ease, pleasuring himself, inch after inch, and mumbled insignificant foibles.

Naughty was the understatement of the year. Teddy was pleasurably wicked with his tongue and sucking. I felt walloped by his lust, windblown and merry next to his skin. My eyes rolled into the back of my skull as my breathing intensified. I couldn't help but to clamp my hands to the back of his head and assist him. Our sexual stride and mellifluous muttering became synchronized. Like a good roommate I bounded into his mouth, certain to delight the both of us.

Before blowing my sticky load too soon, though, I was spun around by his unstoppable palms. My last pair of briefs were tugged free from my skin. And Teddy—no longer angelic, moral, and decent—pushed me to his bed and pried my bottom open with fingers and...

"Your tongue...use your tongue on me, dude." I couldn't help myself, longing for our flesh to link/collide/meet.

Like all fairy tales with believable, rising action, and like all fairies with just the right sprinkling touch of gay magic, Teddy dotted his tongue to my center. A quick dab and lick drove me wild. Another speedy tongue movement caused me to call out his name. A third connection required a gasp and moan. And a fourth embarked on the words, "Use your cock, man....I can't wait any longer."

(Click: I had a variety of photographs that proved Teddy pushed things into his bottom: two dildos, extended fingers, a wooden broom handle, numerous butt plugs, an assortment of beads, a screwdriver handle. Occasionally, he would spread his legs and supply his taut bottom with some dick-jolting ass pounding. Truth was, those were my favorite pictures of the model, ones that caused me to wrap my own steady palms around my hearty pole and take advantage of my skin, shooting many loads onto my...)

Lust was how many inches a guy entered my behind on the first crack. Teddy was totally into me, since he pressed all nine inches of his condom-covered rod into my bottom.

I became anxious beneath his weight, pressed to the edge of his bed. And feebly I closed my eyes because of his titanic girth and length and gritted my teeth in contentment. I clamped palms and fingers onto the bedspread in sheer amusement, pained but in deep hunger for his body inside mine.

Problem seven: No longer was he the Mormon boy-reticent, since he lightly spanked me while plunging his cock into me. My roommate released all nine inches, plummeted them inside me again, and continued that necessary movement for the next fifteen minutes, plowing my pink canal with bliss and stamina. The supposedly shy and straight guy was all over me, inside me, behind me. He licked my back and shoulders, thumping my rump. And in an unruly approach, heaving for breath, colliding avidly with my core, he grabbed onto my hips and drew me close to him for one last rhombic and fiery bolt. Behind me, he confessed, "Ready or not...we're going to cum," and pulled out of me.

Before he exploded I was flipped over. My eight inches of

tool was pressed firmly against Teddy's tool, his hand wrapped around their muscled lengths and hearty widths.

Twinkle-eyed, handsome, and charming, he peered down at me with a glowing smile and recommended, "Let's cum together, Evan."

I was in no position to object, of course, and whispered, "Hell yeah....Bring it on."

Numb beneath his touch, he worked the tools in an attentive and detailed manner. No longer was he rushed and spirited to burst his load. His stroking was calm and relaxed, unhurried and just right. Our cocks' skins kissed, up and down, over and over. His reduced motion seemed to top off the moment, prolonging our sexual agreement. Ardently he moved his right hand north and south, rotating our cocks as he smiled down at me. And majestically I fell under his spell, hypnotized with the parallel movement, wanting to continue it...until the end of the semester.

"It's cumming," he whispered.

"I'm with you," I offered.

Together we held air in our lungs, failed to breathe, and turned pale. Together we bucked our hips in a generous and timely fashion. And together we gyrated and blew our creamy sap upward, six inches or more, watching the droplets explode like fireworks and twirl down to my chest, his hand, and our rods.

We found air simultaneously, eager to breathe again, spew-free. Hovering over me, his weight collapsed against my own and he began to laugh. And, in his arms, post-sexed, heaving for breath, I listened to him confess, "Tomorrow should be interesting, Evan."

"Why's that, Teddy? You're giving my briefs back, right?"

He held my face in his palms, dotted a kiss to my nose, a

cheek, my neck, and breathed in my sweet-sticky-salty skin. He supplied, "Not a chance...I've decided to keep them...and you."

"You're sexually untamed," I admitted with a smile, happy to be in his company.

"You like untamed."

And I laughed, holding him close, knowing he was right, and he was mine...all mine.

Problems solved.

STILL LIFE WITH PHILLIP DELANEY

Connor Wright

I tried real hard to hold still, but it wasn't easy. My left foot was all pins an' needles, my arms were tired from holdin' myself up, an' my feet an' my hands an' my ass were all cold. Why'd I ever say *yes* to replacin' Ginger as the model for this life drawin' class anyhow? I mean, 'sides from the fact that Ginger'd done me a handfulla favors over the last few years an' I kinda owed her at least one.

"All right, time," the lady at the front of the room, Miss Jenkins, said, an' I finally relaxed a little. Notta lot, though, 'cause if I relaxed *too* much I'd be showin' off my bits an' pieces an' I didn't wanna do that. She told me I wasn't s'posed to, anyhow, an' I didn't wanna piss her off.

"If you'd please change position, Mr. Delaney?"

Thank God. "Okay," I said, an' shrugged at her. "Whattya want me to do, now?"

"Um..." She thought about it, then pointed at the wooden box I was layin' on. "Just stretch out on your side, please. And mind your, er..."

I minded my *er* an' did as Miss Jenkins asked. At least I was gettin' *paid* for takin' my clothes off an' lettin' people draw me naked. It was easier work than what I usually did, an' I even kinda liked it—I usually got to see what people drew an' there were some real artists in the class.

There was also this guy. There he was again, sittin' in the back, all bundled up in a coat an' hat an' even a scarf, hunched up an' drawin'. He never let anybody see any of his pictures, an' he always left right after my time was up. It was weird, but I'd figured out that mosta the art students were kinda weird, so I didn't think too much about it.

As I was layin' there, listenin' to the scratchy sound of people drawin' me—it sounded like a buncha mice, really—I wondered what Benny was up to. Whenever I asked him, he just said he didn't do a whole lot, just read or spent time with the guys or somethin'.

I couldn't think about Benjamin Summers too much, couldn't think about the way he looked when he smiled or how he kept our place all tidy or even just the way he smelled, while I was sittin' around bein' somethin' to draw. If I did, Miss Jenkins'd prolly throw me out *an'* call the cops, an' that woulda been even worse than just gettin' thrown out.

Finally, while I was tryin' to decide if I wanted to try countin' to a thousand by three-and-a-halfs, Miss Jenkins clapped her hands an' said, "All right! Time to take a few minutes to rest. Thank you so much, Mr. Delaney; you've been *so* helpful tonight!"

"It ain't a problem," I said, sittin' up an' tryin' to remember what I did with my clothes. Oh, yeah, there they were, by the end of the box closest to the door. There was a shufflin' noise an' I looked up to see the guy scurryin' outta the room like his coat was on fire or somethin'. I took my clothes an' went an' got dressed, then went back to the room an' looked at the pictures for a little while, an' then I went home.

None of the lights were on when I got there, which was kinda strange. I figured Benny mighta gone down to the Cumberland or the boss's office or somethin', so I wasn't too worried about it. Then I turned on the light in the hallway. It ain't a real special hallway; I mean, it's got a floor an' a ceilin' an' a light an' two walls. Tonight, though, there was a piece of paper layin' on the floor an' *that* got me upset.

Me an' Benny, we thump people who need thumpin'. An' in our line of work, paper on the floor ain't a good sign. It usually means a kidnappin', or a killin', or somethin' else that ain't nice or legal or neat an' clean. So I went over an' checked on it an' found out that *this* paper, this one didn't have nothin' on it like that. No, what the paper had on it was *me*. Naked. It was from one of the classes I sat for, one of the early ones, 'cause I was sittin' kinda hunched over, tryin' to hide my dick from everyone.

Except...I got down on one knee an' looked closer. Except in *this* picture, I could kinda see it. I got hold of the paper, real careful, an' got up. A little further down the hall was another picture, from the same class. I was sittin' on a stool, in this one, lookin' kinda like I prolly did when I got sent to the principal's office in school: my heels an' elbows were out, my knees an' my toes pointin' in. An' there was my dick again, right there where it ain't *s'posed* to be.

I picked up the second picture an' headed for the kitchen. When I turned on the light, I found three more, each one of me an' showin' parts of me that weren't showin' when I sat for 'em. I stacked all of 'em together an' checked the dinin' room, an' there was another one right in the middle of the table.

It was different than the others, though, 'cause even though

it was a picture of me, I was layin' on my back with my hands
up by my head, holdin' on to a pillow or somethin', an' my legs
were stretched out wide. My dick was hard, in the one on the
table, an' my eyes were closed, my mouth open. It was...It was
kinda weird an' kinda hot an' even a little bit scary, 'cause who
drew it? An' how'd they get into our *house*? "Benny?"

Nothin', but I didn't really *expect* anything, either. I let out
my breath an' gathered up the picture an' went to poke my head
into the room we called the library. It ain't fancy or nothin', just
a spare bedroom we put some bookshelves an' lamps an' chairs
in. When I opened the door, I could see that Benny's lamp was
on, shinin' on his chair. It wasn't really empty, 'cause there was
a piece of paper on the cushion, but Benny wasn't around.

Me again. Hard, an' this time sittin' on my knees, my head
tilted back an' my hands back behind me, holdin' me up. There
was somethin' new, though: a little line, comin' up from my
head, like in a comic. I was sayin' *Please, Ben, suck me or fuck
me or some*thin*'*...I tried to decide if I should risk goin' to the
cops, 'cause this was just *wrong*. Someone spyin' on us, *listenin'*
to us, an' drawin' pictures of it? Of *me*? I turned around to leave
an' saw there was somethin' on *my* chair.

Me, kinda curled over on one hand an' my knees, the other
one under me, prolly holdin' on to my dick. Another one of
those lines, this time leadin' to *God, I wanna fuck you now,
Benny. Please, can I?* An' I almost missed it, but I looked for
just a few seconds longer an' I noticed a line comin' from the
edge of the page an' some more words. *If you don't, I'm going
to be really disappointed.*

I could almost hear Benny sayin' that, an' then the way he'd
laugh after. Where the hell was he? I headed back out to the
sittin' room an' turned on the light. Two pictures on the sofa an'
one on the low table between it an' the fireplace. I looked at the

sofa pictures first. Me, me, always me. In one I was on my back again, jerkin' myself an' a hand—not one of *mine*, somebody else's—was up against my ass an' all I could think was that there hadda be at least two fingers inside me.

The idea of someone drawin' these an' leavin' 'em for me was still creepy, but I was startin' to get horny, too. The pictures were all kinda rough, but I knew exactly what they were s'posed to be showin', an' dirty pictures *are* dirty pictures. In the other sofa picture, I was layin' there with cum on my belly an' my hand kinda curled around my soft dick like I was tryin' to keep it safe.

The table picture was me on my hands an' knees, again, an' this time there was a dick half-inside me. I was sayin', *Yeah, please, fuck me like that,* an' I could almost *feel* it, could almost feel Benny's hands on me. I tugged at the front of my pants an' wondered what I'd find in our room.

What I found was my lamp on an' one last piece of paper, on the floor right inside the door. It was smaller than the rest of 'em, an' it wasn't just a picture of me. It was a picture of me fuckin' *Benny*, an' it didn't really look like the rest. It was more finished, or something. It also had a little scribble down in the right-hand corner at the bottom, which none of the rest had. A little noise brought my head up an' I remembered that I was kinda worried about there maybe bein' some kinda creep in the house.

There wasn't a creep, there was just—"Benny!" He was in bed, the quilts pulled up to his chin an' no book in sight.

"Hey," he said, an' kinda lifted his chin. "You found them."

"Yeah, but I dunno what to think," I said, wavin' the pictures at him. "I mean, you're about the only one who's seen me naked like *this*, recently."

"Yeah, I am." There was somethin' kinda funny about the

way he said it, an' I looked at the last big picture, really *lookin'* at it, 'specially the writin'. Now that I was lookin' at it, I was pretty sure I knew whose it was.

"You—Benny? *You*...drew these?" They were a lot less creepy an' a *lot* more sexy all of a sudden. "When?"

He smiled at me, duckin' like he does when he's embarrassed. "I did. Over the last few weeks. I was afraid you'd catch me."

"Catch—" I set the pictures on top of our bureau an' crossed my arms. "That was *you*? In the back an' the hat an' everything?"

"Guilty," he said, an' I could *hear* him smilin'. "It was a spur-of-the-moment idea, really. I thought it would be interesting to draw you, but I didn't know if being in the class was the best thing. And then when I was sketching you, I started thinking about, well..." He shrugged.

"Yeah, it's prolly a good thing I didn't know it was you," I said, an' hooked my thumbs under my suspenders. "Hey, Benny?"

"Hm?"

"Tell me," I said, gettin' my suspenders down an' then pullin' my shirt outta my pants, "did drawin' these, y'know, do it for you?"

"Yes," he said, an' moved a little. "Especially the last few."

"Mm, yeah?" I started unbuttonin' my shirt, slow. "Even the last one? The little one?"

"The little one...no." Benny moved again, lookin' at me an' then lookin' at the mirror over the bureau. "Because I didn't draw that one. I, um, commissioned it."

"You what? Had it drawn?" I forgot about my shirt for a minute, feelin' kinda like I did when somebody hits me on the jaw in a scrap. Parta me was kinda pissed, 'cause I ain't interested in sharin' Benny with *no*body, an' parta me was tryin' to figure out who the hell we knew that Benny woulda *asked* for somethin' like that.

Noddin', Benny sat up an' the quilts fell down, showin' me that he wasn't wearin' a shirt. "Yeah. 'Cause I'm not *that* good, and...I don't know, it was one of those things that just kind of took on a life of its own. Uh...Forest did it. I paid him, cash."

"Oh." Forest, of course. I felt silly insteada bein' pissed off, then, an' shrugged. "He's real good, ain't he?"

Benny relaxed an' I kinda wondered just how worried he'd been about me an' that picture an' me knowin' he asked Forest. "Yeah," he said, watchin' me.

"I know somethin' else that's real good, too," I said, an' skinned out of my clothes. Benny slid outta bed an' I saw that he was naked, too, which made my dick happier. He was smilin' at me again, too, which was...I dunno, I ain't that great with explainin' how he makes me feel when it comes to that kinda thing. But I liked seein' him smilin' at me an' it made my chest get all warm.

"And what would that be? Something like, oh...this?" An' then Benny came over an' got down on his knees in front of me, an' when he leaned forward I put my hands on his head. He started off by kissin' my legs an' my belly an' even my knees; he got his hands up on my ass an' squeezed it, some, an' started lickin' me.

"Mm, yeah," I said, puttin' my hands over his. A minute later, Benny started suckin' on me, an' I made a happy noise. His mouth was hot an' wet an' wonderful, an' the way his tongue curled around me, rubbed at me....I closed my eyes an' tilted my head back. "God."

Benny's mouth moved off my dick an' he kissed me, makin' a line up over my belly an' chest to *my* mouth. After we kissed for a while, with him pressin' up against me an' our dicks rubbin' on one another, he bumped his nose against mine. "You're so much better than any drawing," he said. "Come to bed."

"So're you," I said, an' kissed him again. "Only if you're gonna fuck me."

"Sure thing," he said, an' pulled me over to the bed. He kissed me again, an' I pinched his ass, an' he tried to tickle me an' we ended up fallin' over onto the quilts. We kinda wrestled for a couple of minutes, kissin' an' bitin' a little an' lickin' one another, 'til finally I ended up on my back with Benny sittin' on my legs.

"Will you fuck me now?" I gave him my best 'pretty please' look, even though I knew what the answer was. "Please?"

"Of course," he said, and moved over so I could get my legs open. "You wanna start with two?" He leaned over me an' grabbed the lube off his table.

"Yeah," I said, and then, "God, Benny, *yes*," when he gave me what I wanted.

"Phil?" Benny said, a couple of minutes later. He had a funny look on his face, one I ain't seen very often.

"What? Benny, please."

"One of the reasons I started drawing those pictures? Seeing you sitting there made me appreciate just how good you look." He moved up an' kissed my dick an' licked it a couple of times. "How hot, how fuckable you are. Do you have any idea how hard it is for me to wait?"

I laughed a little. "Not really, 'cause I ain't you. But I know how hard it is when I'm fuckin' *you*." Then I rubbed my hands over my chest an' pinched my nipples an' kinda stretched, like I was showin' off for him. I was prolly as tired of waitin' as he was, so I said, "So don't, Benny, don't wait. An' don't make *me* wait, please?"

"I won't, swear to God," he said, grinnin' at me. Then he

moved away from me, lookin' for the lube. Just a little bit longer an' then there was the cool slick an' he was pushin' his cock into me. "But slow, okay?"

"I know, I know." I hated it, but I knew there wasn't nothin' I could do to make him hurry. Didn't mean I wouldn't *try*, though. "Wanna feel you, okay? C'mon, Ben, move."

Benny touched my dick real softly, shakin' his head. "Just a minute." He moved, though, an' I hummed a little as he stretched me.

He ran his hands over me, up the outside of my thighs an' my sides an' across my belly, up to my chest. Benny got deeper as he petted me, an' I wiggled, tryin' to help him out. When he was tight against me, he curled over an' helped me up so we could kiss. It was messy an' slow an' God, it was so *good*.

"Fuck, Benny?"

"Hm?" He opened his eyes an' looked down at me.

"C'mon, please?" He just touched my face an' kissed me again, slippin' outta me real slowly at the same time. Benny pushed inside me again, an' when he was all the way in, I pulled him down an' kinda rose up 'til our lips touched. I opened my mouth an' Benny licked at me, sucked on my tongue, an' moaned at me some. I dunno how many times we did that, him movin' in an' outta me so slowly an' the both of us kissin' like a couple of kids neckin'.

"Benny," I said, wrappin' my legs around him an' movin' under him, "God, *move*."

"Fuck yes," he said, an' made a short little thrust that made me groan. After that, he started fuckin' me for real an' I laid there, lovin' the way it felt. All of a sudden, though, he slowed down again.

"What's wrong?"

"Nothing," Benny said, an' wrapped his hand around my

dick. "I just want you to cum first, that's all."

"Ah." I moaned as he started jerkin' me, fuckin' me at the same time. It took Benny a few minutes to get back into the rhythm, but he did. I couldn't really help him out, much, 'cept by liftin' my ass an' tryin' to fuck his hand. I made noise, every time he hit me just-so inside, an' he leaned over.

"God, I love the way you sound," he said, stoppin' for a second. "Makes this so much hotter."

"Please," I said, movin' 'cause he wasn't, "do it, fuck me."

"Are y'close? Wanna hear you cum, baby, c'mon."

Benny's fist was slick an' tight an' *perfect* around me. "Yeah, 'm close, but I want you t'fuck—"

"Cum for me," he said, an' got me just right inside again, "c'mon, Philip. God, you're gorgeous; so hot and hard for me; love seein' you on the edge like this. You're so close; c'mon, cum for me."

I grabbed at the sheet as he talked to me, as he touched me, my muscles gettin' all wound up an' tight. I was almost there, *almost*, just needed a little *more....* "Ben, Benny," I said, only it was mostly air, *"please—"* An' then he pulled out one more time an' slammed back into me an' that was it, all I needed. It was like everything good ever got stuffed into my head an' then went off like fireworks an' my brain went all fuzzy, when I came.

An' Benny, he had a hold of me an' was fuckin' me, hard an' fast. I watched his face, watched him bite his lip an' the way he got this little wrinkle between his eyebrows. It didn't take no time at all 'til his mouth opened up an' his fingers dug into me an' he shoved his cock into me as far as he could. "Fuck, fuck *yes.*"

He flopped over an' kissed me, sloppy an' lazy, an' I got a hand into his hair. "Mm. Hey, Benny?"

"Yeah?" He lifted his head, some, so he could look at me.

"Was it real good?" I grinned at him an' he laughed, sittin' up.

"Wanna know a secret, Phil?" Benny pulled outta me, gentle, an' lay down alongside me, rubbin' at the blobs of cum on my belly. I nodded an' he put his mouth right up next to my ear. "No matter how good I think it's gonna be, it's always *better*."

I poked him with my elbow an' shook my head a little. "Jesus, Benny..."

"It's true." He kissed the side of my head.

"I ain't gonna argue," I said, 'cause I couldn't think of what to say to that. Sometimes if I think too much about him an' me, I get kinda scared about it—about how *much* we seem to feel. So I leaned over an' swatted him on the hip an' then I sat up. "C'mon, let's clean up an' I'll make you some flapjacks, okay?"

"How about French toast instead?" He sat up, too, patted me on the leg an' then got outta bed.

"Sounds good," I said, an' followed him, glancin' at the pictures as we went by. "We gotta remember to find a frame."

Benny just laughed.

BEAUTIFUL.
DIRTY. RICH.

Clancy Nacht

M att's first runway made him nervous. The show was major, and he was wearing a long, open silk robe with a stand-up collar that made it look like a cross between a kimono and something Sherlock Holmes would wear.

All he had to do was walk. Who didn't know how to walk? But runway was different. It required attitude. He had to *walk*.

At this point, he was just hoping he didn't fall on his ass. But if he did, he'd better make it fierce.

Looking next to him, he saw Gabe, a German model who spoke English better than most of Matt's friends. Gabe's grin was a bit lopsided. That seemed to be fine; male models were rarely asked to smile on the runway. His dark hair stood in stark contrast to his pale face. His lips were rouged, his eyes painted around to give him an exotic appearance. "Don't be nervous. You have it," he said to Matt.

Matt exhaled slowly and nodded. They weren't with the same agency, but Gabe had stood in line behind him and had sat near him during makeup. Matt gestured to the stage.

"So what do you think about while you're out there?"

"Beer."

"Just beer?"

Gabe laughed. "Good beer. Beer I'm going to have at the afterparty."

"There's a party?" Matt played with the long black wig attached to his hat. When he'd looked in the mirror, he'd barely recognized himself. They'd even airbrushed on abs, which begged the question, why did they cast him? There were plenty of bigger guys with six-packs, but he'd guessed their shoulders didn't fit into these clothes.

"Yeah, there's a party later. If this show ever starts."

Without his phone, Matt felt like he was in a vacuum. He had no idea what time it was. "What's the hold-up?"

Before Gabe could answer, there was a loud clamor at the back of the broad, bright room with its rows of empty makeup tables. The double doors flew open, and a striking man in stiletto boots and a leather military jacket swaggered through. His blond hair fluttered in a breeze of his own making; his lush lips curled at the sides. Chin up, he looked haughty, his gray eyes imperious as he surveyed the lineup of men and then the makeup tables.

Matt leaned into Gabe. "Is that the designer?"

"That," Gabe spat, pointing with his glare but obviously too intimidated to gesture at the blond, "is nobody. A big, fake nobody."

The nobody dropped into a makeup chair and sat back as stylists appeared to frantically make him up and undress him. For a nobody, he commanded a lot of attention.

"I'm sure he has a name." Matt couldn't help but be intrigued. He'd been told to arrive two hours early and be prepared to wait. And wait he had, through several touchups. This guy just popped in and was being fitted with a headdress.

"Niko." Gabe rolled his eyes. "I'm so ready for him to be over. He's horrible."

Matt noticed that even with all of Gabe's harsh words about Niko, he couldn't take his eyes off him.

Niko stretched out his arm and pointed toward a table lined with bottles of alcohol that the models weren't allowed to drink. He snapped his fingers. A production assistant appeared to plead with him. Niko sat up, turned his head to give her his full glare, and she shot off toward the table.

It was fascinating.

Gabe snorted. "She's such a bitch."

"Oh! I thought this was an all-men's show." He'd assumed the blond was a man, but his cheekbones were high enough to be a woman's.

"It is."

As if to confirm, Niko stood from the chair in a nude thong. His impressive length distended the bottom of the nylon. He held his arms out, and they dressed him in a very short kimono topped with a corset. He frowned at the shoes they'd chosen and shook his head.

Assistants rushed to offer several pairs to choose from. Niko consented to wear some platforms and stepped into them as the woman who had gone to the forbidden table returned with a champagne flute.

He took a sip and then smiled at the long line of men. The stylists had just finished with a bustle ending in a long train when Niko approached them, seeming not to walk so much as *glide*.

Matt was so fixated on Niko's long, pale legs that he didn't notice Niko staring right at him.

"You're new." Niko smiled. They'd painted his lips black; they were perfect, with a sharply indented Cupid's bow. His teeth were blindingly white, and the black paint around his gray eyes made them eerie.

"Yeah, this is my first show."

Niko's brows rose. "Well, this is a good show for a newbie to book. Are you nervous?"

Matt nodded. His cheeks felt hot. Everyone was staring at him, but that wasn't nearly as intimidating as Niko's eyes roving over his body like he was noting flaws. Matt wished he could look away, but Niko was too absorbing, too ethereal. If Matt looked away, Niko might vanish altogether. "Yes."

Niko sipped his champagne and then handed it to Matt. "Don't drink it; just hold it. I'll be back."

"But I have to—I mean, I'm going to go on stage."

Niko laughed. "You're so cute."

The music was ramping up, and the designer appeared. Niko turned as the designer greeted him. They air-kissed one another and the designer made minor adjustments to Niko's wardrobe. Then Niko stalked up the stairs and onto the stage. The lights hit him, and he glimmered from head to toe. Applause.

Gabe rolled his eyes. "He is such a pig."

Matt leaned forward until Niko was too far down the stage for Matt to watch. "A pig? Why do you say that? Does he get around?"

Gabe opened his mouth to speak, but another model said, "Niko gets what he wants, but he's never wanted Gabe."

The man winked at Matt and returned his attention to the catwalk.

Matt raised his brows. In spite of popular belief, most male models weren't gay. Some experimented, but it broke down about average for the general population; some guys were more sensitive about it than others, so Matt had kept his thoughts to himself. "You like him?"

"No." Gabe sulked and shook his head. "I don't like him. I don't want him. I have a *girlfriend*. He just gets everything handed to him because he's the heir to a lotion fortune. Everyone kisses his ass and acts like he's royalty, but he's not all that."

Niko reappeared and the next model stepped onto the runway. There were only three models ahead of Matt now. It made him jittery.

Niko descended the stairs and plucked the champagne from Matt's hand. He sipped, casting Gabe a quick glance, then focused again on Matt. "Don't worry, babe. You've got nothing to worry about. Just be fierce."

With that, Niko swatted Matt's ass and headed to the racks for his next outfit.

"Be fierce," Matt told himself. Then he was on. The lights hit him, blinding him to the audience. The music pumped a good beat for striding, and he walked, thinking about Niko's graceful strides, the slight swagger in his shoulders, the way he cocked his head.

He hit the end of the runway, paused, looked at the blank outlines of people, and turned, striding back. He wanted to think about beer, but all he could think about was champagne.

Gabe gave him a nod as Matt passed him on the runway, and then Matt hit the steps and it was over. He'd only been hired for one look.

His eyes were still adjusting, but he recognized Niko's voice. "Killed it, Matt. You totally killed it."

Matt's stomach flipped. "How do you know my name?"

Now that he could see better, he took in what little Niko wore. Ornate strips of silver leather wound up his legs, around

his torso and down his arms. Makeup artists struggled to finish
off his look.

"I'm a witch." Niko glanced to the wall where there was the
model board on which each model was featured with a Polaroid
and his name written in Sharpie below.

Matt rolled his eyes at himself. Still, it was a good sign that
Niko had bothered to look him up. "How do you know I killed
it?"

"You really are new, aren't you?" Niko pointed at a monitor
mounted on a rolling cart. The designer was glued to its
screen.

Gabe gave Matt a light shove as he moved past him.

The action made Niko smirk. He followed Gabe with his
eyes and raised a brow.

"In any case, my runway-killer Matt, I should let you tend
to your friend, time for me to get back on stage. Tell Gabe not
to pout too much. He is, after all, closing the show. Though I
imagine he's just *sore* that I got there first."

Niko headed back to the stage, leaving Matt to puzzle over
what *that* meant.

The modeling world was bewildering.

Matt changed into his street clothes next to Gabe, glancing
at him furtively. He'd just met him but felt some loyalty. Or
that's what he told himself. Niko was intimidating; even his
kindness seemed barbed.

Matt finished removing his makeup. In the mirror, he could
see Niko behind him, pulling the straps of his costume off, air-
kissing the designer again, pulling his clothes on.

Gabe got up without a word and went to the end of the line
to close the show. He refused to look Matt in the eye.

Matt watched Gabe moving up the line, wondering what
happened next. Gabe was hot and all, but not of Niko's caliber.

"Wakey, wakey. He's straight-ish, Matt. Don't waste your time on him. Waste your time on me." Niko grinned. Even without the black lipstick, his smile was dazzling. He'd left the eyeliner on, but his lips were pink and glossy. "The champagne here is for shit. Come on."

He tugged on Matt's shirt and gave him a pout that probably got him anything he wanted.

"What about the afterparty?" Matt was already on his feet, following.

Niko smiled over his shoulder. "I'll show you where the real party is."

That was all it took. A smile from those perfectly formed lips, a lowering of those eyes to reveal those perfect lashes, the turn of his head, and the promise of danger. Matt followed him out through the double doors and down the winding hallways until they were outside in the brisk air.

They'd gone out the back to avoid the crowd. There was a red Ducati motorcycle parked against one of the pillars. It looked more like an anime machine than a real vehicle. Matt followed Niko to it.

After unlocking it, Niko straddled the thing and raised his brows. "There's only one helmet, so here you go."

There was something sexy about the rail-thin blond in eyeliner and long streaming hair offering to drive Matt on the back of that machine. Something dangerous. And that's what Niko was: sexy, dangerous, hard to pin down.

"What about you?"

Niko's smirks were the sign of cruel thoughts that were about to be given word. "I'm the dangerous one. You're the one who needs protecting. Put it on; get on the bike. I'm not staying here all night while you try and figure out where you misplaced your balls."

Matt crushed his hair under the helmet, though he wasn't sure how necessary it was. Fashion Week traffic was notoriously slow.

As soon as he hopped on and wrapped his arms around Niko, he was grateful to be wearing it.

Niko gave little warning to the other models milling about or the few fashion people who had spotted them and were coming over to take pictures or chat. He simply revved the Ducati, and then rocketed down the short length of stairs to the sidewalk. Niko didn't even brake. He sped into the traffic and wove between the stuck cars at a speed that made Matt worry he was going to lose a limb.

It was dark out and the lights streaked by like they did in the movies. People honked their horns. Fists and fingers came out of windows, but Niko didn't slow down. His hair whipped back behind him, straying over the edges of Matt's helmet. A few strands got under it, tickling his chin.

Luckily for Matt and the contents of his stomach, they didn't have far to go. Chelsea was only a few blocks away, and at the breakneck speed with which Niko had taken sidewalks, roads, any surface, they were already riding up a ramp into a parking garage.

The building they'd approached was all plate glass and girders, like its wealthy occupants liked looking down on the plebs to see how they lived their petty lives.

Niko lived in one of the top three floors. There were only a few doors in the hallway, all done up in a chilly modern style with polished wood and brushed steel.

The condo was an open two-story plan, windows floor to ceiling on one side. The kitchen was at one end, a television and low couches at the other. There was a loft space on the second floor that presumably held the bed.

Niko headed to the kitchen first, where he pulled a bottle from his wine chiller. Then he pulled a baggie of weed from somewhere in the spice rack. "Anything else you want?"

"Where is the party?"

"*I* am the party." He started climbing to the loft.

Matt fluffed his hair, hoping to look rakish rather than helmet-headed. He checked his reflection in the window and primped until he decided he looked good enough. By the time he got upstairs, Niko was already sitting on the bed naked. The lights of the city twinkled, casting Niko's pale body in shades of blue. He had his back to Matt, leaning on one arm, hair covering one shoulder.

Niko drank straight from the bottle. "Roll me one."

Matt crossed the room, pulling off his shirt. He tossed it to the side and then toed off his shoes when he got to the foot of the bed. Niko sat back to enjoy the show as Matt slowly unbuckled his pants and then pushed them off over his hips.

Niko cupped his hand over Matt's length through his boxer briefs. Then, with a quick pull, the elastic waistband rolled down and his cock sprang from the fabric. Niko pulled again, dragging them down to his ankles. Matt stepped out of them and sat next to Niko, feet resting on the cool wooden floor.

The paper and the baggy sat there among the velvety blue sheets. Once Matt had the joint rolled and lit, Niko traded the bottle of wine for it. The wine was red and tasted like blood and ash.

With half the joint smoked, Niko took the bottle back and set it on the hardwood floor. He passed Matt the joint. Niko dropped to his knees on the floor and spread Matt's legs. With his face between Matt's thighs, Niko grabbed the base of Matt's cock, ringing it with thumb and forefinger to twist at the base. He warmed the tip with his mouth, just breathing on it.

The sensation made Matt's legs tense up, his body on edge for more. He felt loose and happy, open to the possibilities. Niko flicked his tongue along the tip, still ghosting his fingers over the shaft.

Niko looked up at Matt, lips wrapped around the tip. He placed his hands on Matt's hips, keeping him in place so that Niko could moderate how deeply his mouth was fucked. He controlled the pace but took the cock deep into his throat. His cheeks bulged as his mouth filled and hollowed as he pulled away.

Matt dropped the remainder of the joint into the ashtray next to the bed. He held himself up on the bed sheets, but just barely. His grip kept loosening with how hard, how intensely Niko took his cock. Each time he looked down and saw that gorgeous blond head bobbing, those pillow lips clutched tight around his cock, Matt almost lost it.

Niko slurped and released Matt's cock from his mouth. A tiny trail of saliva connected his lip and the cock, then snapped as Niko spoke. "Don't cum yet."

He crawled back onto the bed, pushing Matt down on his way to the nightstand. From there, Niko produced a couple of condoms and lube. "Turn over."

Without question, Matt pressed his face into the pillows, leaving his legs parted.

Niko kissed up Matt's back, his neck, over his shoulders. The blond's erection felt like it was leaving wet kisses up Matt's leg as he crawled up his body.

Already Matt was fucking the bed linens. His hole clenched with want.

The clenching was met with Niko's warm, slick fingers. He rubbed the hole gently, barely breaching until Matt caught his breath. Niko kissed the back of Matt's neck as he pressed his fingers into him. Again he paused, waiting for Matt to relax, then worked his way in. It wasn't the sort of preparation Matt needed, but he appreciated the gesture.

He heard Niko unwrapping a condom and waited until he felt that solid warmth pressing between his cheeks.

"You need to work for the next couple of days?" Niko asked.

"More runway." Matt turned his head on the pillow, trying to look back at Niko.

"I'll go easy then." He bit Matt's shoulder lightly as he angled himself against Matt's opening.

Niko breached him and it occurred to Matt that he had appreciated neither just how big this cock was nor the need for Niko to prep him for it. Matt hissed through his teeth, feeling split wider than he could ever remember being. Niko's body was so thin and angular that his hip bones bruised. He gripped Matt from behind, his arms looping under him for a better grip. His nails bit into Matt's shoulder, but he was careful not to drag welts.

Niko had gone slowly as requested, but he was a lot bigger than Matt expected. Each movement took Matt's breath away. He sweat and grunted with each of Niko's thrusts but pushed back, craving more.

His thrusts took on a slow, sensual rhythm, in no hurry to cum. For Matt, the pain of the intense stretch was giving way to a more ecstatic feeling. Inside of him, there was an itch only Niko's cock could scratch, and Matt twisted to get the head just *there*.

Matt grunted loudly as the sensations mounted. His knees rubbed raw as he scrambled against the sheets to keep Niko's cock where he needed it.

Sweat poured down his temples, and he gasped for breath. His body tightened. He burrowed his face into the pillow to muffle his cries. His balls ached for him to let go; his legs burned.

Matt was trembling, his body surging with need to cum, when Niko sat up behind him.

"Fuck!" Matt said into the pillow. He was sure it was sweat, but he wouldn't have been surprised if the wetness at his eyes was tears.

Niko grabbed Matt by the shoulders and turned him over.

The fucker was smirking.

Matt was about to start shouting expletives when Niko ducked his shoulders in under the backs of Matt's knees and folded him in half.

With a smooth, decisive movement, Niko was back inside him. The shock of loss and resumed spearing left Matt's body confused and sweating. But now he could see Niko's arched eyebrows furrowing, how flushed his face was, and the rivulets of sweat dribbling down his jaw line. His blond hair stuck to his cheeks as he gasped for breath. His eyes closed like he was in a trance, a very intense dream he was determined to get to the end of.

Matt pulled his own cock, watching Niko, thinking about how beautiful he was, how much he needed to cum—how much he wanted Niko to be the one who made him cum.

Matt tensed. His legs tightened again, and he trembled as his body strove towards climax. This time he didn't have to move to get Niko where he wanted him. Niko seemed to know instinctively how and when to twist his hips, when to lean down and kiss Matt, when to bite his lip.

Niko moaned into Matt's ear; his breath was humid and smelled of old grapes and weed. He moved Matt's hand and replaced it with his own, pulling Matt's cock in time to his thrusts. His fingers squeezed hard, gripped at odd angles, forcing the pleasant and uncomfortable sensations to their absolute limit.

Even the pinching, even the twisting of his cock in Niko's

hand felt amazing. Matt's body was so tense now that he felt like he would either cum or combust. His throat was on fire from moaning so loudly; his chest hurt; his body throbbed with each thrust like a heartbeat that started at its root deep inside his body. He closed his eyes and clenched his teeth. The tingling inside him intensified, and then, with shouted curses, he let go, jolting with each jet of spunk that shot from his cock and splattered hot on his chest.

"Fuck. Fuck you, Niko. Fuck."

Before his wits returned to him, Niko had him rolled over, kneeling face-down in the pillow. Niko fucked him hard enough that Matt had to time his exhales with the thrusts or couldn't breathe. Their bodies slapped together like their own applause.

He'd never been fucked so hard or for so long. Matt twisted his face to the side, trying to get fresh air, but he thought he might well strangle from this. He was about to ask for mercy when Niko made a guttural sound.

After a few more hard pumps, Niko dropped on Matt's back and crushed him into the bed.

They lay still for a few minutes; Matt was grateful for the respite to catch his breath. It was like hyperventilating; his lungs refused to work properly for a few frightening seconds. But soon he found his breath again and tried to get it under control.

On top of him, Niko's breathing was steady and calm, so slow that Matt worried he'd fallen asleep.

But once Matt could speak, Niko rolled from him and pulled off the condom. He tossed it on the floor. "There's a party we can still go to if you want."

Matt was too sore and overwhelmed to want to do anything but lay there. "Nah."

He rolled over on his side to look at Niko, who sat cross-legged on the bed.

Niko had found his bag of weed and papers; he rolled a new joint. "Good. Those parties are fucking lame."

He got up and cracked open one of the panes on the giant wall of windows. Chilly fall air freshened the room. Niko blew the smoke out of the window.

Cool wind buffeted Matt's body as he stood to go to the window. He grabbed a blanket to wrap around him like a cape.

Niko didn't look happy or sad. Just distant, like he was waiting for something.

"Hey, Niko?"

Niko startled like he was shocked from a daydream. "Thirsty? I've got champagne. Water? Coffee?"

"Nah." Now that he was here, Matt wondered what he'd thought he'd say to Niko. He felt so dowdy next to him. Sure, Matt was a model too, but Niko was a star. "I guess I wondered why you picked me up. Do you just like newbies?"

Though Matt expected the smirk, Niko shrugged. "Would you believe me if I said you were the hottest guy in the room?"

Matt snorted. "No."

That made Niko smile and he gave him a sidelong glance. "True. *I* was in that room."

"Were you trying to piss Gabe off?"

"Feel free to shoot me if that jackhole motivates anything I do." Niko took a long drag from the joint and exhaled into the night. "You appealed to me. No magic algorithm. Sorry if that's disappointing."

"Really? Sounded like there was something going on between you two." Not that Matt was going to be picky about how he got with Niko. That wasn't a fucking he'd soon forget. He just wanted to know if it might happen again.

"He wishes." Niko grabbed Matt's blanket and yanked him forward. Their bodies pressed together. Niko's skin was clammy from exposure to the outside. He pulled the blanket around them both. "Stop talking about him. He doesn't matter."

Matt took the joint and took a long drag. If Niko said he didn't matter, then he probably didn't. "What does matter, then?"

At that, Niko smiled, his slightly crazy, mostly caustic smile. "Me."

YOUNG
MAN'S GAME

Michael Bracken

I relied on my good looks to get me everything I ever wanted when I was in my twenties, traveling to photo shoots on six of the seven continents and enjoying commitment-free sex with other models and the men attracted to us, but my modeling career abandoned me when makeup artists started taking longer to prep me than photographers took to capture my image.

When the top fashion houses no longer requested me by name, my agent promoted a receptionist to junior agent and made me his first client. The afternoon Delray called to inform me, in his chipmunk-chipper voice, that he was now representing me and that he had booked a one-day shoot for a hemorrhoid cream, I told him he could shove the gig up the same orifice where he might apply that cream, and I quit the business.

Unlike many of my contemporaries—boys who became men in a make-believe world where natural beauty and easy money lead to overindulgence in multiple vices—I had never required rehab to control my urges, nor had I become intimate friends with plastic surgeons in a vain attempt to recapture the youthful appearance that was so obviously escaping me.

I sold my condo in New York City, emptied my bank accounts, and returned home to my family's west Texas cattle ranch, a place that favored hard work over good looks, and during the next two decades I put on forty pounds of muscle and saw the lines on my face that makeup artists had tried to spackle over develop into deep crags. The sun and the wind turned my exposed skin to leather, and a farmer's tan—face, neck, and the lower three-quarters of my arms—replaced the carefully cultivated all-over tan I once had.

The one thing I hadn't counted on when I returned home was the dearth of potential sexual partners so far from any town large enough to have a stoplight. With only three places to meet people at the town nearest the family ranch—a diner, a feed store, and a Methodist church—I resigned myself to taking my sex life in my own hands. And for too many years I did exactly that.

Fifty was safely in my rearview when my past caught up to me.

I spent the morning at the feed store, talking to Carl about an increase in our monthly order of mineral supplements, and stopped at the town's only diner for lunch before heading back to the ranch. I was sitting at the counter, halfway through a chicken-fried steak, pinto beans, and double order of creamed potatoes, when a stranger left the booth in which he'd been sitting and straddled the stool beside me.

"May I take your picture?"

The first time I'd heard that line I'd been sitting at the other end of the counter fresh out of high school and two months away from starting classes at Texas A&M over in College Station, following in the bootsteps of my older brothers. I'd thought the sweating fat man asking the question was hitting on me, but he turned out to be a talent scout who'd taken a wrong turn on his way from Ft. Worth to Amarillo and had driven too far south. A month later I had an agent, my first modeling gigs, and an anemic photographer's assistant giving me blowjobs.

I examined the handsome man sitting beside me and felt my cock rearrange itself in my jeans. Almost ten years my junior, he was slender like someone who watched his weight but was unaccustomed to hard, physical labor. He dressed like a catalog cowboy, though, not like a cattleman, in a blue and black embroidered western snap-front shirt, too-new Levi's jeans, and high-heeled ostrich Justin boots that showed no sign of wear. A black felt Stetson remained on the table he'd just vacated. His dark hair was slicked back and he didn't have hat hair, as if he carried the Stetson rather than wore it. Wherever he was from, he clearly wasn't from west Texas.

I asked, "Why?"

He pulled a business card from his shirt pocket and placed it on the counter next to my plate. "I'm a photographer," he explained as I glanced at the card and learned that Steve Carson hailed from Austin, the liberal center of the conservative state where we lived. "I'm shooting pictures for a coffee table book called *Contemporary Cowboys* and—"

"No, thanks," I told him. I turned away and forked another bite of chicken-fried steak. I dredged it through the creamed potatoes and white gravy and stuck it in my mouth.

The photographer touched my arm, sending an unexpected jolt of sexual electricity through my body that caused my balls to tighten. I turned toward him.

"You're exactly the type of man I've been looking for," he explained. "You look the part and everything."

I wore a blue denim shirt with the cuffs rolled halfway up my forearms, faded Wrangler jeans molded to my lower anatomy, and cow-flop-colored ropers—low-heeled cowboy boots—with unevenly worn soles caused by a slightly bow-legged gait that came from years astride a quarter horse. Unlike the photographer beside me, my apparel wasn't some wannabe Marlboro Man garb ordered off the Internet but the daily attire of a working cattleman. "This isn't a costume," I said. "Not like that getup of yours."

"What's wrong with how I'm dressed?"

Pushed back on my head was a sweat-stained white Stetson made of Shantung straw. I touched it with one forefinger and pushed it back another half-inch. "No self-respecting cattleman wears black felt in the summer."

Then I told him what else was wrong with his outfit.

"Nobody else has said anything," he said defensively.

"Trust me, son," I told him, "they were laughing behind your back."

He considered that for a moment and then asked, "Why aren't you?"

I shrugged. I knew what it was like to be ridiculed by men like my father and my brothers and I knew how hard I'd had to work after returning home before our neighbors accepted me back into the community.

"So what's your name, cowboy?"

"J. C. Beck." It wasn't the name I'd modeled under.

"So let me take your picture Mr. Beck," he said. "Show people what a real cowboy looks like."

"Cattleman," I corrected, dismissing him as I returned my attention to my now-cold meal.

The photographer returned to the booth behind me, grabbed his hat, and left the diner while I tried hard to forget the way I'd

felt when he'd touched me. After I finished and sopped up the
last of the white gravy with the butt end of a biscuit, I realized
he hadn't left but was outside, camera in hand, leaning against
a Japanese-made pickup truck dwarfed by my white Ford F-
350 parked next to it.

I slipped Steve Carson's card into my shirt pocket, left a
fistful of crumpled singles on the counter for Edna, and pushed
out of the diner. As soon as the door opened, the photographer
lifted his camera and took my picture.

"You don't give up, do you?"

"I know what I want," he said, "and I want you."

Squinting against the bright sun, I stared at the photographer. I wanted him, too, but not the same way he wanted me.

So we talked.

Carson spent the night at a motel fifty miles up the road and
drove to the ranch before sunup the next morning. I introduced him to my father and my brothers and told them what
he wanted.

My father looked him over and I was glad Carson had been
smart enough not to try to cowboy-up that morning, instead
wearing jeans, blue T-shirt, running shoes, and a gimme cap.

"We ain't posin' for nothin'," my father told him, "and you'd
best not get in our way when we're working."

"I won't," Carson assured my father, and he didn't. He spent
the morning capturing images of the men in my family as we
went about our daily chores.

That afternoon, after stuffing ourselves with my mother's
beef fajitas and sweet tea, Carson assured me he could drive a
stick. So I saddled up my quarter horse and had him follow me
in my F-350 out to where most of the herd was grazing.

Away from my family things changed.

After we stopped, Carson climbed into the bed of my truck and I circled the truck on my horse. Even though digital technology had replaced film since I had last been on the business end of a camera lens, I still knew how to pose. Moving with the light, I presented my best side to Carson, tilted my head forward and back, turned it left and right, and did all that I could to ensure that he had the best possible shots.

Then I climbed off my horse and Carson climbed down from the truck. He took several more photos of me with my horse and with some of the Herefords, and some of me walking through the mesquite. When the wind kicked up for a brief spell, he even caught a few shots of tumbleweed blowing past me as I held onto my hat.

Working with natural light and without makeup artists, hair stylists, wardrobe people, and the herd of other necessary and unnecessary people I had learned to tolerate at high-end fashion shoots, we didn't stop until the sun had slipped low in the evening sky.

I hitched my horse to the driver's side door handle and sat with Carson on the lowered tailgate of my F-350, leaning close together to view the day's photos on his digital camera's small screen.

After examining several dozen photos, Carson put one hand on my jean-clad thigh, turned to me, and said, "The camera loves you."

It always had, but I didn't tell him that. Instead I covered his hand with mine and slid it up my thigh so that he could feel my rapidly stiffening cock through the thick material of my Wrangler jeans.

Without a word, Carson set his camera aside. I tilted my hat back and pushed his gimme cap off, letting it fall to the dirt at his feet. I covered his mouth with mine, and our tongues met in a fiery dance of repressed desire.

My hands roamed over his still-clothed body, just as his traveled over mine. He was slender but firm, with strong arms, trim waist, tight butt, and a full package. He found my belt buckle and undid it, unfastened my jeans and reached inside my briefs to wrap his hand around my cock.

My eyes snapped open. No man had touched me there in years and I worried that I would be too eager, too quick to cum and I tried desperately to think of something—anything—that might delay that moment. Instead I remembered men and moments from my past—the photographer's assistant, the sugar daddy who wanted to make me his, other models, in the bathroom of a New York City nightclub, in the makeup trailer in New Orleans, on the beach in the Bahamas. That was all behind me, memories I had repressed and needed to repress again. So I pushed those thoughts from my mind and instead concentrated on events happening right then, right there.

Soon I sat on the tailgate with my jeans and my briefs bunched around my boots, and Carson stood before me. I leaned back on the pickup's bed, bracing myself with my hands, my erect cock jutting up like a saddle horn from the graying thatch of my pubic hair.

When the photographer bent forward and took the swollen head of my cock in his mouth, I saw the last vestiges of the sun slip behind the horizon and I moaned with pleasure. He licked away the glistening drop of pre-cum, painted the head of my cock with his tongue, and then slowly took my entire length into his oral cavity.

Carson drew back until his teeth caught on my glans and then did it again. As his head bobbed up and down in my lap, the photographer reached between my thighs, palmed my nut sack, and teased the sensitive spot behind my sack with the tip of one finger.

My hips began rising to meet his descending face, and I wrapped my hands around the back of his head. I held him as my hips moved faster and faster and I knew I couldn't restrain myself much longer.

When Carson squeezed my swollen sack, I came, firing a thick wad of hot spunk against the back of his throat. He swallowed and swallowed again.

He held me in his mouth until my cock softened and withdrew. Then Carson straightened up and stared into my eyes. He said, "I've wanted to do that ever since I saw you in the diner."

"I wish you hadn't waited so long," I told him. "I thought I was going to explode."

I wrapped one hand around the back of his head and pulled him forward. I kissed him again, a deep, penetrating kiss that had me tasting my own cum, and I felt my cock begin to snake back to life.

The closest thing either of us had to lube was a half-used tube of moisturizing cream I kept in the glove box of the pickup. I told him to get it, and while he did I stripped out of my boots, jeans, and briefs and threw them into the bed of the pickup.

When Carson returned, I made him do the same. Then I spun him around and bent him over the tailgate. I smeared moisturizing cream on my middle two fingers and slipped them down the crack of his ass to his tight little sphincter.

I massaged moisturizer into his ass crack until he relaxed and I could slip one slick finger into his shitter shutter. I used my free hand to dribble more moisturizer down the length of his crack and was soon able to slip a second finger into him.

"Quit teasing me, cowboy," Carson said hoarsely.

I withdrew my fingers, grabbed his hips, and pressed the head of my cock against the photographer's sphincter. He pushed back as I thrust forward, and then I was in him. I drew back and pushed forward, holding his hips so tight I left bruises that we didn't notice until later.

I slammed into him again and again and soon discovered that Carson was less familiar with a stick shift than he had let on. He'd stopped my F-350 on a barely perceptible downslope, had left the truck in neutral, and hadn't set the emergency brake. My repeated pounding rocked the truck and it began to roll out from under Carson.

He grabbed the tailgate but couldn't stop the truck's forward momentum, and I couldn't stop fucking him even though I saw what was happening.

"Let go," I insisted as the weight of the rolling truck began to pull Carson out from under me. "Let go!"

As the photographer released his grip on my F-350, I slammed into him one last time and fired a second wad of hot spunk deep inside him.

We stood together, my spasming cock deep in his ass, and watched as my truck rolled about fifty feet, my quarter horse walking calming beside it. The rolling truck startled some inquisitive Herefords that had moseyed in our direction as if seeking a how-to primer in doing it people-style.

Carson started laughing first and I soon joined him. After he pulled away from me and straightened up, I wrapped my arm around his shoulders we walked barefoot and bare-assed to where the truck had come to a halt.

During the following year, Carson and I developed a relationship that went beyond randy sex and runaway pickup trucks. As he continued traveling around the country photographing all manner of contemporary cowboys, we remained in touch via cell phone. When his schedule permitted, he stopped at the

ranch and spent a day or a night or several days and nights with
me. Only occasionally, because cattle don't take weekends off,
I drove to Austin to stay with Carson in his apartment.

The book slowly came together, but except for that one
evening sitting on the tailgate of my truck, I never saw any of
Carson's photographs. He told me he'd selected several photos
of me, including some with my father and brothers, but never
told me how they'd been used. I never saw page proofs and
didn't know until the book was published and a copy presented
to me by my lover that my photograph graced the cover.

There I was astride my quarter horse, a herd of Herefords
in the background, a faraway look in my eyes, looking every
bit the buff, weather-hardened cattleman I had become and
nothing at all like the young fashion model I had once been.

"You shouldn't have put me on the cover," I told him. He
still didn't know that I had once been a professional model.
When I saw the smile on Carson's face begin to fade, I added,
"But thank you."

I thumbed through the book and checked the photo
captions, which, thankfully, identified me by my real name—J.
C. Beck—not as Jase Beck, the name I had used back when I
was modeling. I hoped no one would put the two together.

Two weeks later, as we were about to sit down for dinner—
my parents, my brothers and their families, and Carson—the
phone rang. We all had cell phones and didn't often receive
calls on the landline, so my father stepped into the foyer to
answer the ringing phone.

A moment later he called to me and handed me the phone
when I joined him in the foyer. As soon as I pressed the handset
to my ear, I heard Delray, my former agent-for-a-day. He said,
"You're a hard man to track down."

"I shouldn't be," I said. My parents have had the same number for decades. "Why did you call?"

"You don't know?" he said. "You're hot again. You won't believe how many calls I get for handsome men of a certain age, and that cowboy book with you on the cover is the talk of the town. Everybody in New York wants *you*. I'm the only person who knows who you really are and I have a dozen advertising agencies and three magazines already lined up."

"I'm not interested."

"Not interested?" Apparently Delray had become successful despite losing his first client. "You know the kind of money I can get you?"

"I left all that a long time ago," I explained.

Carson stepped into the foyer and I looked at him. I had finally taught the slender photographer how to dress when he visited the ranch, and he wore a denim shirt, Wrangler jeans, and ropers. His Shantung straw Stetson hung from the coat tree in the hall, next to mine.

I said into the phone, "I have everything I ever want right here."

I don't regret traveling the world as a model, nor do I regret the wild adventures I had as a young man, but fashion modeling is a young man's game. I had no desire to return to the bright lights of the big city. I had traveled around the world just to realize that I could find everything I ever wanted within spitting distance of my front door—wide-open sky, hard physical labor, and a committed relationship.

My former agent continued talking long after I stopped listening. I dropped the handset into its cradle and stared deep into Carson's eyes.

"What was that all about?" he asked.

The phone began ringing again, but I ignored it.

I had a lot to tell Carson about my former life. But that could wait. I took his hand and walked into the dining room where we joined my family.

SWEET CHARITY

Heidi Champa

I can't believe I let you talk me into this, Marty."

"You look great, Wes. Quit worrying. Besides, it's for charity."

"That's not the point, Marty."

"It's a good cause. Besides, you don't want to disappoint your fans, do you? The press release went out last week. People are expecting you to participate. Quit being such a diva, will you?"

"Fuck you, Marty."

Marty smiled as he walked over to the craft services table and grabbed a donut. I was starving, having not eaten all morning. Wouldn't want to ruin my look for the photos. Moments later, his cell phone rang and he answered it immediately, despite having just started a conversation with the set director. Typical Marty behavior. I would have killed him if I wasn't otherwise engaged at the moment. I sighed for the millionth time as the crew readjusted the lighting for the next set of photographs. I just stood still, waiting for them to finish. The makeup girl checked her work, and as her brush tickled against the skin on my stomach, I tried not to flinch.

This certainly wasn't my idea of charity. Charity was writing a check or buying some tickets to an expensive dinner or putting a colored ribbon on the lapel of my jacket. Charity wasn't standing naked in front of a room full of people with nothing but a soccer ball to cover me. The crew was very understanding of my situation, but it was a fact that was hard to ignore. When everyone else in the room is wearing clothing and you're not, uncomfortable doesn't even begin to cover it. It was a nightmare come to life in some ways, the classic dream about showing up to school naked and everyone laughing. Except no one was laughing. They were flitting around, doing their jobs while I just stood there, waiting. With no clothes on. Marty shot me a smile and thumbs-up, but I could only scowl at him as he shoved another pastry in his mouth.

Six months ago, when my agent Marty approached me about posing naked for the soccer league's charity calendar, it sounded like a great idea. But I had forgotten about it until a week ago, when Marty told me to start doing more sit-ups, because the photo shoot was just around the corner. By that time, I couldn't back out and I now found myself getting my abs highlighted with makeup and having oil rubbed on me by a girl with black-rimmed glasses. She took her time, and if I didn't know any better, I'd say she was trying to get my attention. But her caresses were wasted on me. I'm sure some of the other players who were slated to be in the calendar would like her a lot. I just smiled and tried not to move too much.

Marty sauntered over, his phone call just ending. He seemed oblivious to the pleas from the crew to stay out of the way, ignoring them like he did everyone else. As he got closer to me, he glanced down at the soccer ball I was holding in front of my cock and took a few steps back. We were close, but not that close. Clearing his throat, I noticed him stifling a laugh and I broke.

"I'm going to kill you for this, Marty. I swear to God."

"Come on, Wes. Don't be such a baby. It's two days out of your life. They put you up in a swanky hotel suite and they are shooting your pictures tomorrow at one of the nicest beaches in the world. Man, you need to get a little perspective."

He was right, damn him. There were worse things in the world than being objectified for a good cause. But, in the moment, it was difficult to focus on the positives.

"I mean, face it Wes. People want to look at you naked. I personally don't understand it, but if it helps this charity sell a few thousand more calendars, that should make you feel good. And if it helps you get a shitload of new endorsements, all the better. Hell, maybe it will even help you find a date."

"Fuck you, Marty. I don't need any help getting a date."

Marty rolled his eyes at my comment, because he knew exactly how long it had been since I'd had a decent date. Damn him, and his nosiness about my personal life.

"How exactly would it help me do that?"

"I knew I'd get you with that one. There is an assistant over there who has nearly spilled five cups of coffee because he can't take his eyes off you. Don't walk near him, or you'll fall in his puddle of drool. If you weren't so busy grousing, you might have noticed him eye-fucking you from across the room. You've got to focus on the benefits here, kid. So, play nice and it will end up working out. For all of us."

Marty stepped off the set, just in time for the next set of shots to start. Once Marty was gone, I scanned the room and found the assistant Marty was talking about. He was hovering right behind the photographer, his eyes half-hidden by the shadows. He seemed young, like a typical college kid, maybe twenty-two or twenty-three years old. But it wasn't easy to tell with the flashbulbs going off in my face. As they told me how to turn, where to stand, and not to smile, I caught glimpses of him. Marty was right. He stared at me the whole time, looking at me like someone who had never seen a naked man before.

I wasn't one of those athletes so in love with myself that I assumed everybody wanted me. But this kid made it pretty fucking clear that he was interested. When I finally caught his eye, he looked away quickly, but after a few moments, his eyes returned to mine. As odd as it felt, focusing on his face made the whole photo shoot a lot easier. When the camera stopped flashing, he turned away, pretending to be engrossed in some piece of busywork. I could finally see him properly, and I liked what I saw. He was tall and fairly skinny; his sandy brown hair fell into his eyes every time he leaned down. It was my turn to stare at him, and I did so as he moved all around the set, attending to the needs of the increasingly moody photographer.

They gave me a robe to slip into while I waited for the next photo shoot and I found a chair near the back of the set. I tried to ignore all the food sitting next to me and sipped from my half-empty bottle of water. Marty was engrossed in a conversation with a young blonde girl who was helping with wardrobe. The photographer's assistant walked toward me, his eyes shifting all over the room as if he was suddenly uncomfortable. Up close, he was really cute, and when I looked down at his college T-shirt, I knew I had guessed his age about right. That part I had gotten right. His blue eyes settled on me, and I couldn't help but smile.

"Mr. Hollingsworth, Gabriel thinks we're done for the day. We'll be ready to start tomorrow morning around eleven. A car will come to the hotel to pick you up around ten. Is that okay?"

I stood up, anxious to wash the makeup and oil off me and get back into my clothes. The assistant backed up a fraction, and I noticed he was a few inches shorter than I was. His lopsided grin made him look so sweet, and I had an overwhelming urge to run my hand through his messy hair.

"That's fine. And, it's Wes, by the way."

"Okay, Wes."

He started to walk away, but I didn't let him get far.

"I didn't get your name."

"Joe. My name's Joe."

I looked across the room to Marty, who had a shit-eating grin on his face. He flashed me another thumbs-up and laughed. He just might be right after all. This whole thing could end up working out great.

I made Marty spring for dinner. He talked my ear off nearly the whole time about the cute wardrobe assistant and how he'd gotten her phone number. He did pause long enough to ask me about the photographer's assistant.

"So, his name is Joe. What are you going to do about it, Wes?"

"Nothing. I mean, after the photo shoot is done tomorrow, I doubt I'll ever see him again."

"Well, then no time like the present. Come on, Wes. I'm not talking about the love of your life here. Why not just have a little fun?"

"I don't know Marty. I mean, he's cute, but he's just a kid."

"You're a professional athlete, Wes. It's your job to screw around and live the dream. How is anyone supposed to look up to you if you don't hold up your end of the bargain?"

"You're all heart, Marty."

After dinner, I spent most of the evening walking around

the city. Back at the hotel, I started watching some stupid movie on television, and I had just about fallen asleep when I heard someone knocking. Thinking it was Marty, I jumped up and pulled the door open. But, it wasn't Marty. It was Joe. To say I was shocked was putting it mildly. He looked just as sheepish as he did at the photo shoot, and just as cute. I motioned him into the room, and he entered without a word. He looked around the suite before turning around to face me, his hands jammed into his jeans pockets.

"I just wanted to stop by and let you know we're going to be starting the photo shoot a little later tomorrow. So, you won't have to be ready as early."

I took a few steps closer to him, Marty's words ringing in my head. He was right. It had been too long since I'd had any fun at all. And Joe looked like he could be a lot of fun.

"Oh. Okay. But, you know, you could have just called. You didn't need to come all the way over here to tell me that."

I took another step closer to Joe, and he swallowed hard as I continued talking.

"I think there is another reason why you came here, Joe."

"What do you mean, Mr. Hollingsworth?"

"I told you, it's Wes. I saw the way you were looking at me during the photo shoot today."

"Well, I was just...I didn't mean to. I mean, uh, I'm sorry."

"You don't have to be sorry, Joe. It's not like I mind or anything. But I think you came here for something more than just a scheduling change."

"Okay, you caught me. I figured I'd take a chance. I mean, when am I ever going to get an opportunity like this again?"

"That's funny, Joe. I was thinking the same thing."

I put my hand around the back of his neck and pulled his face to mine. A small yelp left his mouth as I kissed him, his hands now out of his pockets and around my back. He went from timid to eager in the span of just a few moments, his hips pushing forward into mine as we stood making out in the sitting room of my hotel. When I pulled back, Joe kept his eyes closed for an extra second before looking at me. I swept my thumb over his jaw, enjoying the feeling of his soft skin. I looked down and saw the bulge of Joe's erection pressing into the zipper of his jeans. His hands kept roaming all over me, touching me anywhere he could reach. It had been a long while since I'd been with anyone so eager and adorable.

"So, why all the pretense, Joe? You could have just been honest with me from the beginning."

"Gabriel doesn't like anyone fraternizing with the models. He thinks it's terribly unprofessional. I really need my job."

"Well, it's lucky for you I'm not a model."

"You could be, you know Wes. You are certainly hot enough. I mean, if the whole soccer thing doesn't work out, of course."

"Thanks for the compliment Joe. And, don't worry. What Gabriel doesn't know won't hurt him. It can be our little secret."

Joe's hands yanked my hips forward, his hands moving to my belt. For a moment, I panicked, suddenly unsure of what I was doing. Joe was a cute kid, but there was a moment of hesitation where the logical part of my brain wanted me to slow down. But, as his fingers fumbled slightly on the button of my pants, the zipper easing down slowly, those doubts flew out the window. His long fingers slid into my boxers, a moan escaping my lips when I felt him touch my hardening cock. He wrapped his fist around me as his tongue moved deeper into my mouth. I gripped his shoulders for dear life, my hips moving forward without thought. I whimpered when his hands left me, leaning forward to nibble his lips quickly before he dropped to his knees in front of me. He pulled my pants down my legs while I tore off my shirt, tossing it aside. I looked down and saw him staring at my cock with worshipful eyes. I couldn't help but moan at the sight.

"Fuck, Wes. What a cock. It's the one thing I didn't get to see during the photo shoot. It was worth the wait."

Joe's hand gripped me tight, his thumb passing gently over my weeping slit. I watched in awe as his delicious lips wrapped around the head of my cock, his tongue meeting my sensitive flesh for the first time. I expected him to be timid or clumsy, but he was neither. His tongue moved over me slowly, but he was confident in all his movements. My eyes shut tight when I felt his lips move lower and lower, the head of my cock bumping against the back of his throat. I couldn't keep my hands out of his rumpled hair, gently guiding his bobbing head as he sucked me hard. It was beyond me to be quiet, my moans filling the large room. His enthusiasm overwhelmed me, his hand gripping my thigh as he moaned with every sweep of his hot tongue. I felt the familiar tremble run through me, as I got closer and closer to cumming.

He pulled his mouth back, standing up to shuck his jeans and shirt off. I stared at him, my tongue itched to taste his sweet skin. I started with each of his nipples, giving them tons of attention. As I moved lower, I stopped to lave over each bump of his abs, his thin body well muscled. My hands explored what my mouth couldn't, feeling his muscles strain and relax as I touched him.

It was my turn to drop to my knees, my face right in front of his young, hard cock. I marveled at it, admiring its every detail. The thick drop of liquid at the tip begged to be licked away, and I obliged. His ragged breathing gave away his nerves, despite his calm façade. I let my tongue swirl over the head of his cock. It felt thick and silky soft, his salty-sweet taste filling my mouth.

I sucked him gently into my throat, easing down slowly. His hands fisted my hair, his hips pushing forward, trying to urge me on. Trying to keep us both on the edge, I teased him, not giving him too much too soon. His ass tensed under my hands, his body a mass of tension and effort. His voice wobbled, but it still sounded so good.

"Oh God, oh fuck Wes."

I just smiled before devouring him fully, my nose touching his flat belly. But his reprieve didn't last long. I pulled back, rubbing my lips against his weeping head, avoiding his advances.

"Please, Wes, I can't take much more."

I went back to what I was doing, but my own desperation was outweighing my need to exact my revenge. After a few more deep thrusts of his cock in my throat, I stood up. His mouth was immediately on mine, kissing me frantically.

He pushed me back, toward the fancy couch that sat against the wall. I sat down and he immediately straddled me, his mouth back on mine before I could say another word. In an effort to slow Joe down, I moved him from my lap, just long enough to find the bag I had thrown near my suitcase. I had made a stop on the way back from dinner with Marty to buy condoms and lube. It was wishful thinking, but I didn't think I would need them until after the shoot tomorrow.

Once I got back to the couch, Joe was right back onto my lap, our hard cocks rubbing against each other as I pulled him closer and took one of his tiny nipples into my mouth. While he was distracted, I popped open the lube and began smearing the liquid onto his puckered asshole. He started groaning and pushing back against my fingers. I strafed his nipple with my teeth, just as the tip of my index finger slipped inside him. I expected him to pull away, but he grabbed my head, holding my mouth right where it was. He squirmed above me, and I

managed to work my finger inside him almost all the way. Joe
sat back, licking his lips as he stared down at me.

"Shit, Wes. I'm tired of waiting. Fuck me."

His brazen words shocked me. Shy Joe was clearly long gone;
his lascivious eyes devoured me as I rolled the condom onto my
waiting cock. He took me in hand and positioned himself above
me, guiding me as the tip spread his asshole open. I closed my
eyes, just for a moment as I felt him open up, a little at a time,
his tight heat covering my cock. Joe was silent above me, and
my eyes went from his sweet face to watch the last few inches of
my cock disappear into his ass. His hand wrapped around his
dick, jerking himself as he adjusted to my cock in his ass.

I put my hands on his hips as I started to ride him, his tight
ass squeezing my cock with each move. He leaned forward and
kissed me slow and sweet, his free hand pressing hard against my
chest. Joe was moving faster than I wanted him to, pushing me
too close to the edge. As much as I wanted to keep watching him
bounce around on my dick, I knew I would blow my wad too
soon if I didn't slow him down. I stayed inside him as I pushed
him down on the couch, flat on his back. I held his ankles in
my hands and slowly pulled my cock nearly all the way out of
his ass. I only stayed still for a few seconds, but Joe whimpered
as if it had been an hour. I smirked at his distress and then
thrust back inside him, repeating the same slow torture a few
more times. He looked down and watched me fuck him, his eyes
transfixed on the place where our bodies met.

"God, Wes. Fuck. I'm so close. Oh fuck."

His hand moved frantically over his cock, jerking hard as
I continued to fuck him nice and slow. His eyes were pinched
shut, the muscles of his body tensed at once, and I watched him
cum all over his sweaty stomach and chest. As the last shot
filled his navel, I couldn't hold back any longer. Putting his feet

on my shoulders, I pounded into him with abandon, pent-up frustration and lust flowing through me as I looked down into his tranquil brown eyes. I came harder than I had in months, his tight asshole milking every last drop of cum and every bit of energy out of me.

I could barely move as I pulled away from Joe, collapsing on the couch in a heap. My eyes felt too heavy to open, my whole body sated and loose. I heard Joe stirring next to me, felt his lips on my neck as I struggled to stay awake.

"That was amazing, Wes. Aren't you glad I stopped by?"

"Absolutely, Joe. Definitely."

We cleaned up and started to get dressed. The heat of the moment had been replaced by a new comfort; all the tension and awkwardness had disappeared. I couldn't resist pulling him close and kissing those sweet lips one more time.

"So, Wes. I guess I'll see you tomorrow. Gabriel has some really amazing shots planned for the beach."

"Can't wait."

He smiled at me one last time before walking out of my room and into the night. I barely made it to my bed before collapsing, my whole body exhausted.

My phone rang around 10:30 in the morning, and Joe's voice brought me back to life.

"Hey, Wes. Bad news. Gabriel has to cancel today's shoot. There's an emergency with his dog. We'll have to reschedule. How does tomorrow look for you? Can you stay another night?"

Part of me was thrilled but a little disappointed that I wouldn't get to see Joe again. Oh well, if it could only be a one-night stand, that would have to be enough.

"Tomorrow would be fine. I'll let Marty know, but I don't think I have anything else going on."

There was silence on the line before Joe cleared his throat.

"Seems a shame to make the charity pay for another night in a hotel room, doesn't it, Wes?"

"It sure does, Joe. But, then where would I stay?"

"Well, I have a nice big bed here in my apartment and an unexpected day off from my job. So, unless of course, our star model has something else to do today...."

"Give me the address, I'll be there in an hour. After all, anything for the charity."

THIRSTY EYES

Stephen Osborne

It had been a long day. Hell, the day was over. It fucking well was officially evening and things were going from bad to worse. The photographer was getting cranky, his assistant was downright belligerent, and the models were getting circles under their eyes.

"It's not working," I said aloud, voicing what I'm sure everyone was thinking.

Sammy, my poor distressed friend who was manning the camera, sighed and looked up at our two models. "Take five, guys," he said. The vampire and his victim broke their pose and relaxed as Sammy, head hung, made his way over to me. "What's up, Matt?" he asked. His tone indicated that he really didn't want to know the answer.

"Our vampire," I said, shaking my head. "He's just not doing it for me."

Sammy sighed, putting his whole body into it. "Jesus, Matt, if we don't finish this shoot by nine we'll have to pay these guys overtime, and they were expensive enough to begin with."

I gazed over at Nick, our erstwhile vampire, dressed in a white silk shirt unbuttoned nearly to his navel, as he chatted with victim Carl by the water cooler. "He's just...I don't know." I needed to just get it out, even though I knew what Sammy's reaction would be. "He's just *so* gay."

"News flash," Sammy told me. "We're doing the cover for a gay vampire erotica anthology."

"I just don't want our vampire to be *that* gay. I know I'm being picky—"

"You are."

"—but he's just not sensual enough. I don't believe he wants to bite Carl on the neck and suck his blood. Suck something else, yes, but neck, no."

Sammy rolled his eyes. "You're a piece of work, you know that? Fuck, we're a small press. No one expects the moon from us. Look, let's get a shot you like and I'll Photoshop the shit out of Nick and butch him up for you."

"It's just that I think we're going to sell a hell of a lot of books this time around and a good cover will do just that much more for us."

"You should have gone with something else, is my opinion," Sammy said, fiddling with his camera. "Vampire erotica is out. It's been done to death."

"Gay vampire erotica?"

"Please. Vampire erotica is always gay."

Exasperated, I ran a hand through my hair, messing it up even more. "We just have to get someone else. That's all there is to it."

Sammy gaped. "We can't! For one, it's too late! And we'd still have to pay the bastard! We simply can't afford it!"

"We'll have to. It's important we get this right." I waved

a hand toward Nick, who was sipping from a paper cup and violating Carl's personal space. "Look at him. Yes, he's pretty, but he doesn't have that look of smoldering, sensual menace that our vampire needs to have. He needs to have thirsty eyes, not a look that says, 'I'm just waiting to hit the boy bars.'"

"You're asking a hell of a lot," Sammy said with a wry smile. "This is Indianapolis, not New York or Chicago. Honestly, Nick was the best thing the modeling agency had available on such short notice."

"Hey!" Carl had attempted, in vain, to try to distance himself from Nick. He had to look over Nick's shoulder to holler at me and Sammy. "Any sign of that pizza you ordered? If this is going to take much longer, I'm going to need food!"

Nick didn't even bother to turn his head. He simply shouted, "And I can only give you another half-hour. I've got things to do."

"Yeah," I muttered so only Sammy could hear me. "Cocks to suck. Balls to lick. Nick is one busy boy."

Sammy chuckled. To the boys he shouted, "We'll get this shot in just a few minutes. Don't you guys worry." He arched an eyebrow at me. "We will, won't we?"

I didn't answer.

Minutes later we tried again. Sammy had Nick stand just behind Carl, arms encircling Carl's chest. Carl looked great. He had just the right look of pleasure and thrill as he tilted his head, exposing his neck for Nick. It still didn't work for me. Nick just wasn't my idea of a vampire.

Sammy clicked a few shots and then glanced at me warily. I shrugged. He sighed and then told the boys, "Okay, we've got it. Thank you very much."

Nick and Carl relaxed. "Thank God," Nick said, rubbing his cheeks vigorously as if the pose had caused them to atrophy.

"I've got to tell my agent not to book me so late in the day. I've got shit to do!"

Carl asked him, "Aren't you sticking around? They promised us pizza."

"Honey, no pizza for me. Too many calories. Gotta watch my figure." Nick put his hands on his nearly nonexistent hips as if to prove his point. He then stripped out of the silk shirt we'd put on him and quickly threw on his own shirt, leaving our expensive garment in a heap on the floor.

There was a knock at the door of Sammy's little studio. Having grabbed his jacket, Nick answered the knock as he made his exit. Seeing the young man standing with a pizza box, he unnecessarily announced, "Your pizza is here!" Pushing his way past the pizza delivery guy, he added, "Contact my agent first thing in the morning. I like to get paid promptly."

The pizza guy entered, looking somewhat confused. "Someone order a pizza?"

I'm sure my mouth was hanging open, and not from hunger for pizza. The delivery boy, although dressed in a most un-vampiric way in torn jeans and a Bob Marley T-shirt, was exactly what I wanted for our book cover. The T-shirt was stretched to the limit across his muscular chest and the arms that held the pizza box looked strong and unyielding. There was a hint of a mocking smile on his face, as if he knew more than any of us mere mortals ever dared to dream. His thick black hair hung over his forehead, just barely brushed off to the side so as to not obscure his dark eyes—eyes that beckoned but yet warned of danger within. He was my vampire.

"See ya, Nick," I muttered, barely aware that he had already scampered down the hall.

No one moved. The pizza boy blinked and looked at each of us in turn. Uneasily he said, "Large pie, pepperoni and sausage." When no one reacted, he looked down. "What? Is my fly undone? Why is everyone staring at me?"

Finally the spell was broken. "Get your camera ready, Sammy," I said. "We've got a cover to shoot."

Sammy had all sorts of objections, all of which I knew were coming. The modeling agency would be furious. We'd still have to pay Nick, as well as pizza boy (whose name was Brian Wagner) and who knew what else Nick's agent would throw at us. "We're probably breaking some union rules by doing this," Sammy said, looking worried.

"I don't think there's a union for models," I said. "The Screen Actor's Guild specifically doesn't cover modeling. If there is a model union I don't think our Podunk little agency here in Indianapolis is affiliated and even if they are, I'll take care of everything." I hoped I sounded confident. All I knew was that I wanted Brian the Pizza Boy for our vampire and I'd do whatever it took to make that happen.

Brian himself took a little coaxing. "I won't have to pose nude, will I?"

I assured him he wouldn't. I explained that we simply wanted him to don our discarded silk shirt and pose with his arms around Carl, a look of lust—of blood and sex—on his face.

"Sounds kind of gay," Brian responded simply. I told him that it was for a cover of a gay volume of vampire erotica. "I don't know," he said, shaking his head doubtfully. I told him what we'd pay him. The shaking of the head immediately stopped. "I'll do it."

My gut instincts were correct. Brian was a natural, and he and Carl struck up an instant rapport that showed in their modeling. Sammy snapped off shot after shot, but we knew within minutes that we had several excellent choices for our book cover. When we were finished Carl and Sammy hungrily snarfed pizza. I was too excited to eat, and Brian confessed that he could no longer stomach pizza. "We get a great discount and I've had my fill of the stuff."

My heart was still pounding a rumba beat in my chest as Sammy and his assistant gathered up their equipment. Carl and Brian had already made their exits; Carl off to his apartment and his waiting boyfriend and Brian back to the pizza parlor, sure he was going to have to face an angry boss for being so late. I told him to have his boss call me if he needed elucidation.

Sammy hovered at the door, his assistant already down loading stuff into their car. "Aren't you coming? We can go out for a drink or something."

"I'm fine," I said, knowing I was too wound up to enjoy being out with a bunch of half-drunk strangers. "I'll just tidy up in here and then get on home. I'll lock up, don't worry."

Still Sammy paused. "I have to admit that you were right about the pizza boy. He looked fantastic!"

"Certainly better than Nick."

Sammy chuckled. "Nick's pretty, but a little too pretty. I wouldn't want to fuck him. This Brian guy, on the other hand..."

"He oozed sexuality, didn't he?"

"Nearly made me ooze just watching him. Sure you don't want to come out with us? We'll be at Sandy's Bar if you change your mind."

We said our goodnights and I closed the door after Sammy. There really wasn't much cleaning up to do but I wanted to stay for a little longer in the small studio. I felt good about finding Brian and I guess I wanted to savor my triumph. I looked around. With most of the lights off and the shades drawn over the windows the studio had a weird feel to it, probably caused by the odd shadows cast by the various props that littered the place. One could easily imagine a spectral hand coming out of the darkness and touching one's shoulder. I sighed, dismissing such macabre thoughts. Just straighten up a bit and head out, I told myself. Maybe I would join Sammy for a drink after all.

I walked toward the long table over by the windows, where I'd set my satchel down. I only walked a few steps before my foot caught on something, nearly making me trip. I cursed and looked down. There, wadded in a heap, was Brian's Bob Marley T-shirt. In the excitement of the shoot I hadn't even noticed that he hadn't changed back and had walked out wearing our white silk shirt. Oh, well. Losing a shirt was well worth the extra book sales we'd get from the smoldering cover that would adorn our little volume!

I leaned down and scooped up the shirt. As I was straightening, a voice came from the shadows. "Sorry. I meant to get that before I left."

I nearly leapt out of my skin. I'm pretty sure I yelped as I spun around to see Brian Wagner emerging from the shadows in the corner. "You scared the piss out of me!" I told him, hand to my chest to keep my heart from thudding through my rib cage.

"Sorry about that." Brian moved closer, his feet soundless on the hard wood floor. He was still wearing the silk shirt, now unbuttoned nearly all the way.

"How did you get in?" I asked with a frown. "I'm sure I locked the door after Sammy left."

"I came back in while he was still here. You guys were chatting and didn't notice, so I sort of just moved into the corner and sat there quietly, waiting for him to leave. I wanted to thank you for asking me to pose for your book."

An alarm bell sounded in my brain as I knew what he was

saying wasn't likely. I would have seen him re-enter and so would have Sammy. The place wasn't that big! Still, Brian had to be telling the truth. How else could he be here?

I found myself not caring about my questions as Brian came even closer. Very close. He put his arms around me and before I knew what was happening we were lip-locked, our tongues wrestling a mad dance. He was a great kisser. His tongue explored my mouth gently but hungrily. We both kept our eyes open, me because I couldn't believe I was being kissed by such a gorgeous hunk of man and I couldn't bring myself to blink in case the whole thing might not be real. I don't know why his eyes remained open. I'm not Quasimodo by any means, but I was hardly in this guy's league as far as looks went.

Brian held me tighter and I found myself melting in his arms. I moaned as I dared to close my eyes. He didn't vanish in a puff of verisimilitude. Impossibly, his tongue continued to roam over my teeth and along the side of my own tongue. After what seemed an eternity he broke away. I looked at him questioningly, wondering if there was more to follow.

He must have read my thoughts because he smiled as his hands continued to caress my shoulders and back. Finally his left hand reached down and grabbed hold of my ass, kneading the soft flesh. "I wanna fuck you," he said, his mouth mere centimeters from mine. "To thank you for the opportunity to pose for you."

"I..." I had to swallow hard to continue. "I'd love that."

Brian moved incredibly fast. Before I knew it he'd pushed me back against the long table, his hands tearing at my clothes. I didn't care. Fuck buttons on shirts! They're overrated. I let him rip the shirt off me while I struggled with my belt buckle. He kissed me, continually pressing me back until somehow we were both on top of the table, scattering papers everywhere.

Somehow I managed to kick off my shoes. I tried to get my pants down, but with Brian's weight on me I could barely shift them. I gave up and clawed at his back. The silk shirt shifted over his rippling muscles. God, he was fit. My cock was desperate for release and I squirmed under him so that my bulge nestled against the one in his jeans. It was as rock hard as mine.

I wanted him in me desperately, if only to reassure myself that I wasn't dreaming. The pain of him entering me would be the equivalent of pinching myself. Breathlessly I said, "Lube and condoms...in my satchel there." I laughed nervously. "Emergency supply, you know."

He laughed, raising himself up by a pushup, taking his reassuring weight off me. Then in once swift movement he was up and off the table. He quickly pulled off his clothes, revealing his muscular body. I couldn't help but stare. There was a bit of a smirk on his face as he fished into my bag. He knew how good looking he was. Normally this was a turn off for me, as I hated super-inflated egos. Somehow it just made Brian sexier.

My eyes were on his cock. It was standing straight up, thick and veiny. I wanted to throw myself off the table and take it into my mouth and suck him until he blew a wad into my mouth, but I couldn't move. Moving might destroy reality. I was in Brian Wagner's world, and he was God. I didn't dare act on my own volition.

He sheathed and lubed himself. "I wanted to fuck you the moment I saw you."

I looked into his eyes. I believed him. There was lust and desire there, along with a fire that blazed brightly. I could think of no reply. Anything I said would just sound ridiculous.

He vaulted back up onto the table, his body lithe, moving with an animal grace. Normally being a top, I must have glared at his cock with a worried look. He chuckled and positioned himself between my legs. "Don't worry. You're going to love this."

"I'm sure of that." My voice was hoarse from anticipation.

Truer words were never spoken. We squirmed around and I lifted my head so our lips could meet. Then he entered me.

Oh. My. God.

It was like we were made for each other. There was no pain, or if there was the pleasure masked it entirely. He began slowly but was soon pumping his cock into me, sending waves of ecstasy through my body. I writhed, nearly unable to endure how good he felt inside me. I wished we were in a comfy bed and not on a hard table, if only because I needed a pillow to bite into to keep from screaming. So I screamed.

"That feels so fucking good! Fuck me!"

"Oh, yeah," he said, his own voice rising. "You like that cock in you, don't you?"

"Fuck yeah." I couldn't seem to breath, or maybe I was breathing too much. Brian was increasing his thrusts and I could tell by his grunts that he was getting close. "I wanna feel you cum," I said as I began jacking my dick.

"You ready for something really fantastic?" he asked, the words coming out in jerks as he rammed into me.

"Oh, yeah." My own voice was little more than a squeal.

I shouldn't have been surprised by what happened next, what with Brian being in the room when he shouldn't have been and the way his feet made no sound as he approached me. The hunger in his eyes. His lithe, athletic movements. But then, I'm a rational man. I ignored the things that made no sense to me.

I couldn't, however, ignore the fangs that suddenly sprouted in his mouth. I couldn't rationalize his sinking his teeth into the soft flesh of my neck.

We both came just as he began to suck my blood through the bite he'd made in my throat.

I yelled out, both from ejaculating and from surprise. His cock throbbed within my ass, shooting out its load. His lips clamped onto my neck and continued to suck. I could hear my own heart, thumping loudly. The world seemed to spin and then everything went dark.

I awoke to the sun shining into my face. There was no sign of Brian. No silk shirt. I located a mirror and checked. There were two puncture wounds on my throat.

I never told Sammy about my encounter with Brian Wagner. He wouldn't have believed me, and I wouldn't have blamed him. Part of me isn't sure that I didn't just have hallucinations from some bad pizza topping. I mean, hiring a real vampire to pose as one for a book cover? Maybe I just hit my head on the table as we shot our loads. Yeah, that must have been it. Vampires don't exist. So I didn't have sex with one. I'm a rational man.

Although if vampires did exist, I could see why being a pizza delivery guy would be a good job. You could scope out potential victims while you made money. Get the lay of the land. And you'd get tips.

If I had been sick from food, though, there had been no other symptom other than seeing vampires. And if I'd hit my head, I managed to knock myself silly without raising a lump on my skull. Still, either explanation made more sense than vampires. I mean, really! And the puncture wounds? Okay, I've got nothing there. Can't explain them. Bug bites, maybe? Unlikely, I know, but better than believing my blood had been a meal for one of the walking dead.

Still, when it came time to do a cover for our volume of gay werewolf erotica, I told Sammy he could do it on his own. I'm not taking any chances.

HEAD SHOTS

Neil Plakcy

I was walking along Ocean Drive in Miami Beach with a couple of my frat brothers when this dude came up to us. He was some kind of old hippie with a ponytail, an earring, and a Springsteen tour T-shirt. "You guys ever think about modeling?" he asked.

He handed us each a card that read Beach Boyz Model Agency. Chuck and Larry were like ready to book, but I fancied seeing myself on the cover of some magazine. "What's the deal?" I asked.

"Give me a call," he said. "We'll take some head shots and see how you look on film. Then I'll see if I can book you any jobs."

"Cool," I said.

"You're not actually going to call that loser, are you, Gavin?" Chuck said, as we walked away.

"Why not? You think I'm not good looking enough to be a model?"

"It's some kind of scam," Larry said.

We were all students at Florida University, living together in the Lambda Lambda Lambda frat house just off campus. It was the only all-gay frat in the country, and we were lucky to have a chapter at FU. At other colleges, gay students still got bullied and teased, but at Three Lambs, as we called the house, we were safe from outside pressure, free to concentrate on studying.

And sex, of course. Most of the guys in the house had hooked up with each other at one time or another. Chuck and his boyfriend Fitz were among the first guys in the house, and they had an open relationship. Most of the other guys in the house were single, hooking up whenever the need or the mood arose.

Every guy in the house was good looking, in one way or another. Chuck had this Asian inscrutability going on, like he was a direct descendant of some Manchu emperor. His hair and his eyes were coal black. Larry was a tall stringy bean pole with awesome abs and a mop of shaggy blond hair.

I flattered myself that I had a kind of all-American wholesomeness. I'd often been told I looked like I belonged in an Abercrombie & Fitch ad. Square jaw, close-cropped blond hair, and a body conditioned by years of high school sports and college workouts.

And the truth was that I could use the money. I wasn't the smartest guy at FU, and my parents were paying the full tuition because I didn't qualify for any scholarships. They kept me on a short leash cash-wise, and I couldn't take on a regular part-time job because then my grades would slide even farther down and my parents would pull the plug.

But I wanted to be able to afford the kind of clothes the rich boys wore, the fancy sneakers and the bits of bling. So Monday afternoon I called the number on the business card. I made an appointment for late that day, borrowed Chuck's old beater, and drove back across town to the beach.

The office wasn't much, just a second-floor walk up over a bodega on a side street a few blocks from the beach. But the waiting room was lined with head shots of good-looking men, and there was a receptionist and a buzzer and everything.

The hippie dude's name was Alfie, he said, when he came out to meet me. "Come on back and we'll take some test shots."

He led me into a room with big windows overlooking the street and lots of bright light streaming in. He positioned me in front of this big white sheet of paper and started fiddling with lights and shades and cameras. "Big smile now," he said.

I smiled, and the camera flashed. He led me through a bunch of expressions—moody, sexy, relaxed, and so on. Then he asked me to take my shirt off.

I pulled it off, and he took a couple of shots as I stretched, exposing my long, narrow chest. My shorts were hanging an inch below the top of my boxers, and he seemed to like that, talking sexy to me and snapping shots.

"You're a natural," he said. "I can tell. The camera loves you."

He put the camera down and looked at me. "I don't want to pressure you into anything you don't want to do—but how would you feel about posing nude?"

"You mean like this?" I asked, dropping my shorts and my boxers with them.

He laughed. "Yeah, that's how I meant."

I felt myself popping a boner, and shifted.

"Yeah, that's exactly how I meant," he said. "Stay just like that."

He brought over a couple of props—a chair, a beat-up calculus text, a baseball cap. Then he posed me in a bunch of different ways—sitting on the chair, straddling it, then reading the text, with the ball cap backward on my head.

"Oh, yeah, this is great," he said. "Love your dick, baby. Touch it, will you? Yeah, just like that, your finger right below the head. Man, that's hot."

After a half-hour of that, my dick was stiff as a rock and ready to explode. When Alfie finally stood up and put the camera down, I wanted nothing more than for him to come over and blow me. But instead, he said, "I'm going to print these up, and see what kind of work I can get you. I'll be in touch."

That was all? No sex? Fuck, I was horny. Even though he was like a hundred years old (probably more like fifty, but it's all the same when you get that old), I was sort of hoping he'd make a move. I'd never had sex with an older dude and I was kind of wondering what it would be like.

But just my luck, Alfie was 100 percent professional. Either that or straight, which was pretty much the same thing to me.

"Stop at the front desk with Tony and fill out an application form with your contact information."

I filled out the forms and drove back to the Three Lambs house. I didn't tell anyone what I'd done, because I didn't want anybody to razz me about it.

I didn't hear anything for days. Finally, Friday morning, just as I was rolling out of bed after a beer bash the night before, my cell phone rang. "Gavin? It's Alfie, from Beach Boyz. How'd you like to make some money tomorrow?"

"Sure. What do I have to do?"

He gave me an address on Lincoln Road, the big pedestrian walkway in the middle of the Beach, and told me to be there at seven the next morning.

"I have to wear anything special?"

"They'll provide everything," he said.

I borrowed Chuck's car again, telling him that I had scored a job that day, though not specifying what kind. The roads through Miami and the causeway over to the Beach were empty that early in the morning. I parked in the garage behind the building and walked around to Lincoln Road.

There was a guy about my age standing at the door of the building, peering at the buzzers. He had the kind of looks that immediately put me on the defensive—he could have been a movie star, with his oval face, high cheekbones, and shoulder-length dark brown hair. "You here for the shoot?" he asked me.

"Yup." I was so stunned by his looks I could barely speak. In addition to his handsome face, he had a body to die for, just over six foot tall, with broad shoulders and a narrow waist.

"Good. I forgot the suite number. You have it?"

I looked at the instructions I'd written down. "302."

"You're a lifesaver," he said as he pressed the buzzer. When the door opened, he held it for me and ushered me ahead of him. Then he said, "I'm Tate."

"Gavin."

"Haven't seen you around before, Gavin," he said, as we waited for the elevator.

"This is my first photo shoot. I kind of don't know what to expect."

"Expect to be bored," he said. "That is, if you have a brain. If you don't, you'll probably love it."

"And do you?" I asked, as the door opened. "Have a brain?"

He smiled. "You'll have to figure that out for yourself."

We got off on the third floor, and Tate confidently walked up to the door to suite 302 and opened it. I followed him into a wide, high-ceilinged room with big picture windows that looked south, over Lincoln Road toward downtown Miami and Biscayne Bay. Various set-ups lined the side walls—an office with a desk, chair, and file cabinet; a king-sized bed; a recliner;

and a couple of other settings. Each one had big sheets of white paper hanging on the wall behind it.

A tiny twenty-something girl with a clipboard came up to us. We gave her our names, and she checked us off on her list, then directed us to wardrobe. A very queeny older guy with a blond pouf said, "I'm Leigh. With an i-g-h. I need to take your measurements before I can fit you. You first."

He pointed at Tate and began measuring his arms as I stood back. "Hey, watch the goods," Tate said, as Leigh ran a tape measure up the inside of his legs. "No free feels."

"Honey, I have felt a lot bigger men than you," Leigh said.

Tate simply smirked. Leigh called out measurements to the tiny girl with the clipboard, whose name was Molly. Or maybe Mali, because she didn't spell her name the way Leigh had.

"Next," Leigh said, motioning me over. "Don't be shy, honey. I don't bite, unless I get paid extra."

It felt funny to have his hands roaming all over my body, and I started to feel myself get hard. Oh, no. I tried to focus on math problems, but Leigh kept up a silly chatter and I couldn't concentrate on anything other than his hands.

Thankfully, he finished and stood up. "All right. Now you wait."

There were a couple of other guys in the room, standing by a water cooler in front of a Japanese screen, so Tate and I walked over to them. Tate knew one of them, a guy named Misha who had a heavy Russian accent. A very regal, very tall and skinny Haitian queen introduced himself as Jean-Jacques, and the third guy mumbled so much I didn't catch his name.

I couldn't figure out what was going on. The photographer, a hard-looking blonde woman named Marta who could have been forty or sixty, moved from setting to setting randomly, calling for us by our looks. "Blond boy," she said, pointing to me. "Underwear. Bedroom." She had a faint German accent that made everything seem even more like a command.

Molly led me back to Leigh. "Underwear," she said to him, then walked away.

"All right, strip," he said. He turned to a table full of clothing and started pawing through it.

"Right here?" I asked. My voice was a little higher than I intended.

"We've all seen it before, honey," he said. I looked over at Tate, who had been summoned for the office set, and saw he was stripping. So I pulled off my T-shirt and kicked off my deck shoes.

Leigh turned back around. "You'll be wearing these," he said, holding up a pair of red boxer briefs.

"That's all?"

He sighed deeply. "No, we're going to photograph you in a tuxedo," he said. "Of course that's all. How do you think they sell underwear?"

My dick was hardening at the thought of stripping down, then being photographed in my undies. "But...but..."

He looked me up and down, then smiled. "I see what the problem is. Don't worry, the camera loves a good hard-on. Now come on, get naked, and get these on."

As fast as I could I pulled down my shorts and my boxers, feeling the rush of air conditioning on my naked body. Fortunately the cold calmed my dick down a bit, and I was able to get myself stuffed into the red boxer briefs. "Go over to the bedroom," Leigh said. "Wait there until her highness tells you what to do."

I stood there, feeling like a fool, for at least ten minutes before Molly came over to me with her clipboard. "She wants you standing, with one hand on the headboard and one leg up on the bed."

I positioned myself.

"Good enough," Molly said.

Another ten minutes passed. I was starting to get a cramp in my leg when Marta finally came over.

"Not like that," she said. "Do you know nothing?"

It seemed like a rhetorical question so I didn't answer. She came over to me and repositioned by hand, tugging it farther along the headboard, turning my head, twisting my body. By that point I felt nothing at all beyond frustration about being nearly naked. I let her move me around like I was a Gumby figure, then she backed away, nodded, and picked up her camera.

She moved around me, snapping shots from all angles, occasionally stopping to check the digital display at the back of the camera. Finally she said, "Good. Back to wardrobe."

Gratefully I reassembled myself, stretching to work out a kink in my back, and then walked over to Leigh. Tate was lounging against the table full of clothes, completely naked, and looking very comfortable. His body was even more perfect than I had imagined when he was clothed: big, flat pecs with tiny dark nipples, washboard abs, and a neatly trimmed patch of pubic hair framing his half-hard dick.

At least I hoped it was half-hard. If it was that big in a resting position I could only imagine what it would swell up to.

"Take those off, please," Leigh said.

I skinned down the briefs and handed them to him. "Don't worry, I'm not going to sniff them," he said. "God knows if I sniffed every pair of shorts a boy gave me I'd pass out."

"What do you want me to wear next?" I asked. It was cold standing there naked, and I couldn't begin to feel as comfortable as Tate seemed to be.

"Don't know yet," Leigh said. "Just wait."

"Like this?" Once again, my voice betrayed me, coming out

half an octave higher than I intended.

"Just like God made you," Leigh said.

"You can't be bashful if you're going to model," Tate said, motioning me over to him. "Around here, we're just meat."

The mention of meat made my dick stiffen a little. Tate looked around. Everyone in the room was busy except us. "Come on, I'll show you how I relax," he said.

He walked back over toward the water cooler. I couldn't help notice the way his sweet ass moved as he walked, and the thin line of hair at his crack. I followed him as he stepped behind the Japanese screen.

Then I was astonished as he dropped to his knees and wrapped his hand around my stiffening dick. My mouth opened wide as he licked the head of my dick, then took it in his mouth.

"Tate!" I whispered.

He waved dismissively at me with his other hand.

The feel of his lips on me was so good I felt like swooning. With his hand, he tickled the underside of my scrotum. I struggled to keep from making any noise, conscious that there was a whole room full of people out there just beyond the screen. And what if Leigh, or Molly with her ubiquitous clipboard, were to come back there? Or the photographer? Or one of the other models?

I frantically waved my hand at Tate to let him know I couldn't hold back any more, but he just suctioned my dick and swallowed everything as I ejaculated into his mouth.

My whole body sagged and I was having trouble catching my breath as Tate stood up, a grin on his face. "That's how we relax," he said.

Then we heard Leigh's gritty voice. "Tate! Gavin! Where are you?"

"Right here, boss," Tate said, sashaying around the screen.

"Just waiting for your call, darling."

I scurried around behind Tate, hoping no one could smell the sex on me. Leigh sniffed a little, but didn't say anything as he handed me a T-shirt and a pair of board shorts. "By the white screen, both of you, please."

There was one big white screen with no furniture in front of it. "I don't get it," I said to Tate as we walked over there. He was wearing a different shirt and shorts.

"They put in the background later," he said. "Like a waterfront or a yard."

"Oh."

Marta posed us a couple of different ways. I felt a lot more relaxed, having shot my load. I guess Tate was right. We worked all day, and by five o'clock I was beat. Who knew it would be so tiring just standing around posing? Finally Molly announced, after conferring with Marta, that we were done.

"But Gavin and Tate, please stay," she said.

I looked at him, and he looked back at me. He shrugged.

We walked over to Molly, who said, "She wants to talk to you."

Marta was busy packing up her cameras, so we stood around and waited. Leigh left, then Molly. It was just Tate and me.

"I do other photography on the side," she said. "X-rated. I see you guys slip behind the screen earlier. You interested in extra cash?"

"How much?" Tate asked.

She quoted us a figure, and I sucked in my breath. "I'm in," I said.

"Sure, why not," Tate said. "You want us to do it now?"

"Now's as good a time as any," she said.

Marta directed us over to the bedroom set. "Now, forget I am here," she said. "Just do what you would like."

"C'mere, you," Tate said. He motioned me toward him and put his arms around my back. Then he leaned forward and kissed me, his lips light and feathery on mine.

I groaned and sagged into him. I could just see Marta out of the corner of my eye, snapping pictures, but I focused on Tate. He began kissing his way along my jaw and then down my neck, and I arched my back, offering my throat to him as if he was a vampire. His gorgeous hair fell in a wave against my shoulder.

He slipped his hands under my T-shirt, tickling his way up my chest, and I giggled and pulled away. He took that opportunity to hoist my T-shirt up over my head. We fooled around and rough-housed a bit, him trying to tickle me, and then I got hold of his shirt and began unbuttoning it, and he tilted his head to the side and smiled.

When his shirt was off, he reached up and took each of my nipples in the thumb and forefinger of a hand, and began pressing. That sent an electric signal to my crotch and my dick stiffened in my shorts. I pressed my crotch against his leg and rubbed.

I heard the click of Marta's shutter. Tate gave up pinching my nipples for sucking them, one after the other, until they were hard nubs of flesh that tingled in the cool air of the studio. As he was sucking my left nipple he began unbuttoning my shorts and then slipped them off.

My dick tented my boxers, the head just sticking out through the slit. I was so horny I could hardly focus on unbuckling his belt and undoing his pants. He had to help me, my hands were shaking so much from desire and anticipation.

Then we were both in our shorts—his boxer briefs, my boxers. We hugged and pressed our bodies together in all kinds of ways, continuing our previous rough-housing. Then we ended up on the bed together, kissing, him on top of me.

His breath was sweet against my cheek, his skin warm to the

touch. I could feel him touching me in a dozen different places, chest against chest, arm against arm, dick against groin. He pushed me up on the bed so I was leaning against the pillows and ducked his head down to lick my dick through the slit of my boxers. I splayed my arms against the pillows and leaned back in ecstasy.

"Lift your hips up," he grunted, and when I did he pulled down my boxers and my stiff dick sprung free. It was already dribbling pre-cum from the head. "God, you are sexy," he said.

His hair hung down around his head like a brown curtain, and he reached around to pull it away so he could focus on sucking my dick. I found myself pushing up against his mouth. I saw Marta moving at the side of the bed, and I snickered at the idea that she was taking a different kind of head shot. Then I saw her put a bottle of lube and a couple of condom packs on the table next to us and figured I was going to get a lot more than head.

Tate saw it too. As she backed away and began snapping pictures again, he reached over and grabbed a condom. With one hand still stroking me, he used his teeth and the other hand to rip the packet open, and the latex sheath slid out and landed on my stomach.

He left it there, then stepped off the bed so he could shimmy out of his boxer briefs. For a moment I got to stare wide-eyed at his physical perfection. I loved the way his broad shoulders rippled with muscle, the way his chest narrowed to his waist, the fat, juicy-looking dick that wagged half-hard between his legs in front of a pair of big, low-hanging balls.

His thighs were solid muscle, his calves too. He saw me eyeing him and struck a bodybuilder pose. I almost came right there.

He reached for the lube as he got back on the bed. Then,

with a quick motion, he had my legs up over his shoulders, and his mouth was at my ass, licking and tonguing it. I sighed with pleasure, grabbing my ass cheeks with both hands and prying them apart to give him greater access.

He squirted the lube on his fingers, then began penetrating me with first one digit, then two. The lube was cold at first but he warmed it up fast, sliding his fingers in and out of my ass as I wiggled and moaned. "Fuck me, Tate," I said hoarsely. "Please."

"Since you said please," he said. He backed off and took the condom from my belly, stretching it down over his dick, which had stiffened by then. It was impressively large and I worried my hole might not be big enough. But hell, I didn't care if he ripped me apart; I wanted that dick inside me.

Then he squirted more lube in his hand. He focused on my eyes as he stroked himself, coating his condom-covered dick in lube. It was so erotic, having him look at me that way, and I hoped Marta was able to capture that look of pure lust.

Then he was in me, his dick pressing against my chute, sending electric sensations through my whole body. My legs were starting to ache from the unfamiliar position, but I didn't want him to stop, just to keep on fucking me. We were both sweating by then, and his hands were slippery around my thighs as he pushed forward.

In and out, in and out. With every thrust my whole body rocked with pleasure. "Oh, god," he said. "Oh, god, Gavin."

He reached between my legs and grabbed my dick, his hand still slippery with lube. He began jacking me madly as he pushed in and out of my hole, and we both were writhing around on the bed in ecstasy.

I began making high-pitched sounds I'd never heard come out of my mouth before as he slammed hard into me, bashing against my prostate. I felt the heat of his cum shooting into the condom. That was all I needed to spurt, and my cum arced out of my dick and splattered my belly.

He pulled out of me, lowered my legs, and then collapsed on top of me, the full condom cold and wet against my leg.

I was no virgin by then, but that was by far the most amazing fuck of my life. I had the feeling Tate felt the same way, from the glazed look in his eyes as he squirmed up to lie next to me, his hair splayed against my shoulder, one hand resting on my abdomen.

"Beautiful," Marta said. I had forgotten she was there. "Amazing. You boys are stars. I will write you checks."

Neither of us wanted to get up, but finally I pushed myself off the bed and pulled on my boxers, my dick and ass still tender from the fucking Tate had given me. He followed suit, and we walked over to Marta's table, where she had us sign a second set of model releases, then handed us our checks.

"I feel like I could eat a whole cow," Tate said, as we walked to the elevator. "Want to grab some dinner and celebrate these fat paychecks?"

"I'd like to eat, then celebrate with your fat dick again," I said.

He laughed and pressed the button. "That can be arranged," he said.

VINCENT
ON THE
HALF-SHELL

Rob Rosen

The room was empty, vacant easels surrounding a plywood box, the smell of acrylic paint and turpentine wafting languidly up my nostrils. I stood at the sink, painstakingly washing my brushes, heart beating hummingbird-fast, fingers trembling, expectantly, as I watched the traces of amber and chartreuse cyclone down the drain. Oh sure, I'd painted nudes before, but this was different. In a classroom setting, things were more, well, clinical. This, though, was no classroom setting; the model and I would soon be going *mano-a-mano*—with him being the first man-o I'd ever painted, nude and alone. I gulped at the very thought of it.

Then I heard him enter, the gulp going on auto-repeat.

"Where do you want me?" I heard him ask, my backside facing his way as I continued with the brushes.

"Oh, uh, on the box would be great," I replied, over my shoulder.

I heard his sandals shuffling, the wood groaning as he jumped up, a lemon-sized pit already forming deep within my belly. "Robe on or off?" he asked.

The lemon pit pulsed, as did my prick, consigned as it was within its cottony chamber. "Um, off," I managed, my voice suddenly all fifteen-year-old boy. I heard the robe drop to the ground just as I flicked the faucet off. I turned, slowly, curious as to what would be greeting me. It would be a gross understatement to say that I was shocked at what I found. Or who. "Steve!" I hollered, dropping my handful of brushes, which clinked as they rolled around on the cement.

"Greg!" Steve yelled in return, jumping off the box to retrieve his robe. Jumping, that is, and then tripping, his lean, tall body slamming into a row of easels, all of them crashing loudly as they collapsed, one after the other.

I watched in stunned disbelief, my roommate writhing naked on the floor, cock flipped to the side, crinkled asshole winking out at me. I almost looked away. Almost, but, come on, this was quite a show, however embarrassing it might have been. Still, I did rush over to help him up. Not that it was any less awkward having him standing naked in front of me, mind you.

"What are you doing here?" I managed, trying (and failing) not to stare. Downward.

"You know I model, dude," he replied, hands trying (and failing) to cover the goodies up.

I nodded, as did my dick. "You're a catalog model, Steve," I reminded him. "Guess what? My paintings aren't going to make it into the new Sears brochure."

He laughed, a flush of red working its way up his neck before splashing across his smooth, angular cheeks. "I, um, do this on the side. In between gigs. Easy money."

Again I nodded, dick at full throttle now. *Bad dick,* I thought to myself. *Down boy, down.* "My money," I amended. "Today, at any rate."

His nod mirrored my own. "Do you still, uh, still want to paint me, dude? Kind of strange, right?"

I couldn't help but sigh. "No choice, dude. Part of my final exam. Recreate a famous nude on canvas. Everyone else is working with female models, mostly in groups."

He chuckled. "Hence my standing naked, alone, with my roommate, in a studio."

I saw his chuckle and raised him several more in return. "Hence. Yes. And it's too late in the game to find another model. So, tag, you're it, Steve."

He shrugged. "My dick is all yours then, roomie," he replied, the blush returning, his face suddenly crimson. "Figuratively speaking, I mean."

I moved out of his way. "Figuratively speaking, dude, get your figure on the box. Time is money."

He saluted and jogged past me, dick bouncing, a sea of muscles flexing as he hopped up.

Regaining my composure, mostly, I let my eyes take him in, more artist appraisal than anything else. Well, more or less. I mean, the guy was stunning, roommate or not. His hair was the color of wheat, eyes so shockingly blue they practically burned a hole right on through you, lips pink and pouty, high cheekbones, barely a trace of stubble. Brad Pitt minus the wife and brood. Then lower down, heavy pecs, eraser-tipped nipples, a light tuft of hair down the cleft that trailed south, nearly lost among a six-pack with two seemingly extra sets of cans. Lower down still, a manscaped bush, wiry, blond, hovering like a cloud above his dangling cock, heavy nuts.

I stifled a groan at the sight of it. I mean, sure we were roomies, but neither one of us walked around the house naked. Plus, he was away a lot, traveling for work. And I was in school, days, nights, weekends. I finished my visual grand tour with his thighs like tree trunks, calves like boulders, his legs the only thing hairy about him. Divinely hairy, in fact. Adonis had nothing on Steve. No way, no how.

"Everything okay?" he asked, eyeing me eyeing him.

I coughed. "Oh, uh, yeah. Just getting the lay of the land, so to speak." I paused, the word *lay* suddenly echoing off the four corners of my brain. I shook the idea free, and then added, "But you're, uh, standing all wrong." I walked in and stared up at him, his prick suddenly at eye level. I breathed in the heady aroma of him, of his musk and sweat and soap. Irish Spring. Manly, yes, but I liked it too. Then I grabbed his hand and placed it over his crotch, my index finger accidentally brushing the soft flesh. He flinched, as did I. "Now, uh, put your other hand over your chest, like you're saying the pledge of allegiance."

He did as I asked. "Fine, dude, but you're covering my best assets."

I nodded and turned back around. *Tell me about it*, I thought to myself. Then I sat down at my easel, five feet away from him, staring out at all that glorious flesh and muscle. Still, I set to work. After all, the view came with a price.

Thirty minutes in and I had the rough outline done. "Doing okay?" I asked.

He sighed. "Bored silly, dude."

I laughed and nodded. "I'm sure," I replied. "How about, to take your mind off of things, you tell me your weirdest modeling story." It was an innocent enough request. Or, at least, it should've been.

A grin shot northward on his stunning face. "Yeah, I got a few of those. You sure you want to hear the *weirdest* one?"

I glanced up, locking eyes with him, a swarm of butterflies suddenly let loose in my rumbling tummy. "Sure, dude. Let 'er rip."

He nodded, itching his calf with the side of his size 12 foot. "Started routinely enough. Fashion shoot for a national retailer. Me and six other dudes vying for the gig. Big bucks. My agent made sure to get me in last, to keep me fresh in their heads. Only, there was no *their*, just a *he*. The photographer made the final call. The six of us had already passed muster with our portfolios. Anyway, I go inside and the guy is completely naked. Head to fucking toe."

Oh, shit, I thought. *Down, dick, down.* "Anything but routine, right?"

Steve nodded. "Amen. Anyway, dude says, since I'm going to be naked, he thought it would make us models feel more comfortable."

I couldn't help but interrupt. "You said it was a fashion shoot."

He shrugged. "Like that matters. Clothes were on the bed. I was naked, covered, but just barely, by an errant sleeve, a well-placed pant leg. Tasteful." He laughed. "Anyway, guy was way hot; so *comfortable*, as he put it, I was not. Better if he was old and fat. Still, you never argue with the photographer."

"Especially when he's naked and hot," I couldn't help but add, already starting in on some of the shading on the canvas, on the finer lines, his body suddenly coming to life.

"Especially," he agreed. "Except the hot naked stuff wasn't what made it weird. See, he gets me into position, the bed covered in clothes, me sprawled out. Well, you get the picture. Then he starts snapping away, telling me to move this way and that. Standard stuff. And then he turns around to bend down, to get a different kind of lens, and I notice this blue, round thing where his asshole should have been."

I gulped, fingers frozen mid-sketch. "Butt plug?"

"Bingo. Butt plug. I spotted it and started to laugh. And then he turns and asks what's so funny. And, of course, I tell him. And he says it helps him be creative. Like, it's hard to get bored with six inches of silicone plugging up your chute."

"Bored?" I couldn't help but ask.

Steve nodded. "Photo shoots can take hours of shifting and shooting, shifting and shooting. Guess the plug kept things interesting for him. So I told him that I could see his point. Gets boring from my end of things, too, I said. I was just making small talk, really. Only, he doesn't see it that way."

Fuck. Okay, boy, just stay up for all I care. "So he helps you make the shoot not so boring, huh?"

Again Steve nodded. "Dude shoots me a wicked-ass grin and then goes rummaging around inside his backpack. Ten seconds later, he's walking over to the bed with seven inches of bouncing pink latex and a raging hard-on pointed my way. I mean, I've had photographers flirt with me before, but this was ridiculous."

I wiped the sweat from my brow, my eyes glued to his crotch, his hand doing little to cover his burgeoning prick. "So you told him no thanks?"

Steve chuckled, cock suddenly at full mast, his hand at his side now. Because, really, it would've been like trying to cover a dining table with a dinner napkin by that point. "Um, I told you the guy was hot. And hung like a mule." Again he laughed, the hand at his side suddenly lifted for a quick tug on his great big slab of meat. "In other words, I lifted my legs, spread 'em good and wide, and told him to show me how un-bored he could make me."

I groaned, my pencil set in a cup, and pushed down on my tenting package. Steve was jacking away now, clearly playing the scene back in his head as he continued the story. "Dude had one long tongue, too. Spit on my hole and shoved it right on in,

slobbered it up good and wet before easing that pink rod up
my ass. Sucker sent my body on fire, a moan shooting through
me. The photographer must've loved my reaction 'cause he's all
of a sudden snapping like crazy, dozens of shots of me jacking
beneath the fabric, barely out of sight of the camera, all while
he's priming the cum up from his swaying nuts."

I started working on my own slicked-up cock now, which I'd
freed from my pants, his randy tale setting my creative juices
flowing, not to mention the ones leaking over my fat prick head.
And still I continued sketching with my free hand. "How did it
end?" I rasped.

Steve sighed, tweaking a nipple with one hand, slapping the
underside of his shaft with the other. "Fucker shot on my chest
while I jizzed up several hundred dollars worth of high-end
merch. Then he yanked the blue plug out, setting it rolling to
the floor. My pink one I kept. A keepsake."

I was still stroking behind my easel. If he saw, he didn't say
anything. "Did you get the job?" I couldn't help but ask.

Steve laughed. "That's the weird part of the story, dude."

I looked up and over at him. "The dildos, plural, weren't the
weird part?"

He shook his head. "My agent called me that night. I asked
him if I got the job. Turns out, I had it the day before. Portfolio
had been enough."

I stopped jacking and drawing. "The photographer set you
up?"

The laughter grew, echoing around the room. "Yup. Knew
all along what he was doing."

"And you weren't mad?" I asked.

He shook his head. "Nah. You should've seen the photos.
Ran in every major market. Me smiling from ear to ear, eyes
closed, secretly cumming for the world to see, with a pink dildo

rammed tight up my ass. Little did they know."

I coughed. "More hot than weird, dude."

Again he laughed, the stroke up and down on his long, thick shaft suddenly quickened. "My parents saw the ad, Greg."

And then I laughed, as well. "Yup, weird, dude. Definitely weird."

But then his laughter abruptly stopped, a silence enveloping the room, save for the sound of my jacking echoing his. "Weirder than this?" he eventually squeaked out.

I nodded. "I see your point."

He grinned. "Dude, you're seeing a lot more than my point right about now." He swung it to and fro, for effect. Which caused me to groan, just barely beneath my breath. "You, uh, you almost finished over there?" he added. "With your sketching, I mean?"

I stood up, baggy pants falling to the ground, my own point ramrod straight, aimed right his way, fist wrapped around it as a bead of sweat cascaded down my forehead, a similar-sized bead of pre-come dripping over my wide, mushroomed head. "Guess I could use a break," I replied, nearly in a pant.

He winked and beckoned me over, his cock released, pointing down at mine, two divining rods. Only it wasn't water they were after. I strode over, kicking my pants to the side, cock swaying as I approached him. Weird, as he'd said, but so fucking hot as to put the sun to shame. And then I stood at the edge of the box, staring up at him, his steely cock just a few centimeters away from my mouth, and then not even that.

I downed him in one fell swoop, salty jizz hitting the back of my throat like a bullet as a gagging tear made a beeline across my cheek. He moaned as I sucked him in, knees buckling, his hand reaching out to grab the back of my head, to coax me down further, until his balls were slamming against my chin.

"Fuuuck," he sighed, pummeling my face.

I stared up, his head tilted back, mouth agape, sweat trickling down the narrow trench between his pecs. Stunning, with a capital S. I popped his prick out, yanking on his swaying balls. "Speaking of which," I rasped. "How about getting on your back for me?"

He smiled and hopped down off the box, then took a seat, feet dangling before he fell backward, legs raised wide, that beautiful hole of his again on display. "Better?" he asked, already with a slow stroke on his fat prick.

I turned and stared, smiling broadly before retrieving one of the tools of my trade, namely a nice-sized paintbrush. "Understatement," I replied, licking and lapping at his heavy, smooth nuts. His knees went up to his chest, cock pushed through between athletic thighs, so that I could suck on the happy trio: cock, balls, and hole. In that order. Hole last, my tongue diving in, spit dripping down as I reamed him out, his stunning ass rocking into my eager mouth.

"Fuuuck," he echoed, repeating the word, again and again, the sound whizzing around my head like a swarm of bees. Horny bees, but still.

Reluctantly, I moved my mouth away. "Just getting to that," I said, sliding my middle finger up and in and back, his hole gripping my spit-slick digit, breath sucked in as I pushed and prodded. He exhaled, released, and my index finger joined its neighbor, all while I tickled his balls with the brush I'd brought back. Not a dildo, but it would do in a pinch, I figured.

He spread his legs wide again, peering down at what I had in mind for him. "Dirty roomie," he chided, grabbing his cock.

I retracted my fingers and spanked his hole with the bristles. "You say it like it's a bad thing," I said, flipping the brush over, the thick round end swirling around his glistening ring.

I crouched down and spit at his hole, then slid it in, one inch, two, three. "Fuck it, you're right; dirty roomie."

He arched his back, eyelids fluttering, breath ragged. Four inches, five. "Filthy, in fact," he amended, voice gravelly, pace picking up on his swollen cock, the head now slick with pre-come. His whole body, etched with contracted muscle, shook and rocked as I assailed his hole, ramming and jamming that brush in and out, in and out, my cock getting a heavy beating of its own as I watched on in anticipation.

"Close," he grunted, pounding his prick lightening fast now, mammoth balls steadily rising.

"Ditto," I groaned, knees already buckling, sweat pouring down, every nerve ending in my body ablaze.

Then the final "Fuuuck" as his body quaked, his cock erupting, heavy streams of molten spunk shooting this way and that, drenching his ripped belly, broad chest, the creaking wooden box, the cement floor, all while the end of the brush protruded out of his perfect ass.

I shot a split-second later, matching him moan for moan, the sound echoing off the walls, my load joining his on the floor, *splat, splat, splat*. My fist pounded away, milking every last drop, until I collapsed on the ground, panting, and then gently retrieved my brush from his hole. He bucked one final time, legs again dangling over the box, cock still at half-mast, sticky with gobs of cum.

"I think I found my muse," I only half-joked, eyes glued to him.

"David to your Michelangelo?" he asked, pushing himself up on his elbows, a wink and smirk cast wide across his picture-perfect face.

"David looked pretty happy, as far as I can recall. Lord only knows what he had shoved up his ass. And Michelangelo worked with a chisel and a hammer."

Steve winced. "Ouch." Then he jumped down and wrestled me to the ground. "Keep the heavy equipment away from my ass, roomie," he warned, lips soon pressed up tight to mine, mouths colliding as we rolled around the studio.

Which is just where we found ourselves two weeks later.

He stood behind me, hand on my shoulder, the finished painting sitting on my easel. "You deserve that A, roomie," he said, with a pat. "What do you call it?"

I stared with pride at my work and smiled. *The Birth of Vincent*, I replied.

He chuckled. "Looks more like Vincent on the half-shell. But at least I know why he has that shit-eating grin on his face. Nice touch making the angels all leather-daddy-like, too." He squinted, face up close to the canvas. "One of them has a brush in his hand, huh? Wonder what he's gonna do with it?" He breathed hard into my ear, biting down on a tender lobe, sending a rush of adrenalin up my spine, my heart beating in double time.

I pushed my backside into him, his granite-solid crotch butting up against me. "Maybe it's the artist's turn for some brushing," I told him. "Why should the muse have all the fun?"

He turned me around and ran his lips across my mouth. "Because the muse gets paid top dollar to have fun, roomie." His tongue snaked its way inside, before he added, "But this one's on the house."

Have at it, boy, I thought, releasing the beast. *Have the fuck at it.*

WHEN GARY MET LARRY

T. Hitman

The leather. Its smell permeated the air inside the warehouse. Rich and lemony up one aisle, raw and masculine, even arousing, down another.

Big Jim Augusta clapped a hand to my shoulder. "I understand you're an accomplished shutterbug."

Not too accomplished, I thought—I was making six bucks an hour standing on my feet all day picking horse supplies. "I guess," I said.

He pulled me aside, into a corner of the same aisle where dressage clothes and leather chaps shared shelf space. "Let me tell you what I need. In the weeks ahead, we're gonna be doing a big push, *big*, getting the Statewide Tack brand out there to the globe. To do that, I need a new catalog—and a new photographer to shoot it. The old approach doesn't work anymore. I don't have a lot of money to pay you up front and I want you to save costs whenever possible, but you could make it up with bonuses in the backend if you give me solid gold.

And, if you do a great job, you get the next one and we'll rene-
gotiate your fee."

The clank and clatter of a metal trolley trundling down the
aisle echoed through the vastness. Driving the cart was a young
man recently hired in anticipation of the holiday season rush
who'd inspired more than one double-take from me. He wore a
Cleveland Indians baseball cap, the bill turned backward, and
hummed to himself while chewing on a pen. Handsome, oh
yeah. A little goofy, but he wore even that well. His name was
Gary. Secretly, I was smitten.

"Do you know what you're looking for?" I asked.

"Something that knocks our customers on their rich butts
and gets them to open up their wallets. We're going to be offering
cowboy hats, men's jeans, real high-end gear in addition to the
usual stuff."

I nodded. "You want to save on the cost of the shoot? Don't
hire professional models. Throw some cash at your handsomest
warehouse workers. Use your best resources for models, like
you're doing for the photographer."

Big Jim folded his arms and nodded. "I like the way you
think."

"I hope you like the way I photograph. Cowboy gear? That
one looks like a cowboy to me." I tipped my chin at the retreating
back of the young man.

"Looks more like an *Indian* to me. I fuckin' hate the
Indians...."

A few days later in another part of the warehouse, I met Larry,
though *met* is an overstatement. He had just been hired and was
riding a forklift, pulling down shrink-wrapped pallets of equine
supplies, when I walked up to the machine. I knew he was the
other guy in my unfolding storyline the instant I stole my first

glance at him. Not as tall as Gary, I pegged him at around the six-foot mark and a few years older than his coworker, though decades in some ways, judging by his hard expression. Gary had dark hair, cut like a baseball player's. Larry's was blond, brush-cut.

Even then, being an amateur photographer who'd shot mostly landscapes and a few male nudes, I'd learned to live through pictures and observe a lot in a short amount of time. Whole lives, in some instances, which was the case with Larry. He wore fatigue cut-offs with big, baggy pockets, and I knew the hard scowl, like his shorts, had come from the military.

I'd already sold Gary on the idea—he'd just about creamed his khakis at the prospect of getting paid to be a model. I wanted this guy with the great set of hairy legs and the length of sweat sock showing at the tops of his dirty steel-toes. I drank in his handsomeness and called up, some thirty feet, to the metal rafters.

"Hey, you up there, can you come on down?"

The legs shifted pose. Blue eyes gazed from a clipboard to me. "Hold on a sec."

The seconds ticked past. Eventually, he gave the controls a spin and lowered.

"You're Larry, right?"

He nodded. His distrusting expression solidified.

"How'd you like to make some extra green in your next paycheck?"

"Overtime?"

"Of a sort," I said. I introduced myself and explained the offer.

"Modeling?"

"This could change your life. I'm planning for it to change mine."

Larry shook my hand, putting enough strength into the gesture to make me wince. I knew I had chosen well. Sometimes, there's a chemical spark that is clear and obvious and just works. Larry and Gary would be the faces of the new Statewide Tack catalog. Neither of the young men suspected they had star power, but I did.

Sunlight streamed through the loading dock. A warm October breeze scattered dry leaves across the pavement. The foliage was a week past peak; a steady rain a few days earlier had brought down most of it. This third day of Indian Summer had baked the afternoon into something pleasant and perfumed with autumn smells.

I approached Gary, who stood at one of the open garage doors, staring out at the almost too bright landscape. I caught a hint of his sweat, clean and masculine, around the October leaves and struggled for my next breath. I said his name. Gary turned around and smiled.

"Tonight, at my studio. Big Jim says you can clear out an hour early, with pay."

"Dude, I'm so there," Gary said.

I could tell that his mind was opening up to the possibilities of a life beyond this warehouse existence. I sensed the night was going to be amazing.

I rented a small house that had an attached garage. I kept my studio in a spare bedroom inside the house but had found a use for the garage beyond simply parking my car. By six o'clock, I had transformed it into a barn, complete with all the props. Bales of hay created the illusion of a working farm. I had a saddle on the stand and a colorful Navajo blanket tacked to the wall. I only needed my two cowboys.

A pickup pulled into the driveway. I saw that Larry was driving. Gary sat beside him in the front passenger seat. Carpooling was a good sign. In order to accomplish what I had in mind, there would need to be chemistry between my models as well.

Saddles, blankets, riding helmets, ropes, and other tack supplies had been the staple of the previous Statewide catalogs. But with this new edition, which would be mass-mailed in advance of the holidays, Big Jim had wisely expanded the business to appeal to a broader audience. I reminded the guys that riding shirts, men's jeans, cowboy hats, and boots would fill space between the glossy pages.

"Since most of the customers are girls and women, Jim wants men of a certain caliber to model the clothes—men who will make a statement and catch the eyes of the customers. Men so handsome, the ladies are gonna cream at the sight of them and sales will skyrocket."

Larry folded his arms. I ordered myself not to look at the big toe poking through the rip in his sweat sock after he'd shed his boots, but failed. Gary perked up.

"You really think...?"

I handed each man a cold longneck. "Think you've both got the goods? Absolutely, I know you do."

Larry took a swig. "How do you know?"

I didn't answer right away. Should I tell them I loved the male physique and knew it intimately, and not just from the other side of the camera, that I'd shot about a dozen men nude in the very spot in my studio where they stood clothed? I settled for "I've got a great eye. Now let's make this happen."

On one of the tables, new jeans, western button-downs, clean white boot socks, cowboy hats, leather chaps, belts, and even riding jockstraps had been laid out, all of it new and waiting to be filled. I told the guys to get dressed and left them alone with the excuse I'd be attending to a few last minute details. Truth was, I'd caught their scent, that clean masculine smell of new rain on bare skin, and didn't think I'd make it through the preparations without throwing an obvious hard-on, likely either delaying or screwing up the shoot.

Several tense minutes later, Larry called my name. I walked back into the studio to see him leaning his ass on the edge of the desk. He was naked except for the pair of black boxer briefs spray-painted onto his waist and the old pair of socks on his size 12s. Those magnificent hairy legs tempted my eyes. On my next breath, my lungs filled with the smell of tooled leather, athletic sweat, men's feet.

"What's up with this?" Larry grumbled. He held up one of the jockstraps. "I don't gotta wear it, do I?"

Before I could answer, Gary said, "Yeah, you didn't say anything about us being photographed with our dicks swinging."

I chuckled, aware that Gary was barefoot, his pants unzipped and hanging open, his T-shirt in a pile beside his discarded socks, and extremely conscious of the thin line of dark hair cutting down the center of his abdomen. "That's because you aren't expected to model underwear. The jocks, like the rest of the clothes, are yours, compliments of Statewide Tack. We're creating a fantasy here, a story of two hard-working young cowboys. Attractive, All-American guys who work up an honest day's sweat and then party down at sunset. The real-life versions of those men wear jocks like the ones in your hands. It's up to you if you want to wear them for the shoot."

Gary absently scratched at the dense pelt visible through the open halves of his pants. "I haven't squeezed my nuts into one of these for at least five years."

He dropped his jeans, taking the tight-whites beneath with them in the process. Time seemed to fall off track, turning seconds into minutes, and the minutes into seconds. Using the camera of my mind, I recorded the image of his dick, a long and hairy tube over a mismatched set of meaty low-hanging nuts.

"Do you think I could model underwear if I wanted?" he asked.

"Better than Marky Mark, man," I said.

About an hour that felt like a full day later, I was down on my knees, recording his dick up close, and sucking down as much of it as my throat could handle.

The photo that would go on to grace the cover, the one that people, male and female, would masturbate over, fantasize about, *cum* to, almost never happened.

I snapped maybe a hundred others, two dozen of which ended up in the pages of the catalog. The rest were posed and stiff shots of the two men wearing their clothes and a few other wardrobe options and, granted, wearing them well, but nothing that would make a great or alluring cover photo. The problem was that they were in the clothes, but not in the characters. I admit, my lack of direction and growing disappointment wasn't helping our cause.

"Is something wrong?" Gary asked.

He more than Larry was clearly disappointed. With the sun setting and a warm October twilight breeze whispering through the garage set, I lied and said no, there wasn't. Larry didn't buy it.

"Come on, don't dick us," he said. "Is it that we're not good enough, because we're not *real* models?"

I caught the worry in Gary's wounded expression. This was spiraling downward, and the time to turn it around was running out.

"I don't know. It's..."

"It's what, dude?"

I set down my camera. Gary tracked my movements, seeing surrender in that one action. "The energy level needs to be kicked up some. Don't get me wrong, you both are, well...you're amazing. I'm not bullshitting you when I say you're a couple of walking wet dreams. It's here, we just have to harness it."

Gary shifted nervously from one foot to the other. "How do we do that? What have you done in the past at other photo shoots, with other models?"

I couldn't tell them that what I did was pump their dicks, lick between their toes, fluff their stiff cocks to get my other models to relax and into character. "I'm gonna take a breather, get my head on straight, and I'll be back."

I walked away with an ominous sense of dread on my shoulders, convinced the shoot was doomed to failure. Under normal circumstances, cutting out was the wrong thing to do. Turns out, in this one case it was the right, best solution.

Gary followed me into the studio a few minutes later.

"Hey," he said.

I smiled and answered with a tip of my chin, that universal gesture of greeting between males.

Gary moseyed over. He looked great in the clothes, even walked with the kind of swagger and strut his character would show while navigating obstacles in his rural, blue-collar world. Neither one of us spoke further for what seemed a very long time. Then Gary said, "I really want this, even more than the paycheck. Tell me how to make this work, man...what to do. What's worked before?"

Not sure why, I opened the file cabinet and pulled out the studies I'd done a few weeks earlier: a dude in a baseball uniform, then *out* of it, his cock hard over two fat nuts. Gary looked at the color photos, wide eyed, and quickly set them back down on the desk, as though they'd burned his fingertips.

"Huh?"

"You asked, I showed you. Look, the problem here, as I see it, is that the clothes are new, but they're *too* new. That's not the man we're trying to create for this cover. We need to loosen things up a bit. Mess them up."

Gary fixed me with a stare, aimed a finger at the photos. "You suck his dick?"

I could have lied. I didn't. "To get him hard and keep him hard, sure."

"Do you think I'm in his league?"

"You and Larry, you're beyond his league." That, too, was the truth.

Gary reached down and unzipped his pants. "Then suck me, dude."

"If you're sure," I sighed, not taking the offer seriously.

But as I watched, his jock appeared. Unable to resist, I reached for his pouch, tugged it aside. Warm balls spilled out. I worked the jock down and freed Gary's hardening cock. I had only given it a few firm upward strokes when the sound of approaching footsteps alerted me to Larry's presence in the house.

"Is this what you expected from us all along?"

"No," I said. "The only thing I want out of you both is whatever comes naturally to you."

Gary grunted. He pushed on my shoulder, guiding me down. I wasn't sure if getting head from another guy was something that came naturally to him, but it was clear he wanted his dick sucked, and I felt fairly comfortable with helping him out.

I knelt in front of Gary and took his cock between my lips. Gary moaned in response. His nuts jumped in my hand. I sucked deeper. A real man's taste ignited across my taste buds. From the corner of my eye, I tracked Larry, watching us at first, a look of disbelief broadcast from his eyes. But then he kicked off his boots, unzipped his pants, and shuffled closer. Without asking or being invited to, I set a hand on Larry's shin. He tensed beneath my fingers. I pulled back on instinct.

"No, it's okay," he said.

I touched him again, finally able to caress his legs. A few more sucks on Gary's cock and Larry gripped my head, guiding me toward him. His balls were hairier, sweatier than Gary's, no less magnificent. The single eye at the crown of his dick's head wept a cloudy tear. I lapped it up before releasing it.

"Wait," Larry started.

But he'd misinterpreted my pulling away. Lowering, I licked him from the top of his ankle up into the hairy thatch running to knee; higher, to inner thigh, to those fat, furry balls. I suckled his nuts one at a time before taking the head of his dick again between my lips. Tangy pre-cum registered on my tongue. Larry uttered a blue streak of expletives and rose to the tops of his toes, forcing his cock down my throat. Only his nuts and the coarse hair of his crotch stopped him from going deeper.

I sucked, tugging at Larry's balls. It soon became quite clear how much he loved having his stones worked. I caressed his legs with my free hand, enjoying the scratch of the hair beneath my fingertips.

Another hand seized hold of that wrist. Gary guided my fingers around his straining tool. "You forget I'm here, too?" he asked. Then, to Larry, he added, "Stop hogging his mouth, dude."

I spit out Larry's cock and moved again to my left. After a few firm sucks, I slid my tongue behind his sac and licked the funky patch of skin between his balls and his asshole.

"Fuck," Gary moaned.

I returned my focus to his dick, taking as much of him down as I could handle without gagging. I grabbed Gary's balls and tugged. Reaching over, I repeated the same on Larry's set. Larry ambled closer. Their dicks crossed while attempting to seize ownership of my mouth.

"Now who's being a hog with his hog?"

The head of Larry's cock slipped in. I imagined their dicks rubbing together, dripping semen, the two loads mixing in my mouth. I sucked harder, yanking on balls, my own dick so hard it verged on painful.

"Suck it," Larry ordered. "Suck on our fuckin' cocks."

I did as ordered. The raw smell of masculine sweat intensi-fied. Gary was the first to turn around and present his beaut of an ass to me, inspired by my brief earlier visit to that part of his body. I spread the muscled halves of his butt and exhaled a warm breath into his hairy crack. Gary trembled.

"Do it," he moaned.

I ran my tongue along one cheek and into the furry hole at the center and toyed with the set of balls dangling between his spread legs. Gary sucked in a hit of air. I licked, growing hungrier with the revolutions.

"Holy fuck, you're gonna make me nut," Gary huffed.

He spun around, stuck his cock in my face, and unloaded. Cum sprayed my tongue while balls slapped my chin. My own dick, so sore, so stiff, suffered. I worked it out, using the flow of my pre-cum for lube, and came while eating Larry's asshole.

The world around me distorted. My entire body wanted to collapse, as though I'd transformed into one giant cock and every one of my cells had ejaculated, all in unison. Sweat stung at my eyes. The smell in the studio was manly, amazing.

Licking my lips, I pulled myself up and stuffed my dick back into my pants. "Larry, Gary," I sighed. "Now, how about we go make history?"

They reached for their jeans and boots. I told them not to because while most times the clothes make the man, others it's the man who makes the clothes, which turned out being the case with the Statewide Tack catalog.

"Dude, look at your fuckin' dick," Gary chuckled.

"I know," Larry said. He gave his wood a squeeze, tugged on his balls, looked up, meeting my eyes, and didn't have to ask for direction. He knew what to do next, and what I would.

I shot them from the waist up, the two young bucks wrestling, dressed only in unbuttoned cowboy shirts and hats. From the waist down, they were naked except for their clean white socks, cocks hard and begging to be sucked. With the shoot successfully completed, I was happy to oblige.

According to that old adage, a picture's worth a thousand words. But as I recall the conversation over the picture that changed my life, Big Jim Evans at first said only two: "Holy fuck."

Jim, who stood somewhere close to six-five in his Keds and was truly larger than life, held the black and white proof in his giant hands, sensing greatness in the image. That picture was going to translate into millions of dollars in new sales for his company.

"I'm not into other dudes," he added, an attractive grin showing beneath his graying mustache. "But it wouldn't take much to turn me gay after seeing this."

This was the potential cover of the new Statewide Tack and Supply Catalog. No "potential" about it, I knew it was the image Big Jim would choose from the images. He'd known it the instant it had crossed from his desk into his hands.

"I have three others to select from," I said.

"No, this is it, *the one*. Fuck, I can't stop looking at it."

"I hear you," I said. Shifting in place, I realized my dick had grown itchy and threatened to swell. I'd already jerked off twice that October Monday morning before our meeting, and that was on top of the incredible events that had taken place following the shoot itself the previous Friday night. If I wasn't careful while leaning over Big Jim's shoulder with the other proofs, I'd stick my dick into his back and there'd be no doubt about my having been seduced by the photo, too.

Hell, you couldn't look at those proofs and not feel a rush of heat, a ripple of sexual curiosity. It wouldn't surprise me if Big Jim shut the door and whipped out his cock, also rumored to be proportionately huge, the moment I left.

"You're sure these are our guys?"

"Abso-fucking-lutely, boss. Larry McCallister and Gary Stewart."

"Stewart's that doofus from the warehouse, the one who wears a Cleveland Indians baseball cap?"

I nodded.

"I hate the Indians."

I leaned away. My cock had hardened another degree. "You told me to put Statewide on the map with a new catalog cover. I'm confident this does it."

Jim went silent for a few seconds. I could imagine his thoughts about the expansion taking place in the Statewide Tack warehouse, which was growing bigger by the week. I tried to not think about my dick or Jim's, which could also be thickening in response to the proof. He reached down and adjusted himself, confirming my suspicion. I didn't know whether Jim was stiff over the new catalog cover photo or the certainty that his business was poised to become an international contender. Maybe it was equal parts both.

"A job very well done," Jim said. "The catalog's yours for as long as you want it."

The image was a black and white study of the two men. Larry was pressed up against Gary, one arm wrapped around his shoulder, the two cowboys who would become the faces of Statewide Tack captured in a moment before or after some form of rough-housing. Gary had the slightest of grins on his face. Larry's eyes were tipped up, looking slightly wounded, completely sexy. Both men had been dirtied around the edges and looked like they'd just worked a hard day's shift. Only we three knew the real story. Hard, all right. It was an honest image. It was perfect.

"Yeah," I said. "I think you've got your catalog cover."

The irony is that I took the job mostly for the money, even though there wasn't a lot of it at the start. Looking at the proof, I realized I had also achieved a kind of love for the assignment that I hadn't dreamed possible on the day Jim Augusta pitched me on the idea. The photo in Jim's hands wasn't a sailor dipping a woman on the street in Times Square or soldiers raising the American flag over Iwo Jima, but it was iconic. It was beautiful.

It was fucking *hot*.

I knew it. So did Big Jim.

"That's the one," he repeated.

ABOUT THE
AUTHORS

GAVIN ATLAS, at age twenty-four, was once offered the opportunity to model for an artist but was too shy. His published fiction includes a story collection, *The Boy Can't Help It.* He lives in Houston with his boyfriend, John. He can be reached at www.GavinAtlas.com.

BEARMUFFIN's fiction has appeared in several anthologies from Alyson and Cleis Press. He writes for *Honcho, Torso,* and *Mandate.* A devotee of raunchy, anonymous sex, Bearmuffin lives in San Diego and hangs out in adult bookstores, sex clubs, and bathhouses in a never-ending search for grist for his pornographic mill.

MICHAEL BRACKEN's short fiction has been published in *Best Gay Romance 2010, Beautiful Boys, Biker Boys, Black Fire, Boy Fun, Boys Getting Ahead, Country Boys, Freshmen, The Handsome Prince, Homo Thugs, Hot Blood: Strange*

Bedfellows, The Mammoth Book of Best New Erotica 4, Men, Muscle Men, Teammates, and many other anthologies and periodicals.

HEIDI CHAMPA has been published in numerous anthologies, including *College Boys, Like Magnets We Attract, Skater Boys,* and *Hard Working Men.* Her first novella, *White Out,* was recently published. Find more online at heidichampa.blogspot.com.

R. W. CLINGER divides his time between Pittsburgh, Pennsylvania, and Tarpon Springs, Florida. His fiction has appeared in various gay magazines and story compilations: *Teammates, Boys Getting Ahead,* and *Men at Noon, Monsters at Midnight.* His novels include *The Pool Boy* and *Soft on the Eyes.* R. W. is currently at work on a new gay novel.

LANDON DIXON's writing credits include *Options, Beau, In Touch/Indulge, Three Pillows, Men, Freshmen, [2], Mandate, Torso, Honcho, Bear,* and stories in the anthologies *Straight? Volume 2, Friction 7, Working Stiff, Sex by the Book, I Like It Like That, Boys Caught in the Act, Service with a Smile, Boys Getting Ahead, Nerdvana, Homo Thugs, Black Fire, Boy Fun, Ultimate Gay Erotica 2005, 2007, and 2008,* and *Best Gay Erotica 2009.*

GARLAND is the pen name of a full-time actor and writer living in Hollywood, California, who has also worked as a model, yes, including as a nude model. Garland's short stories have appeared in *SexTime: Erotic Stories of Time Travel, Teammates, Tented: Gay Erotic Tales from Under The Big Top, Boy Fun, Cougars on the Prowl, The Bad Girl's Sweet Kiss,* and

Ultimate Uniforms. His website is www.garlandserotictales. webs.com.

CYNTHIA HAMILTON's erotic fiction has been published in *Best Women's Erotica 2011*, edited by Violet Blue. She has also sold a dark fantasy erotica story to the anthology *Cthulhurotica*.

T. HITMAN's stories, long and short, have been accepted into a number of new homes, including *Rockets, Swords, and Rainbows: New Tales of Science Fiction, Jack O'spec: Tales of Halloween and Fantasy, Dark Things V*, and Richard Labonte's *Hot Jocks*.

AARON MICHAELS's fiction has appeared in numerous anthologies, including *Skater Boys, Surfer Boys*, and *Hard Hats*, as well as online at TorquereBooks.com. Aaron lives in northern Nevada and can be found on the web at www.aaron-michaels.com.

EMILY MORETON's publishing credits include stories in *Chroma Journal, Foreigness, Ripple Effect, Necking, Making Contact, In Uniform, Cast The Cards, Naughty November, Pour Some Sugar on It*, and *Twelve Tales of Recovery*.

CLANCY NACHT has published several successful gay erotica novels and short stories since 2009 with Loose Id and Noble Romance. She was published in *Smooth: Erotic Stories for Women* anthology in October 2010.

STEPHEN OSBORNE has had numerous stories published in various anthologies, including *Hard Hats, Best Gay Love*

Stories 2010, Queer Wolf, and *Service with a Smile.* He is also
the author of *South Bend Ghosts and Other Northern Indiana
Haunts.* You can follow him (and Jadzia the Wonder Dog) on
Twitter under the name southbendghosts.

ROB ROSEN, author of *Sparkle: The Queerest Book You'll
Ever Love* and *Divas Las Vegas,* which was the winner of the
2010 TLA Gaybies for Best Gay Fiction, has contributed to
more than a hundred anthologies, most notably *Best Gay Love
Stories 2006, Best Gay Romance (2007, 2008, 2009, and
2010), Best Gay Love Stories: New York City, Best Gay Love
Stories: Summer Flings, Ultimate Gay Erotica 2008 and 2009,*
and *Best Gay Love Stories 2009.* Please visit him at www.thero-
brosen.com.

Residing on English Bay in Vancouver, Canada, **JAY STARRE**
pumps out erotic fiction for gay men's magazines and has also
written steamy gay fiction for more than four dozen anthologies.
These include *Best Gay Romance 2008, Best Gay Bondage,
Bears, Surfer Boys,* and *Special Forces.* He is the author of two
historical erotic novels, *The Erotic Tales of the Knights Templars*
and *The Lusty Adventures of the Knossos Prince.*

Despite the fact that **CONNOR WRIGHT** has a deep and
abiding appreciation for boys who skate and snowboard, he can
barely walk and chew gum at the same time. He lives, works,
and writes in the greater Pacific Northwest region with several
helpful cats, none of whom can type.

LOGAN ZACHARY is an occupational therapist and mystery
author living in Minneapolis, where he is an avid reader and
book collector. His stories can be found in *Hard Hats, Taken*

by Force, Boys Caught in the Act, Ride 'em Cowboy, Service with a Smile, and *Best Gay Erotica 2009.* He can be reached at LoganZachary2002@yahoo.com.

ABOUT
THE EDITOR

NEIL PLAKCY is the author of the Mahu mystery series about openly gay Honolulu homicide detective Kimo Kanapa'aka. Books in the series are *Mahu, Mahu Surfer, Mahu Fire, Mahu Vice, Mahu Men,* and *Mahu Blood.* He also writes the Have Body, Will Guard adventure romance series, *Three Wrong Turns in the Desert, Dancing with the Tide,* and *Teach Me Tonight.*

His other books are the Golden Retriever Mysteries *In Dog We Trust* and *The Kingdom of Dog,* as well as the novels *GayLife.com, Mi Amor,* and *The Outhouse Gang* and the novella *The Guardian Angel of South Beach.* He edited *Paws & Reflect: A Special Bond between Man and Dog* and the gay erotic anthologies *Hard Hats, Surfer Boys,* and *Skater Boys.* His erotic stories have been collected in four Kindle editions: *Tough Guy Erotica, Mr. Surfer and Other Gay Erotica, Three Lambs: Erotic Tales of a Gay Frat,* and *Pledge Class and Other College Boy Erotica.*

More from Neil Plakcy

The Handsome Prince
Gay Erotic Romance
Edited by Neil Plakcy

The Handsome Prince is a bawdy collection of bedtime stories brimming with classic fairy tale characters, reimagined and recast for any man who has dreamt of the day his prince will come. Masterfully edited by Neil Plakcy, these sexy stories fuel fantasies and remind us all of the power of true romance.
ISBN 978-1-57344-659-4 $14.95

Skater Boys
Gay Erotic Stories
Edited by Neil Plakcy

Brimming with attitude and sexual confidence, athletic skaters are quick to shed their shirts and show off their beautiful bodies. How could they not be the object of pulse-quickening, gay desire? The characters of *Skater Boys* all have one additional thing in common: a love of hot man-on-man sex.
ISBN 978-1-57344-401-9 $14.95

Hard Hats
Gay Erotic Stories
Edited by Neil Plakcy

What is it about a hot guy with a tool belt? With their natural brand of macho, the sheen of honest sweat on flesh, and the enticements of hammers and pneumatic drills, men with tool belts rank among the hottest icons in gay erotic fantasy.
ISBN 978-1-57344-312-8 $14.95

Surfer Boys
Gay Erotic Stories
Edited by Neil Plakcy

Is it any wonder that surfers fuel sexual fantasies the world over? All that exposed, sun-kissed skin, those broad shoulders and yearning for adventure make a stud on a surfboard irresistible. Get ready for a long, hard ride.
ISBN 978-1-57344-349-4 $14.95

Ordering is easy! Call us toll free or fax us to place your MC/VISA order.
You can also mail the order form below with payment to:
Cleis Press, 2246 Sixth St., Berkeley, CA 94710.

ORDER FORM

QTY	TITLE	PRICE
___	_____	___
___	_____	___
___	_____	___
___	_____	___
___	_____	___
___	_____	___
___	_____	___
___	_____	___

SUBTOTAL _____

SHIPPING _____

SALES TAX _____

TOTAL _____

Add $3.95 postage/handling for the first book ordered and $1.00 for each additional book. Outside North America, please contact us for shipping rates. California residents add 8.75% sales tax. Payment in U.S. dollars only.

* Free book of equal or lesser value. Shipping and applicable sales tax extra.

Cleis Press • Phone: (800) 780-2279 • Fax: (510) 845-8001
orders@cleispress.com • www.cleispress.com
You'll find more great books on our website

Follow us on Twitter @cleispress • Friend/fan us on Facebook